VATICAN ASSASSIN

Mike Luoma

VATICAN ASSASSIN.

ISBN - 1-4116-6531-7

FIRST EDITION

Dedicated to my Dad, who has always believed in me...

Acts 2:20

The sun will be turned to darkness and the moon to blood...

Chapter One

The moon. Our bright light in the night sky. A cratered white orb shining on a field of stars. When she shines full you can see the glint of metal off of mankind's home on her surface, the main city on the moon, Luna Prime.

The Moon. Home for more than a million people. An independent state, not allied with either of the factions in the ongoing war between Earth and Mars.

Both sides in the ongoing war seek Luna Prime's favor. Both sides respect and maintain the peace of Luna Prime. It's one of the few homes of mankind not involved in the war; one of the few places the two sides can still meet as they try to negotiate an end to bloodshed.

When they bother to try.

The Governor of Luna Prime, Meredith McEntyre, is popular with leaders on both sides of the conflict. She's used her position to gain power both for herself and for Luna Prime. Her stature makes her an attractive ally. And an attractive target.

She's using her power to bring the opposing sides together with a peace conference on the moon. A conference gathering representatives from all involved parties: The Universal Trade Zone, the UTZ, who control most of Earth, Near Earth orbit, and who once controlled the moon itself. The Universal Islamic Nation, the UIN, who control Mars

1

and the mag-lev shipping highway connecting Earth space and Mars. The New catholic Church, allies of the UTZ. The NcC, with a small "c" to represent "catholic" in it's broader sense, the new church which includes all of Earth's Christians (except for the Mormons) ever since the Great Reunification of 2104, five years ago.

Representatives from other faiths are also present at the conference, invited to participate by the governor. Many faiths are now based on Luna Prime, forced or otherwise driven off Earth during seventy years of fighting between the Christian UTZ and Moslem UIN. The governor has invited the representatives of these other faiths to attend to hopefully cool some of the heat between the two foes. The war has been raging hot and cold since 2041, since the destruction of Jerusalem. It's still not really clear who was actually responsible for the destruction of the Holy City, but each side naturally still blames the other.

After Mecca was destroyed in 2070 there was no turning back.

The war has heated up of late, and for the first time threatens to spread to the Moon. The governor hopes to stop this. This conference is a start.

The representatives are gathering in the main conference center on Luna Prime, the great hall used for the moon's affairs of state. The conference has all comers on their best behavior. People who would otherwise shoot each other on sight sit silently at tables across the auditorium from each other awaiting the governor's keynote speech.

Some stare out the giant windows on the long side walls of the hall, out at the gray lunar landscape, at the other domes, tubes and buildings that make up Lunar Prime, and out at the infinite carpet of stars. Some stare at the empty dais and podium and the giant picture of the moon that hangs on the wall behind the dais. Some simply stare at each other.

The Moslems from Mars all wear red colored variations on their ancestors' traditional desert garb. They have been driven from their homes on the Earth but maintain their ancient ways defiantly in the face of those who destroyed Mecca and stole their home. They glare, ignore, and sometimes nod at others in the crowd.

The UTZ delegation are all in business suits. In a way they, too, honor their own ancient traditions. The suit, the tie, the ancient garb of the businessman.

The NcC delegation next to them in the great hall is also in traditional dress, a Cardinal in red, other priests in black, dark purple, blue and green with clerical collars. Their group deliberately ignores the Moslems across the way.

The tension is palpable in the air, electric, you can almost smell the ozone, as if lightning were just about to strike.

The governor waits in the green room for her cue. About a minute left before she's to go out and make her speech to the assembled crowd. To open the dialogue. She has engaged both sides in less public dialogues as well.

The UIN have been very reasonable, nice people, she thinks.

They seem willing to talk and work together. David deals with some of them, and they seem sane enough. The UTZ are all business, no warmth. And the NcC Cardinal and the Vatican delegation are almost a joke. You can't talk to him about public policy. Although they do have a new man up direct from the Vatican. David says he's dangerous. A dangerous priest! He popped in here by mistake just a minute ago and he seemed nice enough. Ah, there's the cue.

The governor walks into the auditorium through a door to the right of the dais. The low buzz of conversation fades as she's seen, as she walks up the dais to the podium. She stands behind the podium and looks out at the crowd.

Some of these people's fathers and mothers fought each other. What chance does anyone have of bringing them together? What chance do I have? Well, somebody has to try. Here goes...

"Welcome, everyone. Thank you all for agreeing to come here, for agreeing to see each other in peace, arms put aside for the moment to talk. Attending this conference is the bravest act yet on either side in this war. I applaud you."

The governor steps back and applauds. Her solo clapping is joined by one of the rabbis in the crowd, and then the applause spreads. The spontaneous ovation drops off after about a minute, as the governor smiles and again approaches the podium.

"We are right to cheer this hope for peace. We begin with hope. We put the battle aside for the moment for this chance at peace.

"Luna Prime is often in the middle of these battles. We haven't been hit physically in this last long round of conflict, but we've been hurt by this war all the same. Hurt by both sides. No side is blameless.

"Luna Prime remains neutral in spite of our pain. Because we are so close to the Earth, the Universal Trade Zone exerts untold pressures upon us. As their only refuge in Earth space, we also feel extraordinary pressure from the Universal Islamic Nation.

"The Moon... " She stops. A puzzled look crosses her face.

She falls.

She collapses like a puppet whose strings are cut. It happens fast.

Governor Meredith McEntyre looks up at the moon, the picture of the full moon on the wall up behind the podium she had just been standing behind. Standing on the moon. Her Moon.

She lies flat on her back, losing consciousness.

What was she thinking? The UTZ war with Mars and the Universal Islamic Nation puts the Moon in the middle too often. Her Moon.

My moon. The moon in the middle...

What?

She can hardly hold her thoughts, hardly keep her eyes open.

She looks up and sees the moon. Her moon.

She rolls her head from side to side, sees less and less

of her moon. There are people rushing around her, grabbing her arm... people are trying to help her as she lies on the dais.

She sees the Moon one last time.

Then nothing.

"The Governor is down! Call a med squad! Get me more security! Close this place off, now! Nobody leaves without answering to me first! No one gets in, either, without my say so!"

Lieutenant Governor Marc Edwards finishes barking orders and looks down at his boss, his friend, Madam Governor McEntyre, lying on her back.

His aide is checking her pulse.

"How is she?"

"I think she's dead, Mr. Edwards... there's no pulse!"

Edwards pushes his aide out of the way. He reaches down and feels for a pulse along McEntyre's neck. Nothing.

People are beginning to crowd in.

"C'mon, c'mon, a little space, please!"

Two men in blue med uniforms rush up the stairs of the dais to the edge of the group gathering around the Governor.

"Medics, Mr. Edwards... "

"Make room! Let them in here!"

The EMTs work on the Governor. Edwards watches as they pound her chest, send tubes down her throat, and scramble to try to revive her.

Edwards looks around the room; diplomats, envoys from the UTZ and UIN, representatives from every religion practiced on Luna. They look on in shock.

The Governor is not responding to any of the EMTs ministrations.

They defib her, but she doesn't respond.

They keep trying... three, four, five minutes.

They do all they can.

She's gone.

Edwards looks up from her still form at the crowd staring back at him. The delegations are looking at him and the scene on the dais, but they also glare at each other as they mill about, waiting for news, waiting to leave the auditorium. Waiting for it to sink in.

Chapter Two

This is not fun. This is not where I want to be right now!

Who would want to be here? Sunk up to my knees in sewerage, recycled fluids, and God knows what else, in one of the waste transport tunnels under Reagan Station. Beautiful place, try it on your next weekend getaway...

It smells like steaming, decomposing garbage, shit, rotting tomatoes, sulfur, urine, dirty socks, disinfectant and vomit... what else do I smell? Shouldn't dwell on it. A wonderful bouquet.

I'm trying to keep remembering that it's of vital importance that I be here doing this right now. Trying to remind myself I do the Lord's work, right? Yeah right, that matters. That makes it different, makes it special. The LORD'S work! Who's Lord? Who am I kidding? They've got me, so I do this for them, for whatever reasons and excuses they make up. Sure, this is for the Lord. Whatever. God thinks I should kill and then wade through this crap, huh? God's pretty fucking twisted, then.

The shit is filling into my boots and seeping up the legs of my pants. Not only does it smell like hell it's burning my skin, too! It's a torture all its own. The Big Guy would probably say using this tunnel as an escape route is my penance. Even though I'm supposedly doing the Lord's work, I must atone for my sin. Forgive me, Lord, for assassinating the governor of the moon. But I did it for you...

It's supposed to be easy this time, a quick hit, fast exit, quick change and back into the hall before any grow wiser. It has to be flawless... the Governor is a major target for the OPO.

I got in and administered the toxin quickly and effectively. Arrived with The Cardinal for the reception, ducked out to use the bathroom after establishing my presence, stepped past the men's room to the green room where the governor was waiting.

"So sorry, ma'am, just lost, new to the place... By the way, I'm the new public relations aide to The Cardinal, Father Bernard Campion..." extend hand with small killbots on fingertips, shake her hand and exchange the killbots, send them off to do their work. "Nice to meet you, Father. The men's room is right over there. You're about the fourth person today to do that!" She laughed, seemed nice. Too bad. She had to be eliminated, for the greater good, to save lives. This is what they tell me, anyway. She's UIN, or at least a sympathizer. We can't let her give them the Moon

All the recent UIN attacks have been launched from Mars. The UIN only have a few stolen transpace ships that are powerful enough to make the trip between Earth and Mars fast enough to be effective. If she delivers Luna to them, they can launch attacks from here. They could bring a lot more of their less powerful ships to the Moon from Mars, and use the moon as a staging base for those ships. Then when they attack us, their ships won't have to travel so far. And they'll be able to use a lot more of them against us at once.

We can't let her give them the moon.

But as the Big Guy would say, ours is not to question why. I did as I was instructed. I did the Lord's work.

After I left the governor, I went back out and into the men's room, and dropped down here through a maintenance hatch. Then it was supposed to be a quick trip down this access tunnel to the next hatch. But where's the next fucking hatch?!

It's here somewhere... right here! No, just a random access panel. It's gotta be here somewhere. It's in the plan. I'll find it. The plan. Let's see...

When I find the hatch, I'll go up and out through a maintenance closet off the main mall, near the rest rooms on the opposite end of the conference hall from where the *governor was. I'll change into my spare clothes I stashed near there and head back to the conference. I'll be seen coming back from the opposite direction from where the governor was, for misdirection's sake, strike up a quick conversation or two on the way back to establish my presence. Then I walk back into the hall into the chaos which has ensued. The Plan.*

Man, this sucks. I made a fast exit, all right, nearly slid under the surface of this gunk when I slipped down the access hatch out of the bathroom... I knew I'd run into something down here but this is disgusting. Glad I've got the change of clothes hidden near the other rest rooms. I knew to expect some slime but this...

The next hatch should be right about here, should lead to that closet and those other rest rooms, but I don't feel it. Damn tunnel wall's so smooth! This tunnel is carved right out of the lunar rock, marble-smooth walls, ceiling and floor, all rounded for easy slippage and falling on one's face or ass into the combined excrement of the Moon's largest settlement.

Oh joy, Oh bliss.

The glorious life of an agent of the Office of Papal Operations, BC my boy...

I can almost hear the Big Guy, the Old Man, in my head, see him in the robes of his office as he speaks words that seem somehow wrong coming from such a blessedly adorned figure:

"She must be eliminated, my son, so that many more will not die. It is God's will, you see. You, as always, Father Campion, are merely His instrument."

Instrument. Hmph. I am feeling pretty played right about now...

Light and sound break the dark silence. Alarms. Flashing white and red light. A voice saying something unintelligible.

Shit, what's that? An alarm? Wonderful. Nice light show. Something's talking, too.   Amplified, but still muffled. Some kind of warning.

Great. Just great. Hallelujah everybody. Too far away to see it yet, but it sounds like an automated security bug. No human Lunar Security Cop would want to come down here.

Ugh! The smell is getting worse! I didn't think that was possible! The security robot is getting closer. It's making a sizzling noise. Must be sweeping around the tunnel with lasers, superheating the sludge whenever it fires down into it. Oh no. Oh man. I can feel the waves of warm shit flowing down past my legs through the sludge, superheated by the security bug's lasers. Heating up the shit. This just sucks.

At least the announcement is getting clearer. There's a positive, huh?

" ...non-standard behavior, including unauthorized access to these maintenance tunnels, is to be reported, investigated and resolved to the satisfaction of Lunar Security. Unauthorized access to this area is covered under the Lunar Emergency Powers Act, and is classified as highly suspicious. Extreme force is authorized, even automated extreme force, as provided under the War Codes . A General State of Emergency has been declared by the Lunar Free Colony. Any nonstandard behavior, including unauthorized access to these maintenance tunnels, is to be reported, investigated and resolved to the satisfaction of Lunar Security. Unauthorized access..."

The robot's getting closer. I can see the white strobe flashing, the red laser sweeping a webbed pattern around its perimeter. Man, I can hear the sludge bubbling and sizzling. It's definitely getting hotter. Still can't find the damn hatch!

"...highly suspicious. Extreme force is authorized, even automated extreme force, as provided under the War Codes. A General State of Emergency..."

Finally! There's the rim of the hatch. It's about chin-high.

Let's see what the sign on the hatch says... "Access 14/Lunar Reclamation System Tunnel 28-C." Ahoy, me maties, thar she blows! In the nick of time, too, damn goo is getting too hot, damn... where's the control panel? There!

10

Clicks. Good sound! Whirring gears inside the hatch. And another click.

The hatch swings in. BC pulls himself up through the hatch as lasers from the security bot start to reach him. A red beam slices into the bottom of his right boot before he pulls it through the hatch.

Damn!

Red and white light flashes and splays chaotically across the hatch as he shoves it closed behind him.

He's in a small space, a meter and a half square around with no visible ceiling. It's another tunnel carved right out of the lunar rock, this time leading up. There's a ladder carved into the wall in front of him.

He climbs up easily in the light lunar gravity.

There's another hatch in the wall at the top, just above the last rung of the ladder.   *Locked!*

He takes out a small silver cylinder. His handlaser. It glows red on the end as he fires it up. He focuses a short, intense beam and runs it along the seam of the hatch. The seam smokes as his laser cuts through it. He works his way around the hatch door.

He braces himself, his back against the tunnel wall opposite the hatch, and kicks the hatch in.

It falls with a soft thud.

That's wrong. Clang, yes. Soft thud, no...

He looks through the hatchway. The hatch has landed on something.

On someone, actually.

It's hard to see. Dim emergency lighting in here. It's a maintenance closet. A storage area, toxicological suits in lockers, broken old cleaners piled off to one side...

And a woman lying on the floor under the fallen hatch door.

Is she all right? Is she unconscious? Why is anyone in here anyway?

He climbs through the hatch, drops to the floor next to the woman. She's wearing a uniform.

Wonderful! A Lunar Security Cop! All right, God... How

about a little help here? Could you work out a helpful coincidence for a change? I'm not looking for a miracle, just a little help here. C'mon.

I wonder if that security 'bot sent out an alert. Shit! Why else would she be here?

He checks her pulse.

She's still alive, just knocked out. Should be fine. Looks like she took a good whomp on the head from this thing, though.

That's good. I do try to limit my killings to just one a day. Any more than that and I'd begin to think it was becoming a bad habit... hmm, bit morbid...

She's pretty... like a sleeping Latino angel... hope she stays sleeping for a while.

Damn, though, this is not in the plan. I'm leaving too big a footprint here, now. She's bound to report this, even if she never sees me. And this is taking time I don't have.

Gotta move.

He picks up the hatch and props it back up in its original position.. He puts the handlaser on a slightly lower setting and runs it back along the seam around the hatch, fusing it back into place.

The Lunar Security Cop on the floor begins to stir as he finishes. He slides past her across the room in his damaged shoes and soaked pants. She begins to move her head. BC reaches the closet exit and tries the door.

Locked!

He uses his handlaser again. The door's lock gives a good fight but loses. BC burns through and pushes the door open.

The door slides halfway open then stops.

Shit! Well, it'll have to do.

He slides through.

If I'm doing Your work, why won't You cut me any slack? Huh?

He's in a small side corridor off of the main dome of Reagan Station. He edges down the right side of the corridor toward the atrium, tries not to look suspicious covered in sewer sludge and smelling as bad as he looks. He pulls his priestly collar off and pockets it.

No need to look _that_ suspicious.

BC leans out of the corridor to visually scan the area ahead, the edge of the central atrium for Reagan Station. Groups of tall pines tower over, stretching to the starry roof of the dome.

Like a forest in a mall. Pine needles and plastic. My bag should be just over by the trunk of that huge pine...

I don't see it from here. Good hiding job. Let's hope.

He ducks out of the corridor and into the first stand of pine trees in the atrium. He tries to nonchalantly search around for sign of his bag.

It's not here! How can it not be here? Is this the wrong group of trees? No, right trees...

He pokes around under the pines and walks into a sprinkler hidden by the needles. He feels his left ankle twist the wrong way and he starts to fall.

Ouch! Damn!

He breaks his fall and plops down onto the pine needles and grass. He sits, massages his ankle and looks around for any sign of his bag.

Looks like it was stolen. There's an indentation in the bushes under the trees where I left it. It was here. It should be right here, these _are_ the trees... c'mon, any helpful coincidences?

Who would steal a priest's clothes?

Chapter Three

Reagan Station began as a military outpost. Now, as Luna Prime, it thrives as an independent city state, a hub of commercial activity, a cosmopolitan capitol and neutral territory in the war, home to over two million people. More than just a moon base, Reagan Station is a city unto itself. Built off the main dome are over fifty separate neighborhood areas, engineered and designed to be aesthetically pleasing and diverse as well as functional.

Most of Reagan Station was constructed in the last half of the 21st century, after a UIN missile strike back in 2062 destroyed most of the first Reagan Station, originally built by the old United Nations as a military security and Mission to Mars base and later ceded to the UTZ. The UIN's missile strike gave them control of the Moon in 2062.

The UIN took over the moon after their attack forced the UTZ off. They began rebuilding, making improvements and adapting the base to their needs. Nine years later in 2071, the war shifted, the UTZ regained control of the Moon and reestablished Reagan Station.

Though still technically a military base, the rebuilt Reagan Station's entertainment facilities and landing facilities became commercial ventures, subcontracted to corporate members of the UTZ. The UTZ is driven by commerce, and finds ways to make money in any venture. The facilities became incredibly popular, a gold mine for the subcontractors. The entertainment facilities' growth soon outpaced the UTZ military's developments on the Moon. The Moon became "civilized".

The employees of these facilities were the moon's new working class. Luna's new backbone. Many of the workers were non-Christians from Earth, who moved to the Moon to escape the war. As this population increased, as Reagan Station grew, the independent nature of the people of the Moon grew as well. The moon became a refuge for those party to neither side in the bitter conflict. An interesting and independent place, intentionally diverse and tolerant.

In 2082, Luna became an independent state under UTZ auspices. Reagan Station has been growing ever since. Though more city than station, the name has stuck. The Independent government calls Reagan Station "Luna Prime," but just about everyone else still calls it Reagan Station.

Reagan Station is lived-in. It's like any other city, with good sections and bad, old, broken-down dark areas and shiny new construction.

Independent and united in their neutrality, Luna's populace segregates itself into its own smaller, separate areas: The Jewish Section, The Pagan Enclave, The Universal Temple, Chinatown. Their separate sectors spoke off the central hub of old Reagan Station proper and the Main Dome through a series of interconnected corridors and airlocks.

The Main Dome is at the center of the old station and the city, a giant atrium nearly a mile across, the central hub for the station. Three floors of residences and shops circle the atrium. The dome atop the atrium is clear, allowing a breathtaking view of the stars and Earth.

Artificial gravity supplements the moon's weak attraction on the floor of the main dome. At the center is a wide, roughly circular pool almost a half a mile in diameter, deliberately overgrown with vegetation and teeming with aquatic life. It's designed as a part of the environmental systems and also to be "aesthetically pleasing." The pool is crisscrossed by two broad walkways lined with trees and bushes. Maples and pines, oaks, elms and Douglas firs, and ferns, hedges and dogwoods, all can be found under the moon's Main Dome.

There are lilac bushes and stretches of grass surrounding the central pool. Artificial breezes circulate.

We try to bring Earth with us, to recreate it best we can. It's been recreated well in the Main Dome of Reagan Station.

BC is in a deserted part of the Dome. There are cleaners and other maintenance robots around, but no people. This is part of BC's plan. This immediate area has no shops or residences.

And now, no bag. Not a part of my plan. And my ankle hurts!

I thought my bag would be safe around here. Maybe it was picked up by Maintenance. That might be worse than getting stolen. They'll make a record of it.

I think I hope someone stole it. Twisted. Huh, like my ankle. Bad pun. Is that a pun? I don't know...

BC looks back at the wall of the Main Dome. The circular outer wall of this level of the dome is blank, but above him, on the second level, he can hear the din of people and commerce.

Where I need to be. The reception hall entrance is back up there, on the other side of the dome.

I can't go up there looking like this, all in black with my collar off, legs dipped in shit and the rest of me splattered. Real fine company.

Then there's the Lunar Security Cop I knocked out. She'll be waking up. I gotta get outta here. Gotta get some new clothes, fast, too. Time to move.

He walks through the pine trees and heads for the center of the dome, towards the central pool. He walks along the pool's edge until he sees a line of shops ahead on the dome's outer wall. He scans the signs of the shops until he sees the one he needs. Men's clothes. Just ahead.

Men's Shop. Perfect. Now, I've gotta kind of casually walk out of the trees and into the open, covered in shit. Hum dee dum dee dum...

He ducks out of the wooded section and heads for the Men's store. There are a few people around, but most don't notice him or try not to notice him.

I haven't been here long enough for anyone to know me yet, thank God. Most of these people seem pretty calm, too... I wonder if the job is done? Should be by now. Should be mass pandemonium, people running crazy... well, maybe not, but some kind of reaction, anyway. Maybe they're just keeping it quiet for now.

BC makes it into the men's clothing store without incident. The sales assistant eyes him warily as he walks in. He's young, impeccably dressed. He arches an eyebrow as he tries to look down his nose at BC. His nose wrinkles as he begins to smell him.

"Can I help you?" His voice virtually drips with disdain.

"I need a new suit. I'd like to have these clothes I'm wearing incinerated in your recycler, too."

"Our fitter is down, should be back up later on. Why don't you come back later?"

I don't have time for this...

"I thought you asked if you could help me?"

"Well, I..."

"...Didn't really mean it. I see. Tell you what, you help me out with something off the rack, burn these clothes, and I won't lose my temper. How about it?"

The sales guy tries to says something but just stammers. BC continues.

"You don't want me to lose my temper here, do you? Not dressed like this. What if I lose it and run all over the store, rubbing myself all over these nice clean pretty suits of yours?"

"Uh, look, sir, uh, wah..."

BC stares him down, then tries to reassure him somewhat.

"Look, I'm gonna pay for everything, so just sit back, I'll find what I need, you take care of my old stuff, and I'll be gone. And then you can forget all about me..."

...And you'd better. I'd hate to have to come back and tie you off as a loose end. Or maybe I wouldn't hate it so much, little prick... Just doing the Lord's work... You'd rather not find out...

This is already taking way too long, and I'm losing

patience fast.

The sales assistant weasels out of the confrontation,"You just go ahead. I'll help with those clothes of yours when your done." He wrinkles his nose again at BC and his soiled suit.

BC finds a dark suit. Not black, but close enough for off the rack. He pays for the suit with an OPO secured credit card, untraceable. He changes in the store after cleaning himself up in the store's refresher. The sales assistant incinerates the remnants of his sewer crawl in the store's molecular recycler and doesn't speak to BC again.

Fine by me. See ya.

BC walks out of the store a new man.

Much better! Mmmm, clean clothes... Just wish I could do some mind trick and make that little prick forget I was ever in there.

Not the right clothes, though. This suit won't pass. I still gotta get into dress blacks.

And get back to the auditorium.

He heads for the center of the dome, and crosses over one of the walkways to the dome's other side. He steps nonchalantly out of the Main Dome, but then gingerly runs down the corridor towards the Vatican's Lunar Holdings, still favoring his left ankle.

Slight modification of plans...

He gets to his room. As the door closes behind him, he kicks off his shoes and rips off the new suit. The tie almost chokes him as he pulls it over his head.

He grabs a suit off his rack, the traditional black, an identical suit to the one he wore earlier. He pulls on the pants, the shirt, fixes the collar... he looks at the clock. Time is ticking away, and he's way off plan.

Time pressure. Got to get back to the reception hall. Gotta cover tracks, too.

BC dumps suit he just bought through the waste panel in his room and incinerates his brand new clothes.

Some tracks covered.... As long as that sales guy forgets. Figures I'd find one of the few places on Reagan

Station with a human attendant. Too bad I couldn't have killed him right off. Would've look suspicious. His lucky day.

BC runs back down the corridor, still limping a little. . He saunters briskly out of the Vatican holdings, through the Main Dome again, then up a level to the reception hall, whose doors are blocked by Lunar Security Cops. A crowd is forming outside the hall.

Good signs. It must have worked.

He makes his way to the front of the crowd. A guard blocks his way when he tries to walk past and into the hall.

"I'm sorry, Father, I can't let you in there."

"What?" BC plays dumb.

"Nobody's allowed to enter or leave the reception hall for right now."

"Oh, but I'm supposed to be in there. I just left to go to the bathroom."

The guard thinks for a second. "I still can't let you in there, even *back* in there. Orders."

"Why not? I'm with The Cardinal. He may need me."

The guard thinks again. Hard.

Straining with the effort. C'mon, buddy.

"C'mon, Buddy. You help a priest, you go to heaven..."

"Aw, Father, I'm Jewish. I'm not sure we even have the same heaven."

"Same God, same heaven... Jesus was Jewish! You still get credit."

The guard laughs, "Hold on a sec, Father." He opens the doors to the hall and ducks half inside. BC can hear him talking to someone. The guard leans back through the door and looks at BC.

"Okay, Father, you're in, but you might not wanna be."

"What?"

"Go ahead in. You'll see."

BC walks through the doors into some of the chaos he's been expecting. People running around. Other people, important-looking people, milling about. Med techs all over the stage. The Cardinal is being escorted back down from the dais.

BC makes his way through the crowd, to The Cardinal. The Cardinal looks up as BC approaches.

"Well, Father Campion, you picked a fine time to heed nature's call. Just as the Governor began her speech, she collapsed. She passed away on the spot, poor thing. I offered last rites but her husband seemed almost offended. Said they weren't Catholic, 'not even new catholic with a small "c"'. He was distraught, of course.

"You should have been here. They're younger, he might have responded better to you."

"Of course, sir. My apologies."

Mission complete.

Chapter Four

BC stares out the window of the Cardinal's office, zoning out on the sharp contrasts of light and shadow in the monochrome gray lunar landscape as The Cardinal drones on. He sees the lights of several ships streak up and away from the surface into the stars. UIN ships by the look of them, their diplomats leaving Luna Prime. The peace conference is over before it began. The governor is dead.

So far, BC has pulled off the assassination without detection despite setbacks.

So far.

So far the most hazardous part of this job is avoiding being bored to death by the Cardinal. I guess the sewerage ranks a close second, though...

"The Governor's death could jeopardize our entire mission..."

The Governor's death was my entire "mission", Cardinal, but I do enjoy the double meaning. I suppose I'm a mission-ary of a different sort...

"Are you listening to me, Father?"

BC turns to face The Cardinal.

Cardinal Andersen glares up at BC from behind his ludicrously large, fakewood desk.

Everything about the Vatican Mission on the Moon is sort of large and ludicrous and fake.

The entire enclave of Vatican staterooms and offices on the Moon is bedecked in a rich gold and red color scheme. Ornate iconography decorates most of the walls, a mishmash of images and relics from all the different Christian strains now unified in the NcC, from Eastern icons to the New Risen Lord of the NcC and every revisionist view in between. The Cardinal's own decorator touch, BC had been told when he'd cracked a joke about it just after arriving. The Cardinal, though not large, certainly was, in BC's opinion, fairly ludicrous in his own right, and usually bedecked in red and gold himself.

"Well, are you listening to me, Father?"

"Absolutely, your holiness. How is our mission jeopardized? The Vatican Mission here is fairly well established by now. You've been here, what, five years yourself, right?"

"Almost five. And we were starting to get somewhere here, Father Campion. The Vatican Mission just being here is in itself testimony to that. We had been discussing a new alliance between the UTZ and Luna..."

"Don't you think it was natural causes?" BC asks.

The Cardinal shakes his head.

"She was so young, just a few years older than you, Father Campion. Does it seem natural to you?" The Cardinal looks down and briefly distracts himself in some of the scattered sheets on his desk.

BC presses on.

"Who would want her dead?"

The Cardinal, agitated, looks back up at BC and continues.

"Well, she was negotiating with both the UTZ and the UIN. And she allowed us to beef up our mission here. The UIN might see that as a threat."

"Really? Are we that threatening?"

The Cardinal stops. He looks down his nose at BC.

"Some of us are."

Dangerous ground you're on, Cardinal. There's stuff you really don't want to know anything about. Guess it's time for some of my famous spin...

"We do the Lord's work, Cardinal Andersen, even the OPO. The Holy Father sends us as his personal emissaries into the world. Do you find the OPO... dangerous, Cardinal? We but serve God's representative on Earth, Pope Peter the Second. We are only 'dangerous' in our devotion to The Lord."

"So was the Inquisition, Father. Torquemada said much the same thing as you, you know."

Better watch yourself, Cardinal. You don't want to be on the wrong side here...

"We're on the same side here, Cardinal. Please don't forget that. Pope Peter assigned you to Luna personally, didn't he? Aren't we all the Pope's men?"

The Cardinal nods. "We are at that, Father Campion. Maybe some more than others, though, eh?"

Careful there, Cardinal...

"There are those who could view your assignment here as my new Public Relations Officer from the OPO as, well... a threat. You know they spread rumors about the OPO. Those people could have very well reacted to your arrival with this possible assassination."

" I really don't think my arrival would have even drawn their attention, much less their anger. I'm not nearly so important. I'd be surprised if they even noticed. And, still, it's only *possible* foul play, your eminence. We must trust in God. Maybe it was just her time."

"Perhaps. But I don't know whether God had anything to do with this. I'm also not the only one thinking there may be more to this, Campion. Governor Edwards and his people are very suspicious. It did look like a heart attack to me at first, but you never know. They do let those *Muslims* wander the halls here, still, even with the war. The price of neutrality, I suppose. Maybe you should watch *your* back, Father Campion."

"I will, trust me, sir. We should all be alert. It is a time of war. After all."

"The UIN may very well have killed McEntyre to derail our negotiations. If they'll kill her, they'll not hesitate to remove those they find threatening who are *less* visible. Be careful. I don't trust them. Bad enough we have to live among them here on the moon. They're naturally violent, and they seem to hate absolutely everyone else."

BC nods.

Jeesh, the guy's almost rabid.

The intercom dings.

"Cardinal?" His secretary on the com.

"Yes?"

"Governor Edwards is here to see you."

"Send him in."

The door opens. Edwards enters.

"Hello Cardinal."

Luna's new governor is visibly nervous as he walks in and shakes hands with the Cardinal and BC. His handshake is quick and uncertain. BC takes quick stock of him.

In his forties, probably. Stocky, about 6'2", short dark hair... looks military, or at least recently ex-military. Maybe he was Lunar Security, a cop, before moving up. Have to do some digging.

He looks like a man suddenly in over his head... like I was in that tunnel, I suppose.

"I would guess you're Father Campion?"

"Yes... or you can call me BC."

"Father Campion is New Unified Reform," The Cardinal interjects, explaining BC's informality.

"And also a ranking Vatican official, I understand," Edwards said.

Hmmm, maybe he's sharper than he looks.

"Nice to meet you, Governor Edwards"

Edwards flinches.

"I'm not used to that, yet. Sorry. The 'governor' thing, I mean..."

Edwards looks down for a moment then comes back to himself.

"I, uh, have some news that may concern you."

Uh oh.

"UIN warships have been detected just a short distance from us here on Luna. We've never seen them get this close, even before..." He stops, thinks a moment.

...Before, when they were attacking us back on Earth. Right, Mr. Edwards? Still, I didn't expect that that was his news.

"What I mean is, before, they stayed pretty far from us when they hit Earth targets. They have people here, too."

I wonder how many of them are still here? No wonder they were so keen on getting out of here after the shit went down.

"Would that really stop them from attacking?" the Cardinal sneers.

Edwards seems surprised by the Cardinal's bitter contempt for the UIN. BC is as well, though less so after their earlier exchange.

"I don't think they'd risk their own people's lives..." Edwards says.

The Cardinal stands, visibly shaking.

"Of course they would! All glory to Allah and all that! They'd just be martyrs and celebrated back on Mars, like killing them did them a favor! And they'll twist it so it sounds like we killed them, you'll see."

Edwards is taken aback by the Cardinal's vitriol. He stares at The Cardinal as if seeing him for the first time. BC watches Edwards, watches his reactions.

The Cardinal's getting all fired up! Christ, he'd applaud my mission, if he only knew. Wonder how he got so bitter? Even I don't hate the Moslems like that. God is Love? Over the fucking top. Could freak out Edwards. I've got to find a way to moderate the situation.

"Our holdings have never been attacked here on the Moon, but we've been hit repeatedly by UIN forces back on Earth and in orbit, Governor Edwards. How close are the UIN ships? Should we worry? Head for shelters?"

"We don't know they're a threat, yet, but with the governor dying so suddenly and the ships showing up at the same time, well, I just worry it's too connected to be a coincidence. Do UIN ships behave a certain way before they attack? Do they get into any formations, or assume any telltale flight patterns?"

BC and The Cardinal look at each other, then back at Edwards.

"I'm afraid you're asking the wrong people about

starship battle tactics, my son," The Cardinal says and smiles, falling back into his patronly pastoral mode. He sits back down and wipes his brow with a red kerchief he pulls from an unseen pocket somewhere in his robes.

Time for me to buy a little bit of confidence from Edwards with a little bit of knowledge. Help reinforce the idea that we're on his side.

"Governor, I've been told they approach single file, spreading out in four directions as they reaching optimal firing range. Then, they rotate while firing, like the blades of a lethal pinwheel. Or at least that's what I've heard. Something like that."

Edwards is surprised.

"Oh. Okay. Thank you, fa, um, BC. Well, yeah, these ships are forming up single file."

"Are they moving this way?"

"Not yet."

"If they do come this way, governor, and they stay single file..."

"Yeah?"

"...we should probably hit the shelters. Reagan Station does have emergency shelters, right?"

"We have some, but they're old. I don't know what kind of repair they're in. And there's nowhere near enough space for everybody in and around Luna Prime. There'll be riots, panic, people getting crushed to death... This could get ugly."

The Cardinal clears his throat and fixes his stare on Edwards.

"They're taking advantage of your inexperience, governor. Because you're new, they threaten and test you. Are these the actions of friends of Luna?" the Cardinal asks.

Whoa, you're spinning it harder than me, Andersen. Easy there, old man, don't ruin it. Edwards is close to losing it on the Cardinal.

Edwards shakes his head.

"Look, your holiness, you're not helping. Save your hate, okay? I just need some helpful advice. I thought that's what you," he looks back and forth at both of them, "are supposed to provide. Am I wrong?"

Got to turn Edwards our way. The Cardinal is blowing it completely.

"I'm trying to help, sir. If there is anything the Vatican can do for you, Mr. Edwards, let me know. And please, let me know if those ships move this way?" BC tries to reassure him.

"Yeah, I'll try to."

Edwards turns and moves to leave, "I've got a lot going on right now, please excuse me."

After he's gone, BC turns to the Cardinal.

"I don't think you helped our cause there any, your *eminence*." BC lays a little sarcasm on the last word.

"Eminence? Please. I haven't been called that since the reunification."

"Actually, I like saying it. Eminence. Em-ih-nence. EMINENCE! Sounds powerful, doesn't it? We must maintain appearances, mustn't we, your eminence?"

"Please stop that! The Muslims are a dangerous and angry people, Campion. They don't think as we do! I know they *say* they count Christ as a prophet, whatever they mean by that, but they do not respect life as we Christians do."

How do I answer that? Sure we respect life. Sure we do. Me, especially, that's what I do for the church, respect life. Best not to think about that too much, huh?

"Do *you* think they killed the governor, Campion?"

"Well, sir, we still don't know that she was killed. Maybe we shouldn't make that assumption."

"I wouldn't put it past them. This whole thing stinks of the UIN. Kill the governor, create chaos, then move in and take advantage. They're infidels and they want us, you and I, Father Campion, they want us dead. Make no mistake. I wanted to emphasize that for our new governor. I think he could be on our side."

"Well, he might be, if you don't scare him away."

"He needs to know the danger in the situation."

Time to build some confidence with the Cardinal. Let him in a little.

"The OPO heard rumors that Governor McEntyre was holding secret talks with UIN representatives here on Luna."

"Really? I saw no evidence of that. Still, it all makes a certain sense, though. And those who think they can bargain with the devil always get burned," the Cardinal chuckles at his own wit. "Are you certain?"

"That's what we heard. Just rumors."

"Is that why you're here, then?"

"Do you really want to know? Do you want to question one of Peter's men as to his calling?"

"No. I suppose I don't want to know. I'm sure it's all in, ahem, God's Name?"

"Absolutely, your eminence." BC lays a little sarcasm on the last word.

The intercom dings.

"Governor Edwards on the line for you both."

"Yes, put him through. Governor?"

"They're moving in closer, single file, just as you said, Father Campion. Could you both meet me in my office immediately?"

Chapter Five

The governor's suite on Luna Prime is strategically located, positioned to catch "earthrise" in most of the windows in it's outer wall along the long strip of meeting rooms, offices and staterooms. BC and the Cardinal now sit in the governor's main office and conference room as the Earth hangs on the short horizon outside.

BC stares at the Earth, large in the window behind Edwards, who stands at the end of a long table shuffling through some papers.

There are officials from the UTZ at the table, and, judging by their uniforms, some Luna Security people as well, people BC hasn't met yet. Conspicuous by their absence are any members of any group affiliated with the UIN.

Edwards clears his throat and begins.

"Thanks for coming with no notice."

Edwards looks nervous. He keeps adjusting his tie. He fidgets with his wristband. BC notices he's changed his clothes.

Probably sweated right through his last set.

"Luna has attempted to stay neutral in the war between the UTZ and the UIN. We have opened our arms to both sides in hopes of being peace keepers and unifiers.

"With our arms open, and the Moon vulnerable, one of the parties we had thought to be our friend now seems to be showing different colors, showing themselves, maybe, to be our foe. As I speak, transpace warships from Mars, from the Universal Islamic Nation, are closing in on the Moon in attack formation. The war may be on its way here.

"We've never asked for the UTZ or the Vatican to join

in our councils before. I thank you for joining us now. We may need allies. We seem to face a clear and present danger from the UIN at this time, which I believe warrants reevaluating our policy of neutrality."

Wow... Jackpot! We couldn't have hoped for better! He's sold already, or playing a very clever game.

Is he that smart?

Edwards is interrupted when a Luna Security Cop enters the office. BC recognizes her. She's got a bruise on her forehead. She's the LSC he knocked out earlier, getting out of the tunnel! He pretends not to notice her.

She looks at him strangely, but quickly moves on and over to Edwards, presenting him with a sealed report. He opens it, grimaces.

"She was killed."

Edwards starts shaking. He brings his hand to his brow, pinches the bridge of his nose, takes a deep breath. Composing himself, he continues.

"Someone, um, assassinated Governor McEntyre. There were neurotoxic traces on her skin and in her blood. Someone murdered her.

"I think, maybe, we can see now who." Edwards is almost talking to himself. Then he looks up at the group around the table.

"Hey, um, I need a minute or two, okay?"

Edwards sits down, motions to the LSC. "Could you, uh, get me the latest reports on the position and disposition of the UIN ships? And could everyone take five?"

The group around the table mumbles and nods assents. They get up from the table and head for the office door.

As they leave the governor's office, the Cardinal turns to BC.

"I told you. They killed her! Now they're coming in to finish the job! You wait here and help Mr. Edwards, Campion. I'm going back to the mission. If the governor needs me, let me know, but I think this is more your area of expertise."

"So I'll be able to reach you in the mission's shelter, then, Cardinal?"

"Yes! Ah... I see, you got me there, Campion. Excuse me."

Just outside the office door the LSC from before taps him on the shoulder.

"Excuse me?"

"Yes?"

"You look familiar, father... have we met?"

"I don't think so. You are?"

"Nita Bendix, Luna Security. You sure we've never met? Do you go out at all?"

"No, not really," BC says, gesturing at his outfit. "I'm a priest."

"Yeah, but you're New Reform, right? You can party and everything, right?"

"Well, sort of, but no, I just got here recently."

"You're kinda cute. Do you have to stay celibate?"

Man! Didn't expect this...

"Well, not technically."

"I see. See you later, father. Father... ?"

"Campion. Bernard Campion, but you can call me BC."

"Okay, Father BC."

"Just BC."

"Okay, just BC. Bye, for now, anyway." She gives him another strange look, turns and takes off down the corridor.

Little flirt! Probably hasn't been right since that clunk on the head. Nice body, anyway...

A tall, blond haired man in a beige suit storms down the corridor towards BC, past Nita Bendix as she walks away. He brushes into BC, almost pushing him out of the way, and begins hitting the greeting buzzer on the governor's office door repeatedly.

A fixed look of anger scrunches up his face. His red-rimmed eyes don't seem to be looking at anyone or anything. He keeps pounding on the buzzer.

The door opens after about the fifteenth buzz. The

man surges in before the door even opens halfway.

BC hears, "Daniel!" as the door closes.

Must be McEntyre's widower. The angry, grieving spouse. Daniel McEntyre. Just got the news, I suppose. He's in with the UIN, too, according to our reports. Possible future target. Has a weakness for very young Asian women and very old scotch. Our reports are pretty damn thorough... Know your enemy, one of the most basic rules. Too many skeletons to hold office himself, so he worked beside his wife. Family affair, how sweet.

He's all worked up. I wonder how much of his grief is real and how much is him trying to salvage the situation for his friends in the UIN?

He's probably in there trying to undo all the confidence and trust I've been working to build up in Edwards. The UIN doesn't want him cozying up to the OPO!

Almost three minutes now. I'll just mistakenly reenter early...

Daniel McEntyre is shouting and waving with his back to BC as BC opens the door.

" Of course this is an assassination, Marc! They killed her. She's gone! They took her from me. Took her away from me! From all of us! And now you're taking their side?"

Daniel McEntyre doesn't hear or see BC enter, but Edwards does.

"Father Campion! Please, excuse us, I'll let you know when we'll reconvene."

I don't think so. Time to see what this McEntyre guy's all about.

"Mr. McEntyre? I'm sorry about your loss. I'm sure you want to blame someone..."

"Damn right I do! This time you and your UTZ puppet masters have gone too far! Was it you? It probably was you! You're Campion, right? I heard all about you. You're OPO. You're not really even a priest! You used to be just a rip-off scam artist, a fake minister until their so-called "reunification" legitimized you! I know all about you, Campion! You and your type make me sick! You call yourselves Christian!"

"Clearly you're distressed, sir. And you must have me confused with someone else, certainly. I can understand..."

McEntyre drowns him out, yelling and moving towards him with his hands balling into fists at his sides.

"You and your UTZ butchers won't get away with this! You won't!"

"David!" Edwards finally tries to intercede, getting up from the table to move between McEntyre and BC.

Best if I just say nothing at this point. Be the calm beside the storm.

"You bastards are all so smug!" McEntyre shouts at BC, face to face. BC doesn't flinch, absorbs the rage.

Edwards approaches, tries to calm McEntyre, pulls him away from BC's face.

"David, you're overwrought, you gotta calm down! Please."

"That's it!" McEntyre turns and charges BC.

Shit! He's crazy!

BC drops under McEntyre's charge, arms up in front of his face. McEntyre flies over him, into the door frame with a loud "slap." He shakes it off, gets back up and turns and grabs BC by the collar as BC gets up.

Edwards muscles in and gets his arms around McEntyre from the back to pull him off BC. McEntyre drops BC's collar. When McEntyre's arms come down, Edwards shifts his hold. He wraps his arms around McEntyre, pinning his arms at his sides, holding him in a steady bear hug.

Wow, Edwards didn't look that big at first. That looks like some law enforcement style hold he's got on him, too. Let's hear it for proper training. And good reflexes.

"Let me go, Marc!"

"Daniel!

"Let me go, Marc! They're the killers!"

"C'mon, Daniel, calm down before I gotta call security..."

"Marc!"

Edwards doesn't say anything. He doesn't relax his hold on McEntyre, until McEntyre finally relaxes and gives in. He stops fighting and sucks in some deep breaths.

"All right. I'm all right, Marc. You can let me go now. Just let me finish talking with you." Edwards relaxes his hold, and McEntyre steps back away from Edwards.

"I think you're finished now, Daniel. We'll talk more later when you're more together. Your loss has you distraught. You're not thinking right, right now, Daniel. We'll talk later. I'll call you."

"No! They're twisting you with their lies, can't you see that, Marc? Send me away now and they win, don't you see? Listen to this *priest*," he spits out the word with bitterness and sarcasm, " and they win! He's one of them! Why do you think here's here now, why do you think he came in here when we were talking? Huh? He didn't want me exposing the truth! He's a fake, a phony priest, and you're buying his shit! He's the real enemy! They're the enemy! And you're letting them win!"

Edwards just stares at McEntyre, eyes dead and emotionless.

"C'mon, Marc," McEntyre pleads again. Edwards calls out to his com.

"Security."

"Shit. You're letting them win, Marc," McEntyre stares at Edwards but points at BC as he turns to go. "You're selling out Luna, Marc. You're betraying Meredith and all she stood for."

An LSC guard enters the office.

"Take Mr. McEntyre to the infirmary and see that one of the meds gives him a sedative so he can sleep tonight. He's taking his wife's death very hard," Edwards says to the guard. Then he turns to McEntyre, "I'm sorry, Daniel. We can discuss this tomorrow. Please?"

McEntyre just storms out, the guard on his heels. The other LSC reenters with the requested reports.

What was her name? Nita something or other. Benzyne or something. Bendix! She's cute. Looks like trouble. I like that. Good trouble.

She tries to both stand at attention in front of Edwards desk and look behind her at the departing commotion.

"Officer Bendix, you'll pull a muscle if you twist yourself around any more than that." Edwards says.

BC smiles at her.

She blushes a little as she turns to entirely face Edwards.

"Sorry, sir. Here's the latest reports on the UIN ships, their disposition and their current position. Commander Cushman said to tell you they've stopped advancing and are holding position just beyond our more sensitive scanner's range."

Edwards takes the report from the LSC and looks it over. He dismisses her with a wave.

"Thanks. Get the door, would you?"

She turns, gives BC a little nod, and leaves, shutting the door behind her.

Edwards looks again at the report.

"I don't know. Maybe they're not here to do anything but establish a presence..."

"A rather threatening presence, don't you think? And maybe they're just waiting to see how you'll react, governor."

"Maybe. Hey, look, Father, I'm sorry about Daniel. He's not himself, what with everything and all. I'm sure he'll calm down with what the meds give him. I hope it calms him down. I've never seen him like that. Are you okay?"

"I'm fine, really. He's just lost his wife. It's natural for him to lash out in his anger and his pain. The McEntyre's weren't catholic?"

"No." Edwards gives a nervous chuckle, "hmph, as you've no doubt figured out by now, we won't be asking you to do the funeral tomorrow. They're agnostic. She was agnostic, I mean. He still is, I suppose, but, never mind, I'm babbling. It's been one hell of a day, if you'll excuse the "h" word, Father. Let's hope those ships stay put so we can at least get some rest tonight."

"I'm afraid I won't rest too well with them hanging out there waiting to pounce. I've been in places the UIN have attacked. I know what they can do. They can be merciless, Mr. Edwards. I don't think I'll rest too well with them out there."

"Sorry, Father. I'll let you know if there's any change. And I want you to know, I do appreciate your input about their tactics. But I've also learned not to trust either side in this war. You both have your blinders on. And, Father, if I may?"

"What?"

"All that stuff McEntyre was saying about you... was any of it true?"

"Huh. Well, sort of. It was pretty distorted. He may as well have blamed you for killing his wife so you could become governor, then called you a two-bit security hack with no right to govern the moon."

"Hey!"

"It's the same sort of distortion, see? I make no secret of the fact I come from the streets. I wasn't a traditional 'priest'. I did the Lord's work in my own way, with a small independent church that joined in the reunification, thereby making me a priest, as all we men and woman of God in each different variation of the faith came to be called. As for the rest, I work for the public relations arm of the Vatican, The Office of Papal Operations, or OPO, as some call it. There are some who spread rumors about the OPO, but we usually disregard them. The pen is mightier than the sword or the laser. We're spin doctors and diplomats, governor. There's the kernel of truth in everything he said, but it was cruelly twisted and distorted."

"But why did he know it at all? Why should he care about you at all, Father Campion?"

"I hesitate to offer my guess as to why."

"Why?"

"I don't want to sound paranoid."

"No, go ahead. Now I'm curious."

"I was thinking of Shakespeare. You ever read the Bard, governor?"

"No, I don't read. I've seen some of his plays in short form. Why?"

"Methinks he protesteth too much..."

"What?"

BC musters up all the false modesty he can and tries to sound convincingly uncertain.

"Usually, those things he said about the OPO? The UTZ controlling the Vatican and such? You hear that from UIN sympathizers. And to know details about a new Vatican functionary seems strange, unless he's gathering information on all UTZ personnel on Luna and just added my folder to his files... I'm sorry, that just sounds paranoid..."

Edwards shakes his head.

"I don't know, that does sound kind of farfetched, Father, if you'll pardon me for saying so. Besides, if he was with the UIN, why would they kill his wife?"

"I don't know, Mr. Edwards. I just don't know, and it doesn't make sense. Unless you know something else, too. There is something else I know that I really can't share too much of."

"What? Don't get all mysterious on me now, Father."

"Well, there is a confidentiality, a trust involved. To tell too much will expose the one who told me what she told me in the secrecy and trust of counseling. Suffice it to say Mr. McEntyre is not, sorry, was not, always faithful to his wife. Nor was he always kind and gentle with women... I fear I may have said too much already. You may know the woman who I learned this from, and she came to me for counsel once back on Earth expecting anonymity, after leaving here in disgrace."

"I think I do know the girl you mean. I heard what happened. I, um, won't say anything."

The room grows quiet.

Edwards mumbles, "But I am beginning to see your point."

Chapter Six

BC leaves the governor's office and heads for his rooms to rest.

It won't be easy to sleep with those UIN ships just hanging out there. Well, at least I've got Edwards starting to think our way... gave him a lot of food for thought. Let him chew on that all night. A little knowledge is a dangerous thing... I've planted some dangerous seeds. Let's see if they take root.

Back in his rooms, BC reviews the file on Daniel McEntyre.

You sir, are scum. No matter whose side you're on. Ah, fuck this for now.

He lies down with the lights off, tired, and tries to sleep.

I really don't like the idea of those UIN ships out there. I wouldn't put a surprise, sneak attack past them. There's probably a target on my back, if McEntyre's any indication of UIN suspicions. Sure was handy knowing about McEntyre's little flings. One of our men took that girl's tearful confession, and now I've used her just like McEntyre did. I think I feel like I should feel worse. But, you know, I don't want to think a lot about what I feel. I don't want to think about it so much, I just want to sleep, just turn it off... gotta try to get some sleep...

BC tosses and turns through a restless night. He rises early to get ready to face Daniel McEntyre again, this time at his wife's funeral.

Hope he's all doped up. I know, not so Christian of me, sorry. The guy bothers me. Good thing the church never took that love your enemies thing too seriously. I suppose if they did I wouldn't have a job...

Most of the representatives and dignitaries on Luna from Mars and Earth, and several orbital concerns, wait in the governor's reception hall for the funeral. BC surveys the crowd as he makes his way to his seat. The crowd looks almost the same as the one yesterday morning, but the mood, the dress and the whole general atmosphere is darker, subdued, more hopeless.

Hmm. Looks like most of the UIN reps are still here, anyway. At least for now.

Those who had gathered for peace just a day earlier now gather to bury the embodiment of the hope for that peace. And, most likely, to bury any hope with her.

Still, it had to be done. Otherwise the war would have gone the wrong way. The other way. She provided only false hope, or hope for the UIN, I suppose.

Space in the reception hall is at a premium, so the general public cannot attend, but several recorders carry the funeral live to millions on the Moon, in orbit, back on Earth, and maybe even on Mars. BC is privileged to attend beside the Cardinal. They watch as Edwards officiates a short ceremony, followed by a clearly drugged Daniel McEntyre being assisted by an LSC...

...that Nita woman again...

...as he takes the cylinder containing his wife's ashes over to the emergency airlock built into the reception room. Its alarms have been silenced for the occasion. He opens the inner door, places the ashes inside, then closes the door again and cycles shut the airlock. An LSC Officer out on the surface of the moon opens the airlock from the outside, removes the cylinder and, closing the airlock behind him, turns to bound across the surface to a launcher of some kind set up on the surface and pointing out into deep space. The LSC drops the cylinder in, then bounds back to the airlock.

Daniel McEntyre is directed to the launch switch, presses it, and sends his wife's ashes off into the stars.

There are poems and music, but they all wash over

BC. He's studying the people, especially Daniel McEntyre.

Edwards must have him on some hard stuff. Looks like we do win this one. Still depends on what they plan on using those ships out there for.

Edwards seems nervous.

I worry about Edwards. He's not holding up so well. Not as hard as he'd like to seem.

After the funeral, Edwards calls BC aside.

"Father! Father Campion!"

"Good morning, governor. Not too much good about it, though, I suppose."

"No. A sad day. Daniel was still not doing so well this morning, so he's still under medical supervision."

So I noticed...

"Do you have a few minutes? I'd like to talk to you in my office."

BC and the governor go into the governor's office. Edwards reassures him right off.

"The ships are still holding the same position. That's not what I want to talk about."

"Okay."

"I contacted the UIN after you and I spoke last night."

"Really. Was that wise?"

"Hell, I don't know. Figured it was worth a try. No offense to you."

"Don't worry about it."

"Anyway, I contacted them to demand justice, an explanation, or a denial over all this. I thought they deserved a chance to answer officially to all this."

"I guess you had to. What did they say?"

"That's what's strange. They didn't say much of anything, really. They just about blew me off. We're talking a major assassination here, and they seemed, I don't know, almost distracted."

"That is odd."

"They almost seemed like they were too busy to bother to answer. Just said their diplomatic office would send a reply shortly, thanks, bye."

"That's not a good sign, Mr. Edwards. Governor Edwards."

A low muffled boom shakes the room like a maraca.

"Neither is that!"

The com starts shouting.

"Governor, we are under attack! The UIN ships are spreading apart and firing at us!"

Edwards responds to the com, barking instructions, "Mount a counter offensive! Activate all defensive batteries. All Lunar Security to duty posts now! Order all residents in the direct path of the attack into shelters. Inform all others not to panic. Let them know that only those in the path of the assault are getting into the shelters right now. Got that?"

"Yes, sir."

Time to bring it home.

"I guess they've just been waiting to attack. They were too busy getting ready for the assault to even talk to you. Nice folks. At least they waited until after the funeral."

"Hard to know who your friends are these days, Father. Don't start thinking I trust you yet, either. You have been helpful, though, I'll give you that. Look, I've got to get to my command center. I'd like you to join me."

"Sure. I'd be honored to. But I've got to check on the staff of the Vatican Mission first. I want to be sure no one plays hero for no good reason, make sure everyone gets to the shelters. Then I'll join you."

"I'll make sure they clear you through. Thanks."

BC heads back to the Vatican Mission. He does send the stragglers he finds down to the shelter level, but then continues on his own way. Muffled booms followed by rough shaking continue sporadically.

The section is just about empty when BC gets back to his room. He locks the door. He reaches over to the air vent in the wall and works his fingers under the vent cover. He pops it off and pulls out his CCU, the OPO standard-issue Covert Communications Unit, the small box that lets him stay in touch with those back home. Time to finally contact

HQ, Vatican City, the actual Office of Papal Operations. He unfolds the CCU and it hums to life.

"Come on."

Something's wrong. The instalink isn't snapping on. The screen keeps flickering, lighting up and going out, trying to connect and disconnecting.

BC tries audio only, "Jove, Diana here, are we good? Keep sending tha..."

"Diana, this is Jove, we are under attack, I repeat, we are under direct attack.Try again later, Jove out." The screen blanks out one last time. Another serious vibration shakes the room.

The UIN has hit some church targets but never Vatican City itself. I can't believe they're hitting the old city! Do they know We iced McEntyre, or just suspect it? They had to have already been ready to go with this assault before we took her out, though, if they're here now. This could just be the UIN trying to expand the war.

The room's com unit comes on.

"Father Campion?"

Shit! It's Edwards.

"Yes, Governor?"

"Could you join me at the command center ASAP? Five minutes?"

"Sure. Just getting the last stragglers into the shelter. Be right there."

Another boom and vibration toss BC to the floor. He gets up, dusts himself off and starts to head out of his rooms.

They're targeting this section! Good time to leave! I've got to try the Vatican again, later, though. This is new UIN behavior. New and different. That always bothers me.

Chapter Seven

Vatican City is home to the newly unified Christian religion, The New catholic Church, small "c" intentional. The current Pope, Peter the Second, oversees a church brought together only five years earlier in the Great Reunification of 2104. The unified NcC is allied with the Earth-governing Universal Trade Zone, though the alliance has never been made public, never formally acknowledged. Pope Peter himself enjoys power equal to the directors on the ruling council of the United Trade Zone. But now thanks to the power of the NcC and their alliance with the UTZ, Vatican City is under siege by the Universal Islamic Nation.

The UTZ had pressed the Christian churches in the past to unite. They felt this would strengthen the UTZ hold on Earth, as the various Christian churches traditionally supported UTZ war efforts. Christians had been the targets of UIN terrorism many times. They generally supported the UTZ's policies against the UIN. The UTZ directors calculated that if the Christians united as one church it would focus their efforts, and their support would strengthen and help sustain the UTZ. But they underestimated the strength the unified church itself would wield. And so, as the churches united, the UTZ found itself sharing power with the new church rather than having power over it, a new equal voice among them. Especially since the elevation of Peter the Second three years earlier.

The old city has been home to Popes back to the first Peter. It was home to a rapid procession of popes right after the recent unification. All died in office, five pontiffs in two years, until Pope Peter came in under murky circumstances and restored stability.

Pope Peter the Second is the first black pope. His street preacher background brought a real change to the church. He began the Office of Papal Operations, the OPO, and turned it into his own elite force of assassins and saboteurs.

At first the OPO just took care of Peter's church "business", but soon Peter had the OPO taking care of some of the UTZ's dirty work covertly as well. Who would suspect a priest?

There's no doubt the UIN has suspected the church to be directly involved in the fight against them, but they possessed no proof. Perhaps until now, possibly leading to the current attack on Vatican City.

Orbital fighting platforms belonging to the UIN drop fighter bombers down through the clouds, which in turn drop their own payloads, fiery blossoms of orange, yellow and red that rip into and through the ancient structures of the Vatican.

The Vatican has few defenses. St. Peter's will be protected, this is certain, but not much else. UTZ forces have been requested, have been dispatched, are on the way, small comfort as another blast lifts the floor and drops it down again. Another ancient stone facade crumbles in the fighter bomber onslaught.

The OPO, the Pope's own men, are not equipped to handle such an assault. They are masters of subterfuge, not such blatant violence as this.

The sound of UTZ fighters arriving, and their ensuing blasts, sound like armies of avenging angels to Peter the Second. He's been readying a retreat to the Vatican Shelter, but has resisted to this point. With the UTZ arriving, his First will not have an easy time convincing him to retreat into the bowels of the earth.

"The UTZ is trying to repel this latest incursion by the UIN. The UIN are hitting many fronts at once, even the Moon. The UTZ security forces have their hands full, but they've managed to send a few squadrons in defense of

Vatican City. They're arriving just about now."

"Yes, yeah, I hear them. About time. At least they're here."

"We've already got report of heavy damage to some of the outer buildings. Our limited defense net is working, but can only dissipate so much energy. It's working overtime."

"What's happening on the Moon?"

"Our man there has been in touch, but we cut it short because both here and there were under attack. There was too great a risk of discovery, of them stumbling across our com."

"Have they been hit?"

"Sounded like it, but he was all right. And it looks like McEntyre is dead, and the Moon is blaming the UIN. This new attack should only reinforce Luna's suspicions."

"Campion does good work."

The First chuckled.

"Yes, sir, yes he does. But then, he does the Lord's work..."

"Yes, he does, doesn't he at that.

"You said the UIN is attacking on many fronts. Where else besides here and the Moon?"

"New York, Vienna, London and Tokyo are all reporting attacks. There have been reported terrorist bombings in Lima and Berlin. It's pretty widespread."

"Any pattern yet?"

The ground shook again, knocking both men sideways. The lights go out, then come back on again.

"We're still analyzing the information, sir. Your eminence, we should get out of here. This attack will pass, but we're still in danger now. Let's get out of here."

"No sense of adventure, First?"

"I'd like to think of it as a sense of self-preservation, sir. Instinct, maybe."

"Very well, let's go. Order all staff to the shelters. Let's get going, then."

The First opens the door for Peter, then follows him out as they leave the office for the shelter.

In the now-empty Pope's office a com unit's incoming alert light pulses red.

Where are they?

BC had started for the door, had meant to go see Edwards, but decided at the last second to double back to try the Vatican again. The CCU is just sputtering, no connection.

"Jove, this is Diana, are you there?"

"Campion? I thought you were already on the way here?" That's Edwards on the room intercom, not the office back on earth. Wrong answer. Not the one he's been waiting for.

What did Edwards hear over the com?

"Please report to Luna Operations immediately. Edwards out."

Shit.

His CCU isn't working. He's getting no response from the Vatican. He tries signaling them one more time. Then something feels wrong, the air in the room shifts.

The door is open.

In the open doorway, looking at BC and the com unit, stands the LSC he'd knocked out earlier. The cute one, Nita something.

She's recording him! She has some kind of recording device focused on him and his com unit.

Shit again!

How long has she been there?!

BC dives at her. She turns and runs and BC hits the door as it closes behind her.

He gets up and tries to get out after her. The door won't open.

Great, she jammed it! I can get it open, but, damn, that's getaway time.

BC pulls his handlaser, blasts the lock, and the door opens. He races out into the hallway, looks both ways. Muted thuds and echoing explosions sound around him, but the LSC isn't in sight. He runs to his left, out toward the perimeter of this section of Reagan Station. She'd probably head out rather than in to the city center, it offers more routes to take and get lost in.

She's just ducking around another corner when BC spots her. She's doubling back towards the center, towards the main atrium.

Gotcha.

BC runs after her. Down a long sloping corridor towards the main dome, then to the left, around the area environmental treatment center. She runs out into the main mall, into the atrium.

When he turns the corner into the dome BC tucks away his handlaser and tries to look like a priest as he crosses through the crowd, moving as fast as he can without attracting undo attention, trying to keep the LSC always in sight. She bumps and dodges her way through the dome, crowded with panicky residents trying to figure out where to go to escape the UIN assault. Her uniform makes her rapid transit through the mall look natural.

BOOM! BOOM-BAH-BOOM-DOOM!

Several people scream, distraut in blind panic, as distant blasts shake the foundation of the station. BC looks around as he dodges through the crowd, hoping he doesn't look too out of place racing after her.

If they even notice me, maybe they'll think it's a church emergency. Last Rites or something. Hey, that's kinda funny, I'll give her last rites...

She's ducking down one of the remote access tunnels!

BC tries to casually edge up to the doorway to the access tunnel. He looks around.

Good. No one seems to be paying me too much attention. She could be right inside that tunnel just waiting to blast me. Gotta be careful.

He sneaks a peek around the tunnel door's edge. The LSC is still running down the tunnel. BC ducks into the tunnel, pulls his handlaser back out and blasts a shot towards her feet.

"Hey! Stop!" BC yells.

She looks back once at BC, then runs faster.

BC follows her down the tunnel. At an airlock the tunnel branches off from the main buildings to run independently across the lunar surface. The airlock is closing, shutting off the tunnel as BC gets there. He manages to reverse the door function and opens the door back up. Before it's even fully open he jumps through. He stops the airlock from cycling, opens the door on the airlock's other side and runs on down the tunnel.

The tunnel runs across the lunar surface to some outer buildings. The tunnel is shaped like a hexagon, with the three top panels clear. He can see the lunar surface on both sides and the stars above. UIN ships flash overhead, blocking out the stars as they approach and fire at the buildings, as BC runs along the tunnel.

Looked like that last ship was over our section. They're probably targeting the Vatican holdings here, too. Hard to tell for sure from here.

There she is!

Another airlock closes in BC's face. He can see the LSC through the closing door as she runs on ahead. He tries to remember the structural diagrams he studied preparing for this assignment.

These independent surface tunnels on the Moon have airlocks every hundred feet or so, as a safety measure. Damned inconvenient measure...

BC reverses the door function again.

This tunnel leads out towards the remote landing facility, if I remember right. Where the hell is she going? This running isn't normal Lunar Security behavior. Of course, neither is recording me in my room. She's more than LSC, probably a UIN spy! A cute little spy, but UIN all the same. Where is she going?

Another thought occurs to BC as he turns a corner and runs along the access tunnel.

I wonder if she's the one who took my clothes? Gotta wonder why she was there in the first place, now.

The tunnel continues on, out past the most distant launching area. The curve of the tunnel prevents BC from getting a clear shot at her.

What was her name? Nita Bendix? And I thought she was nice. Sure, BC, all spies are nice. It's their job. You're nice. On the outside.

The LSC reaches a large juncture ahead, a major airlock. It's a small, sealable room joining their tunnel with two other tunnels. She gets in and closes the airlock, closes off BC. He catches up at the airlock door and tries to reverse the door's function.

She's jammed the controls. They're frozen. He can see her inside the airlock, working to open one of the other doors. BC tries to force the door. It won't budge.

If I blast the door, the safety features might not let me get through. I could lose all the air in this tunnel, too. Damn! Have to short it, somehow.

BC opens the maintenance panel next to the door and rewires the door lock.

Still nothing.

He narrows and focuses the beam on his handlaser and uses it to do some quick and messy soldering. The door hisses open.

BC steps into the airlock juncture. The door behind him slides back into place. The LSC is already gone, through one of the two doors in front of BC.

Yeah, but which one?

Like the tunnels, the upper half of the airlock juncture is transparent. BC can see out through the top part of the juncture into the two tunnels ahead. The LSC is in the right tunnel, leading even further out across the lunar surface. There's an outbuilding ahead, nothing else. The end of the line.

BC tries to open the door to the tunnel. She's jammed the door once more.

Naturally.

BC notices something else out beyond the outbuilding, hovering just above the Moon's surface.

A UIN bomber! Shit! Right on top of us here! That can't be an accident! She is way too hot! If she was only a humble

LSC she would've stopped, filed a report, and had me brought in already. She's gotta be UIN. No way around it. Deep cover spy. The bomber clinches it.

The UIN bomber begins firing at the juncture and BC. All BC sees is a bright blue flash.

BOOM!

That was right next to me! Shit. C'mon door, open! Got to get to her. Hope she's not too expendable to them. Then they won't fire on me, if I'm right there next to her.

BOOM!

Another one, damn close. C'mon door... Nice!

The door hisses open. BC races through the door, turns just long enough to close it behind him.

BOOM!

The UIN ship's fire hits the juncture, throwing BC forward down the tunnel on his face and stomach.

"Explosive bolts to detonate in five seconds," A computer's voice says.

She's turned the explosive bolts on! Fuck me! They'll blow this tunnel right off the juncture! Blow it wide open, too. Wonderful!

The LSC is gone. She went through the door at the tunnel's end, into the outbuilding. BC gets up and runs down to the door to the outbuilding. Another jammed door.

She jammed the door and set the explosive bolts on this end of the tunnel, too. Not very creative, but certainly effective.   I will get through this door... How about a little help here, big guy?

BOOM! Then another BOOM and hissing as the UIN Bomber fires again and the explosive bolts fire at the juncture end of the tunnel, and the tunnel starts detaching from the juncture.

I have to get through... through!

The door swings inward into the outbuilding and BC dives through as the tunnel starts collapsing behind him. Another BOOM! throws him hard against the floor of the outbuilding.

It's a storage bunker, a long building with a row of

windows on each of the long sides and doors on the shorter ends. BC struggles to get up. He leans on the door he fell through, trying to both close it and stand up at the same time. The hatch clanks into place.

Through the windows BC can see the UIN ship hovering just outside the storage bunker.

The motherfuckers are landing!? What the...

Oh, precious. There she goes...

The LSC is suited up outside the other end of the storage bunker. He sees her walk to the UIN ship. She gets in and the ship takes off, leveling blasts at the juncture, the tunnel, and the storage bunker as it heads out.

BC hits the ground, but the bunker remains intact.

"Air supply approaching minimal, dropping rapidly," a computer voice informs him.

"Damn, where are the controls..." BC is talking to himself, but the bunker's computer answers.

"The controls are located next to each doorway of this storage facility. Air supply is nearly exhausted."

BC runs down to the other door.

It's jammed OPEN! What a bitch!

BC fights to breathe as he tries to shut the airlock door. He can feel the air being ripped from his lungs, the strain of trying to breathe greater and greater as he struggles to close the door. Finally he works the door closed, and the computer speaks at him again.

"The atmosphere of this bunker is no longer being released. There is, however, only five minutes of breathable air for one person remaining in this bunker. Four minutes fifty-nine seconds, four-fifty eight, four fifty-seven, four fifty-six..."

"Computer off! Wait, computer..."

"Computer on. Four minutes fifty seconds..."

"Cease countdown!"

"Countdown has been halted. The air supply continues to run out, however."

"Thanks. Thank you so much. Establish communications with Edwards, Marc."

"Unable to comply. Communications from this location have been disabled."

"Damn!"

"Air supply now at three minutes."

"I ordered the countdown off."

"The countdown continues silently for your safety. Also for your safety, you will be informed of the silent countdown at one-minute intervals."

"Does that make any sense?"

No answer.

BC stops arguing with the computer and surveys the storage bunker's contents. Seven EVA suits. BC checks each of them. They're all ripped and damaged beyond easy repair. Every air unit is emptied, gauges on red. The LSC planned ahead well.

BOOM!

BC's thrown to the floor by another blast.

Damn UIN ship must be taking one last shot before they get out of range. Hope I live just to spite them. Uh-oh, I'm not doing so good here...

BC tries to get up, falls back to the floor, face against the bottom of the bunker. He looks up, out the window, looking for the UIN ship. Just as he starts to black out, he sees something else. A different ship. It looks human, but not UIN or UTZ.

Huh? What's that? Am I hallucinating?

"Computer, contact that ship! S.O.S.!"

BC goes out. Out cold.

After a time, he slowly, groggily, begins to wake up.

Where am I? On a ship. Looks like an LSC transport. How'd I get here?

"Wha?" BC tries to speak but his tongue feels three feet wide.

"Easy there, Padre. We're getting you back to Reagan Station. Don't know how you ended up out here... you get lost during the raid? Don't answer, you've got aftervac syndrome going on, a touch of it anyway. A lot of your surface capillaries burst... your tongue's gonna be swollen for a few days, and you'll look like one giant bruise for a bit, but you're lucky we got to you when we did."

"Howthdidyoufinthme," BC tries to ask. Damn tongue.

How did you find me? Why even look?

"We got a coded military alert to come get you. Thought it was the UTZ, but I don't know. I'm not supposed to know, you know? Somebody up there likes you, Father."

Chapter Eight

BC is laying on a couch in the Cardinal's office, basking in the warm glow of sympathy from The Cardinal and Governor Edwards, and obsessively wondering who could've saved him.

I should be dead. That's a sobering thought. But someone did save me. Maybe that last ship. It had no markings. I've never seen anything like it before. It could have just been a hallucination, but then why am I still here? What's he saying?

Edwards has been talking, "...and we're all surprised she was able to maintain her cover for so long. We're lucky you found her communicating with the UIN ships when you did. You probably stopped more killings."

BC motions for the styli and screen to write his response.

I can still spin it my way, as long as I can write...

"She was very nice to me," BC writes, "I'd never had guessed she was a UIN Agent."

"She seemed to like you, Father Campion," the Cardinal offers, reading BC's response.

"She did at that," Edwards adds, "probably just looking for information."

BC erases, writes and turns the screen so the others can read it, "Ouch!"

"You should rest, my boy," the Cardinal says. "You found the killer! It had to be her! The whole attack was just to get her out of here!"

Jeesh, the Cardinal should work for the OPO... he's doing my job for me! Not that I can't use the help just now.

"Too bad you couldn't hold her. She did quite a job on you."

BC holds his "Ouch!" back up again.

Edwards laughs. "I value your help, Father Campion," BC tries to protest, Edwards corrects himself, "I mean, BC. But you shouldn't have tried to chase her down yourself. You should have called in Lunar Security."

BC erases the screen, writes, "She was LSC. Who could I trust?" and holds it up.

"She was an exception, BC, not the rule... Never mind. You need some rest. Near vacuum is no fun! All you can really do is rest up and get better. Thanks for trying to help."

BC erases, writes, and holds up, "You're welcome!"

"He'll be fine with some rest," the Cardinal says. "Your excellent medical staff worked on him for hours. Now it's time for prayer, time to let the Lord do His work,"

"Yeah. Well, thanks again, BC. We'd never have suspected the UIN had infiltrated our security forces. It's disturbing. I don't know how Governor McEntyre could have let this happen."

BC erases his screen, writes, "Remember what I told you. She might have known."

Edwards shook his head, "I still don't know about that, Father Campion. This all has happened so fast, I don't know what to think. Plus, I've got a moon to run now. I'm a little overwhelmed. You're a little injured. Let's talk about this when we can both talk some more, huh?"

BC nods. Edwards turns and leaves BC alone with the Cardinal.

"You should get some rest, Father Campion. Stay here on the couch if you like. Your rooms were pretty badly hit. Stay here for the time being. I'll have someone look in on you. You know, I don't think we've heard the end of this one, Father Campion."

I know we haven't. This is only the beginning, Cardinal. Only the beginning.

Chapter Nine

BC lies in pain on the couch in the Cardinal's study.

Stuck here for more than a week, now. This sucks.

The study is quiet. BC turned off the entertainment center a few minutes ago to listen to Luna Prime, to listen to the sounds of a station alive: the barely audible murmur of people passing outside the study doors; the low-pitched hum of the environmental systems keeping the air fresh and warm like Vatican City on a sunny spring day. And every so often, the entire place trembles and a humming, bass-y buzz is added to the other more constant sounds as a ship passes overhead.

Luna City is vastly more entertaining than the so-called entertainment center. All the same crap, all the time. Stupid UTZ advertising, most of it. Buy this, buy this, and of course, buy this.

BC stares at a painting of a black Jesus, one of many varied portraits and interpretations of Jesus Christ that hang on the walls of the study.

Wonder where the Cardinal bought this stuff? That painting there's a hundred years old, if I read the date right.

Next to the black Jesus on the wall, to the right, is an ancient Orthodox icon of a bleached white Jesus with pinched cheeks dressed like an eastern bishop. To its left hangs a gory medieval oil painting of Jesus on the cross, bleeding and writhing in agony.

Man, I can sympathize! Okay, I don't have nails through my hands and feet, or a spear in my side. I only feel as if my skin had been pierced by nails, every inch of it, all over! This sucks, but in all fairness, I suppose it's not as bad as a crucifixion... I'm still alive, anyway. Gotta be realistic.

But I've never felt this kind of pain before, and all over, too! I don't think I have any part that doesn't hurt. My mouth still tastes metallic. And my tongue's still swollen.

I did almost get killed out there.

I still don't know how I survived. Not much has come back to me, not really, not even after three days. But my surviving might have had something to do with that ship I saw.

That ship out there I didn't recognize, hovering outside just before I passed out. It was further off than the UIN ship, out beyond the limits of Luna Prime. The UIN ship didn't seem to detect it. Probably too busy blowing me up to notice.

I've checked through the station records and port authority logs to try to find some record of the ship. There is no record of it. Nothing at all. It could have been a hallucination, except that this hallucination may have saved my life. Whoever they were must have let someone know something or I would be dead! The LSCs who picked me up got a call from someone. Maybe it was them. But, then, why save me?

Man, I am tired of not being able to talk! Tired of writing everything I want to say down, too. Thank you for all this, Miss Nita Bendix, wherever you are. Whoever you are. Thank you so much. Lovely woman.

"How are you, BC?"

Governor Edwards stands in the doorway to the Cardinal's study.

BC grabs his stylus and screen and writes, "Fine," and holds it up for Edwards to read as he walks in.

"Great! They told me you were doing better. Told me you still couldn't talk, but they did say you should be up and about in the next day or two. Maybe even talking by then, too."

BC nods.

"I just wanna apologize again for, well, your being almost killed by one of our people."

BC writes, "Thanks. Again."

"I'd like to treat you to lunch when you're all better."

BC tries to laugh, writing, "Wow, makes up for everything (sarcasm)."

Edwards almost seems hurt, "Hey look, Father, I'm just trying to..."

BC waves his arms, writes, "JOKING!" and holds it up. He shrugs, then writes, "Thank you. Next week?"

"Sure. Next week'll be good. I really just wanted to stop by and see how you were. I really feel kind of embarrassed. I feel bad that someone we trusted betrayed us, and you, too, obviously. We trusted someone we shouldn't have."

BC writes, "I'll survive," shows Edwards, then writes, "I'm still here!"

"Good! Next week for lunch, then."

"Get better, BC," Edwards says, and leaves.

BC shifts on the couch, trying to get comfortable, but everything is sore.

Ouch! Everything hurts. Can't even really laugh. God, I can't wait until I can talk again! Got to report in to the Vatican, too. I sent them a coded written report, but it's short on detail. I've got to talk to them, explain things. I'm sure they want some answers. I need to ask some questions, too. I've seen the news reports.

The Universal Islamic Nation's recent attacks on the Earth and the Moon were repelled with some success, but according to news reports the Vatican took a beating, hardest hit of all the Earth targets. And of the areas on the Moon that were hit, their section, the Vatican Mission, was hit the hardest. BC's rooms were nearly wiped out.

They're now attacking the Vatican directly. The UIN has finally decided that the New catholic Church is provably, beyond a doubt, in bed with the Universal Trade Zone. Well, duh. It's been a long time coming. The OPO's been working with the UTZ for what, five, six years? I gotta hope no one I know was injured in the attacks. Gotta find out more, check in with Pope Peter. Wonder what the old man's take on all this is. We are definitely being targeted. Strange behavior from the UIN these days.

I really don't think these attacks were in response to the McEntyre Assassination. They came too soon after. Their ships had to be on their way here well before I did the hit. Good timing, though. Thanks to the proper spin, the public thinks they killed the governor. Beautiful!

The news reports on McEntyre's assassination have been decidedly positive for the UTZ and the Vatican. Nita Bendix has been cast as the assassin, the betrayer.

She makes a great scapegoat, running just when it attracted the most suspicion and blame.

The Cardinal enters the study.

"How are we today, Campion? Better?"

For the hundredth time, BC writes, "Fine" on his screen, and holds it up for the Cardinal to see.

"Good, then, good! Better and better each day, eh? We've got you in the daily prayers at Mass, Father. There's some good folks praying for you. I do have some bad news, though. The UIN has attacked the Vatican again, earlier today! Pope Peter is fine, but they've damaged more of the priceless architecture of Vatican City. They're barbarians!"

Again?! Well, this one they might blame on me...

BC writes, "Anyone hurt?"

"There were a few casualties," the Cardinal pauses, thinking, "Oh yes, and the OPO called for you! I told them you were injured, couldn't speak. They'd like you to check in with them when you can talk again."

Wow, if the OPO is contacting the Cardinal to get to me they must be desperate! This new attack, probably. They must figure it's Bendix getting back to the UIN with her "proof", exposing us. I've gotta talk to the home office, see where I stand, make my case.

"Did you hear me, Campion?"

BC nods.

"Did you know, the UIN is maintaining a media blackout? They still haven't said word one to anybody about any of this. 'Unusually Silent' the reports are all saying. Bloody Muslims. Probably just trying to 'cultivate mystery'. Keep quiet except for blowing us up."

BC nods again. The Cardinal seems to enjoy the fact BC can't answer back.

"Their 'jihad', hmmph, all that hatred for us Christians. Supposedly, they worship the same God as we do. They're supposed to. But Allah doesn't sound like Our Father, if you know what I mean."

BC shrugs.

What can I say? Nothing, obviously.

"You know Campion, I like these one sided conversations. Almost enjoy your silence! Ha, too bad you'll be talking again in no time... I'm kidding, of course, Campion!

"Laughter is the best medicine, so they say! I'll check in again later."

Wonderful. Just ducky. Can't wait...

Chapter Ten

Time passes slowly for BC. The next two days seem to take at least a year to go by. All he can do is watch video or stare at the walls, the red and gold, the pictures of Jesus from all the world's faiths. The Cardinal's study is fine, but it's not his style.

Finally, after two days, an LSC comes to the Cardinal's study with the news BC's rooms are ready. BC is up and able to walk short distances, and walks himself back to his quarters.

The glare from the gold on the walls of that study was beginning to hurt my eyes and give me headaches... Thank God I'm finally getting back into my own rooms. Can't talk right, yet. But I've still gotta try to get through to the Vatican.

BC opens the door to his stateroom and gasps. His Covert Communications Unit is out in plain sight, sitting on his folded-out desk. It's sealed tight, looks like a small chest.

The repair crews probably didn't know what it was when they came across it. But seeing it just sitting out there in the open made my heart jump a beat.

He surveys the rooms, his surroundings. They've done okay, though he can see several spots where panels were replaced and seals rejoined. His bedroom is entirely new construction.

Would have been bad dreams if I'd been here when they hit. Good thing I got to go on that wild goose chase. Right. Sure.

BC sweeps the room for bugs and sets a scrambler. He can't be sure there *weren't* UIN agents in the construction crew.

Never can be too paranoid in this business.

The room checks out clean. He opens up and switches on the CCU. The screen lights up with the waiting pattern. He opens the voice channel, turns on the visual.

"Jove, this is Diana, are you receiving?"

A face appears on the screen, an old black man wearing a white skullcap and robes. Pope Peter the Second.

"Well, hello, Diana, I was walking by the receiver as you signaled in. Nice of you to finally call. You know it's not nice of you not to call your father once in a while. Especially your holy father."

Holy shit! The old man himself!

"Hello, sir. Good to see you. I haven't been able to speak, you see..."

"Yes, yes, heh, you sound like you've been drinking! Don't worry about it. I heard all about your accident from the Cardinal. Now... what's the real story?"

BC tells him about Nita Bendix recording him as he called in on his CCU, his chase after her, and her escape on the UIN ship. He decides to keep the unknown ship to himself, for the time being.

Peter stays silent, considering, as BC spins his tale. There's a long silence after BC finishes. Then the pope rebukes him.

"They know you did the hit, Campion, they must, or they wouldn't be hitting us back."

"With all due respect, sir, they were already on their way to hit us, before I even did the hit. The timing is wrong. One couldn't have triggered the other because they were already on their way to attack."

"Is that so? That may be true for that first attack, but, as you've probably heard by now, they've hit us again, just last night. By now there's been certainly enough time for them to have digested the information that woman must have brought to them. *You've* brought them down on us this time!"

"I'm... I'm sorry, sir. But it's not my fault entirely, sir, You know this is certainly a situation that's been brewing..."

Pope Peter cuts him off, "Did she get anything else?"

"Well, I'm not sure, sir. She might have."

"How so?"

"Well, when I was coming up from the access tunnels after doing the hit, I hit her with a hatch door I was opening. I thought I hit her over the head and knocked her out, at the time. I thought it was just random coincidence, that she was in the wrong place at the wrong time when I kicked the hatch in. It was the first time I had ever seen her. I wondered why a Lunar Security Cop was there, figured she was on rounds. Now, obviously, I can't be sure of any of that."

"This is bad, BC my boy. They may have you. Your entire mission could be compromised. Your cover could be blown entirely. I thought you were better than this."

Holy Shit.

"Pope Peter, sir, look, they haven't even said anything. They're maintaining media silence. Wouldn't they have blown this open? If they had me on this, they'd be broadcasting it loud and proud, getting all the mileage they could out of it. Their silence says they don't have anything more than they've had before, even if they're attacking us straight on. C'mon, sir, you know I'm better than that. Father, forgive me!"

"Don't get cute on me, boy, I won't have it," Peter snaps at BC.

"Sorry. But it's not right to pin this all on me!"

"Of course it isn't. But I've been wanting to blame somebody, and you're elected. Plus, you've been incommunicado, and that's been frustrating. I had to let you have it.

"Tough love, my boy. Tough love," the old man chuckles to himself, then looks BC in the eye across the miles.

"Look, your cover may well be blown, BC. They may just be waiting, holding on to the information, holding on to any damaging evidence they have, waiting until the most damaging moment possible to let it out."

"Then why not now, to justify their attacks, to turn the tide in the war by making us out to be murderers?"

"I don't know. We can't know, can't be sure. But they are hitting NcC targets. They've got to know about Vatican involvement in UTZ war efforts, BC."

"With all due respect, sir, who doesn't?"

Pope Peter lets out a small laugh. "Some know we are involved... but most could never guess to what extent. If you've opened us up, exposed us, the general public most likely will not understand or sympathize with our means to achieving their ends."

"So, then... what now? Should I come back?"

"No! No, that would be suspect, too suspicious. What I want you to do right now is forget about the OPO, just for the time being, and get under your cover, completely. For the time being, I want you to be the best Public Relations flack the Moon has ever seen! Issue some press releases, follow the Cardinal around every day, accompany him to every event. Be the spin doctor you're supposed to be!"

"I guess I can do that, sir."

"You will do that, Campion, those are your orders, make no mistake. In the meantime, I'll have the office find you some low-key, low profile assignments that keep you off the UIN radar. All they'll see is the public you, the flack-hack.

"We'll be in touch soon, Diana. Jove out."

"Diana Out."

Damn. This is gonna suck. Tough love, my ass. By Jove.

Chapter Eleven

Two weeks. Two Fucking Weeks!

BC has heard nothing from the OPO in two weeks.

In the two weeks, the Vatican's been hit one more time, another barrage as fierce as the last two, another UIN sneak attack. The Moon has not been hit again.

BC has done his PR flack job, standing loyally by the Cardinal's side, issuing four press releases in the two weeks, and generally playing his role as the Vatican PR Man.

He's laid low, not even taking the governor up on his lunch invite as of yet. And with the OPO out of touch, BC's only been getting the UTZ approved version of events from the news reports.

The UIN continues its media blackout. The media speculates on the motives behind the UIN attacks. Most news reports attribute the new wave of UIN attacks, including the hits on the Vatican, to further religious extremism on the part of the UIN. The analysts, warning against repeating the mistakes of the past, say the UIN has gone beyond politics, bringing religion into the war.

But it's always been in it, religion has. It's what it's been all about. Well, religion and money. Nothing changes. We're still savages, cavemen in nicer pelts, when you get right down to it, no matter how much technology we use, no matter how far into space we go. Cavemen in space. Heh, like that one. Clubbing each other over the head with our high tech clubs.

Ah, yet another fun-filled day of flackery...

As he enters the Cardinal's office he sees the Cardinal is waiting for him.

"Ah, Campion, good. You're a wanted man today, you know."

Wanted? What the fuck?

"What?"

"Yes, you see, the Pope himself has requested a call from you. And the Governor says you're supposed to do lunch sometime, and he'd like to know if you can meet him today. You're wanted by some pretty fancy company, Campion."

You bastard. Wanted, my ass. No need to scare me like that.

"Thank you, sir. Would you excuse me?"

"Certainly."

"I'll check back with you later, Cardinal."

BC heads back to his rooms to check in with the Vatican, his heart beating faster than normal.

Wanted! Geesh, when he said that I felt my stomach flip. Didn't think it was the good kind of wanted. Getting too paranoid. Hope it doesn't show.

Glad to hear the Vatican finally called. Through the Cardinal again. Must be to keep up appearances. God, I hope there's a new assignment! And I guess I really should have lunch with Edwards. He's not so bad. I actually kind of like the guy.

Cardinal M'Bekke answers when BC powers up the CCU and contacts the Vatican. M'Bekke is an old friend of BC's, one of his first instructors in the OPO.

"Campion! How are you? I heard you got banged up pretty good?"

"I'm okay, M'Bekke, I've had some time to heal. Seems like years..." BC plays up a yawn for dramatic effect.

"Well, this should cure your boredom. I have an assignment for you."

"Am I coming back to Earth?"

"No, we want to keep you in your current PR assignment on the Moon for now. The less waves you make, the better. We still don't know how much the UIN knows about you."

"So, then... What? Another assignment here on the Moon? Wouldn't that be just as risky?"

"No, not on the Moon, or on Earth. We need you to

66

travel from Luna to one of the old orbital stations. Used to belong to the Sultan of Brunei."

"No kidding? Who's it belong to now?"

"Nobody, really. It's been officially deserted for years. Place is called Fortune Station, built almost a hundred years ago. We're sending complete info via courier, already on the way. Look for a package tomorrow."

"So, if nobody's there, why are you sending me there? There are easier ways to get rid of me, M'Bekke!" BC laughs.

"BC, would we ever do something like that to you?" M'Bekke says in a falsely sweet tone, then laughs, "Don't answer!"

"Flattery will get you nowhere..."

M'Bekke's tone darkens, "The station's been taken over by a Neo-Christian cult. They've been squatting the station for over five years."

"A cult, huh? What do you want me to do, evict them? Why now?"

"We don't care who lives there. But their leader has become a threat."

"How so?"

"He's a charismatic former Cardinal whose followers are devoted to him. His radical interpretation of the Bible marginalized him back in the nineties in the Roman Catholic Church, part of the whole back to the roots thing ten years ago. Something in him snapped during the reunification and he broke away from the church. He later gathered his followers and left Earth for Fortune Station, after Al-Salid declared Jihad on the Earth."

"So, they've been there five years?"

"Just over."

"Guess they'll know the place pretty well by now. Are there any plans, blueprints, anything?"

"Yeah, the courier has them."

"So, you want me to take this guy out?"

"Basically. But, Campion... "

"Yeah? I don't like the sound of that 'but', M'Bekke..."

"We've already sent two other operatives in. We

haven't heard from them. It's been a month since the last one went in. They might still be alive in there, we just don't know. The place is pretty isolated, high orbit, sealed up pretty tight. His followers are probably his best defense, and we don't know how many of them he has up there with him. There's a lot of unknowns."

"Sounds like. You sure you're not just trying to get rid of me? You still haven't really explained why he's a threat. Good cover for tying up my loose end..."

"No. We want this man gone. We hear he's killing his followers. He's probably killed our two guys, too. We don't know where his loyalties lie, and the feeling here is that he may throw in with the UIN, give them a base to work from in exchange for territory somewhere on Earth after the war. After we're all dead. If he's killing his followers I'd say he's capable of anything."

"Why do people follow people who kill them in the name of God?"

"I don't know... but we certainly don't want to get into a discussion on the morality of killing in the name of God now, do we, BC?"

BC shakes his head in agreement as M'Bekke continues.

"We've hired a ship to take you to the station. The details are in the package. The pilot's a good NcC man. Treat him well."

"Did this same guy bring the others to the station, too?"

"No. The other operatives left from Earth. This pilot and his ship are based out of Luna Prime. Why?"

"Just curious. And you say he's a Christian?"

"There are some of us up there, Campion. You should know! You're supposed to be ministering to them!"

"Thanks, M'Bekke, I'll try to remember that..."

"Be careful, BC. Don't blow your cover any worse than it's already been blown!"

"It's not... "

"Campion, please. This assignment will help you to

keep laying low."

"Or get me laid low."

"It's not you we want dead at the end of all of this."

"That's a comfort. What about just laid?"

"Funny. Watch for the package, Campion. Jove out."

"Diana out."

Two weeks before the Vatican finally calls back. Finally. And this is the best they can do? Two weeks of being the Cardinal's lackey.Two weeks of being a good little PR flack. Two weeks before they finally call back. Finally. Two weeks of waiting for my head to either implode or explode. And this is the best they can do? A wacked out cult leader on an old station out in the middle of nowhere. What kind of threat is that? A threat to me when I wade into the vipers nest to try to choke the life out of the king snake, that's what kind of threat it is. The Vatican doesn't want me dead, but I'm sure at this point they wouldn't mind somebody doing them the favor of my removal. Hope I can stay alive. Have to do some research of my own before that package arrives.

BC's contemplation is cut short by the buzz of his intercom. A priority signal punches through.

"Father Campion? BC? It's Marc Edwards... you available?"

"Audio only, com on. Um, sure, governor. Just a second."

"How about that lunch? I'd like to keep my promise."

Can't keep putting him off...

"Sure. Let me check the schedule to see if the Cardinal needs me anywhere, okay? Hold on." BC takes a deep breath.

Shouldn't snap at the governor. Not good.

"Sure, I'm okay today. When do you want to meet?"

"Could we make it soon? An early lunch? These days my schedule isn't entirely under my own control. I've got appointments jammin' me all afternoon. Why don't you come on over and meet me at my offices. We can head for this seafood place I know on the third level of the atrium, looks out over the central pool, really nice. How about it?"

"Sure, Governor, I'll be there in about twenty minutes. I'm still moving a little slow these days."

"All right. See you then."

BC packs away the CCU. He checks his appearance in the mirror then heads out to meet the governor. He crosses the main mall of the atrium as he walks from the Vatican section to Governor Marc Edwards's offices, taking in the smell of the fresh cut grass.

It almost smells like the outdoors here, almost like Earth. 'Course, on Earth the gravity makes the pine trees pointy cones. Here, they just shoot up, even all around. They look like big green brushes. Weird looking things. At least they smell right.

A monitor in the mall wall near the entrance to the Luna Prime government center blares a news report as BC passes.

"...has finally spoken, today claiming that it has been attacking Vatican City along with UTZ and Lunar holdings because it has proof the Vatican has been collaborating with the UTZ in attacking the UIN."

Oh Shit.

BC stops to watch the report.

"Most observers on Earth and the Moon are dismissing the UIN statements as attempts to deflect blame from the UIN themselves in the wake of the killing of Luna Governor Meredith McEntyre. This is the UIN's first statement since their intensified campaign against targets on the Earth and the Moon began after the governor's death two weeks ago. This latest round of finger pointing by the Universal Islamic Nation rings rather hollow in light of their recent activities. In other news..."

That's it? No hard facts, no mention of me, or the OPO, just general statements of blame? What do they know, then? What do they have?

BC keeps walking. When he gets to Edwards's offices, his secretaries send BC right in.

"BC! How are you? How's the tongue?"

Funny question. Guess he means well...

"I can talk again, thank you. How are you doing, Governor?"

"Call me Marc. I'm calling you BC, after all."

"Okay, Marc..."

"I found out something I thought you'd like to know. We did some digging on that 'Nita Bendix'. It was taken for granted she worked here, but she was never hired! It looks like she just showed up two years ago. She was never officially cleared as a Luna Security Cop. She had forged credentials, stolen uniform, the whole spy deal. She infiltrated, and she fooled us. We look and feel pretty stupid, here. I'm sorry, BC."

"Two years? And no one suspected a thing?"

"She's been on rosters and personnel charts. She was good. She came in right after McEntyre was sworn in, as far as we can pinpoint."

"That's some curious timing."

"I know. After everything you told me, that sorta stinks. I've got some of my good people looking into this. People I can trust, you know?

"Hey, let's get out of here, whadya say? You hungry?"

"Sure. You said seafood?"

The Captain's Table Restaurant on the main mall's third floor overlooks the atrium, the central pool and the pines. BC and Edwards sit at a table at the window. They speak of sports, recent movies, BC's recuperation and other small talk. Over the course of the meal, Edwards apologizes a few more times, which BC eats up along with his swordfish and salad.

I like this guy. He's real. In a way, I'm working him, working to build his confidence to my advantage, but the affection is genuine. He's a good man. I'll try not to fuck him over. Hope they don't ask me to.

Over coffee, Edwards asks, "BC, can I ask you a favor?"

"What is it?"

"Well... I could use the help of someone with your insights and experience. I know there's stuff you can't tell me, things we can't discuss…"

Edwards hold up a hand as BC starts to interrupt and protest.

"No, let me finish. I respect you, Father, and would appreciate anything you might be able to share with me, information wise; I don't expect to hear state secrets. But I'm hoping you can help me as a sort of unofficial advisor."

Wow. I can't believe I've gotten to him this completely. They'll be happy with this back home. Can't be over enthusiastic, though…

"I'm honored, Marc, I really am. I just don't think I can. The Bible isn't too big on letting a man serve two masters. I'm not sure the Vatican would approve, to be honest with you."

"I don't expect to be your 'master', BC. I'm looking for friendly advice and good counsel."

"This is unexpected, Marc. But I'd certainly like to help you. Tell you what. If the Vatican says it's okay, I'll be glad to give you any advice I can. I can tell, all politics aside, you're a good man, Marc. You'll be a great governor. I'd like to help you."

"Well, now *I'm* honored, BC. Thanks. Thank you. It means a lot to me. I'm still trying to get a handle on everything. This is not something I asked for."

"That's why you'll probably do a better job than someone who would ask for it! A lot of times the best leaders are the ones who are thrust into greatness, or have greatness thrust upon them, when they least expect it. Somebody famous said that. You're doing fine. How's that for counsel?"

"Don't flatter me, BC, just advise me. But thanks."

Now, I've got to explain my going away.

."Marc, I've got to take care of some business for the Pope in the next few days. There are always gonna be times I have to take off, and I can't and won't be able to tell you what I'm doing. You have to understand that. The cost of my cooperation, I suppose. And coming up is one of those times."

"I understand that, I think. Whatever help you can offer, BC, you know I appreciate it."

Edwards takes care of the check and stands to leave. "Thanks for lunch, Marc."

"Thank you, BC. I gotta run, but I'll be in touch. See you when you get back."

Unofficial Advisor to the Governor of the Luna Free State. That'll look good on the ol' resume. Not bad! I hope I can trust him. He seems to trust me. It doesn't feel like a setup. We'll see.

Back in his rooms BC does a little freelance research on Fortune Station. He checks in the history files. The computer gives him general background information.

"Many wealthy individuals began building orbital retreats in the early teens to escape perceived overpopulation on Earth. This "overpopulation" was mostly a marketing tool used to scare paranoid wealthy individuals into buying orbital getaways.

"At first, only the very wealthy could afford to build, staff and maintain these luxury stations. Most rotated to provide artificial gravity, using systems that required small crews to maintain and run them. These crews had to be fed and housed. The necessities of life had to be provided for on each station, for both the crew and the inhabitants. All these people had to live, eat and breathe on the station, an expensive proposition at the time given their level of technological advancement. In some cases, the crews were shipped on and off a station between long shifts, but this alternative was also costly."

"History off."
Too general.
"Anything on Fortune Station itself?"
"One Entry. Brief Description."

"Tell me about it."

"Fortune Station. Built in 2012 for the Sultan of Brunei. Abandoned by the sultan eight years later in 2020. Renovated and restored by STSC, LIC in 2028, absorbed by the United Trade Zone in 2031. Used on and off until the end of 2062, when it was again left abandoned. Its high orbit and off-the-beaten path location make it an unattractive target for future renovation and redevelopment. Fortune Station is currently still abandoned. End of entry."

Out of date entry, evidently. Might as well wait for the info package. My profile's gonna be low, all right. Very low. Place doesn't sound like it would make for much of a base for the UIN, but I guess any possible foothold has to be eliminated. Life remains interesting.

Marc Edwards really surprised me at lunch today. He could be just playing his own game, I don't know. Maybe I can trust him... course, I never assume that.

Chapter Twelve

BC gets the package for his assignment early the next day. He reads through it as he packs a light travel kit.

Fortune Station was built by the Sultan of Brunei in 2012. It's now occupied by "The Light" and his followers. Like M'Bekke told BC, this guy was so conservative he was radical. His brand of Christianity was akin to old communism, according to the OPO briefing. He and his followers live, the cult claims, as the first Christians did, with common possessions and no hierarchy, aside for the preeminence of "The Light."

Just another utopian wet dream. His interpretation's not that far from the truth, though, from what I've heard. I've always thought Jesus was a commie. Kind of liked him for it.

When the Roman Catholic church finally joined in the Great Ecumenical Reunification it drove the Cardinal out of the Church. He refused to acknowledge the New catholic Church, and retreated with his followers to the Midwest of North America. When he declared himself "The Light," he claimed the NcC was heretical, and declared that he himself was the only "true Light of Christ" left in the world.

The OPO report describes his followers as hardcore loyals, loyal to him personally. He's a "charismatic, highly persuasive individual," according to the report.

The package has BC's transportation details as well. He's chartering passage on a light freighter equipped with a small passenger section. The ship's called the Paladin IV, captained by one Adrian Longeux, described in the package as "a devout follower of the Pope and the NcC." There's a picture of the captain, identification for security purposes. BC studies his face.

Looks honest. Sure, don't we all.

BC's stateroom com buzzes; it's Edwards.

"Campion! I need to see you ASAP!"

"Um... sure, governor. It's just, well, I'm just getting ready to leave on that assignment."

"This is pretty important, Campion. I'd like you to get over here just as soon as you can."

"Okay, sure. Sure. I'll be right over."

He sounds pissed! Better get over there.

BC is sent right in when he arrives at Edwards's offices.

"Come in, Campion," Edwards say to BC, then he calls to the room's security unit, "lock and secure this room. Thank you."

BC can hear the whirs and clicks around him as the room is secured.

Woah, this is weird. Maybe this is his game. Take me in to his confidence and then get weird on me. Let's see how it plays...

"Precautions, Marc?"

"Precautions. I've received some serious shit about you, BC. Serious shit."

"Such as?"

"Such as you kill people. You're an assassin for the Vatican, not some high level PR guy!"

"That's crazy. Who made these allegations?"

"Daniel McEntyre provided me with a confidential dossier on you. UIN property, Top Secret. Says a lot about you, how you were a con man minister who was legitimized to do the Pope's dirty work. And it says you're an assassin! He says it proves it was really you who killed Meredith! How do you answer that?"

"I say it's crazy, Marc! I mean, consider the source! The first time Daniel McEntyre met me, he physically attacked me, even then trying to blame me for his wife's death! It's fiction, some kind of UIN fabrication meant to discredit me."

Holy shit... got to think fast...

"He's still trying to make people think I somehow had something to do with her death, so he must have had his friends in the UIN doctor up some records to make you suspect me. Think about it! You've just taken me into your confidence. He sees that as threatening! You and I spoke in a public place about it. Word could have gotten back to McEntyre. Look at it! Right after we talk, he gives you a supposed dossier on me. What timing! And how could he get his hands on such a thing, did you ask him that?"

"He said he couldn't tell me how he got it. But it looks authentic! There are newspaper clippings of political killings, with reports tying you to several of them: diplomats, reporters, politicians. They were all pro UIN, all killed by 'unseen assailants'. There are even pictures of you at the scenes! It pretty damning evidence."

"It would be, if it was real. It's not, Marc. Doctored photos and fake stories, it's all part of their game. Psychological operations, covert warfare. They're obviously trying to make you stop trusting me."

How do I play this?

"Marc, you know I am more than a simple priest and PR flack. Can I trust you to keep my secrets if I tell you more?"

"That depends on what you tell me," Edwards says, then pauses. "I want to believe you, BC, but this evidence is hard to ignore."

"Marc, I work for the Pope in a less than overt capacity. McEntyre's challenged my credentials as a priest before, and accused me of assassination before. I didn't deny then and I won't apologize now for the fact I became a priest through some less than traditional circumstances. I do the Lord's work, make no mistake. I am not a cold blooded killer."

It is not I who kill. I am only the instrument of the Lord, after all. Truth of a sort.

Edwards takes it all in and stares at BC, considering. He starts to say something, then stops. BC can see the questions in his eyes.

"We're at war, Marc. You've only had a small taste of it here. We've been at war for years back on Earth. On and off, terrorist attacks and bombings, raids and assaults. The UIN have been trying to kill us, the Christians of Earth, for years! They'd like nothing better than to see me and every other Christian dead! We've been trying to not let them succeed at that. As Christians, we in the NcC are targets. The Moslems have always lumped us in with the UTZ, no matter the fact that there are no official ties. We've been 'accidentally' hit by UIN attacks in the past, but now they're doing so openly. You've seen the reports, they've hit the Vatican itself twice in the last month! Thank God the UTZ came to our defense. The Vatican has no defense of its own. Except for the Office of Papal Operations.

"The Pope started the OPO to provide security for the church, for the NcC. We look out for the interests of the New catholic Church. Essentially, the OPO gathers information and relays it back to the home base. Information is power, and Pope Peter, with God's guidance, we hope, wields that power for peace. We don't want war, so we try to protect ourselves by averting war. People like me, priests who work for the OPO, we watch and we report. We've been called spies, but scouts would be a better term, I think. The OPO watches."

Edwards is still quiet, listening to BC tell his tale.

I can't read him. I've got to let him in a little so he'll trust me again...

"Some of that information helps bring us the protective power of the UTZ. The UTZ enjoys the moral support of the NcC, and they have come to our aid, but we have no formal agreement. Aside from their emergency assistance, we're on our own. As for me? I was sent to the Moon to watch the McEntyres."

Edwards is surprised. "Really?"

"Really. The Vatican's been keeping close tabs on both of them. They've been in close and repeated contact with the UIN. Governor McEntyre had been trying to draw the Cardinal in, making official overtures of friendship, but the actions of her and her husband spoke louder than her words. We were pretty sure she wasn't being sincere with the Cardinal. Pope Peter sent me up here to see if I could find out what they were up to. I didn't think I was going to see her die in front of me!"

...and I didn't...

"So you're a spy? For the Pope? But not a killer, huh? That's still a lot, man."

"Well. Now you know all my secrets."

"I sincerely doubt that," Edwards says and begins to laugh, "but I've heard enough. It really comes down to you versus Daniel. You, I've only known for a short time. I've known him for a couple of years, but I really don't 'know' him that well. I knew Meredith better. I liked her. She was a good woman. It's hard to believe she worked for the UIN, like you say. I think I trust you more than I trust him, but neither of you has me entirely convinced."

"Look, Marc, the OPO knew both the McEntyres were working with the UIN. But what if Meredith had stopped? What if we were wrong, and her overtures toward the Cardinal were for real? It might explain why they killed her. Daniel's probably still working with them! How did he get that fake dossier, huh?"

"That's a good question."

"He's got to be UIN, Marc. While I'm gone, you should be careful. Keep him under close watch. He's poison. I don't know if you still want my advice, but I hope you'll take it this time."

"I still like you, BC, and still trust you on some level. I'd still like your advice. But trust is a rare commodity, I don't spread it around easily."

"I don't blame you. Neither do I. I usually don't trust anyone. But I like you, Marc, you're my kind of people, and I can trust you on some level, too, I think. So if you want my advice, you've got it.

"I've got to get going, if we're okay. I've told you all I can about what I'm doing here on the Moon."

"Not exactly a simple priest... "

"Will you keep my secrets?"

"Sure. It's a deal."

Edwards stands and extends his hand. BC leans across the desk and shakes it.

A strong, solid handshake. Good sign.

"Open the office!" Edwards calls to the room's security unit. The room whirs and clicks again, and the office door pops open. "Give me a call when you get back here, BC."

"I will."

BC leaves the office, heads back through the atrium and back to his rooms. He notices he's breathing a little heavy and his heart is racing.

That was too close. McEntyre's dead when I get back here. He'll be trying to undermine me the whole time I'm gone, I'm sure. I hope I've convinced Edwards not to listen to him. He is poison.

Chapter Thirteen

BC goes back to packing for the trip and the job ahead. He reviews the space station plans and maps out strategies in his head as he checks the charge on his hand laser. He throws in a wrist-worn dart thrower and a small box of poison darts for good measure.

BC hides the CCU away in his rebuilt room, behind a wall panel that used to be a small closet door. The closet remains, but BC disguised the door to look like just another innocent wall panel.

This hit is a little more primitive than the hit on McEntyre. No killbots, nothing that sophisticated. Might be just brute force, blunt trauma... have to play it by ear as I go. Ah, violence is so not my style. Still, this is the least political job I've ever had to do. If this guy is killing people in the name of God, then he already plays by my rules. And under those rules, I am God's instrument of vengeance for those he's killed. I am the right hand of God, come to put the Light Bearer back in his place. His nemesis come to punish his hubris... but now I'm mixing my mythologies.

BC packs an airhypo, air cartridges and tranks and toxins, and tucks the blueprints and plans away as well.

That should do it. Now it's off to see the Wizard...

He throws in some clothes, zips up his cases, powers down his rooms, locks his door and heads for the Reagan Station Spaceport to meet Captain Adrian Longeux and board the Paladin IV.

"Father Campion! Over here!"

BC recognizes Longeux from the security photo. He's kind of a squat man, heavy set, with gray hair and the round face from the picture. He's dressed entirely in green, a one piece jumpsuit with "Paladin IV" stitched in gold above the breast pocket. He's also got a big gold crucifix hanging down around his neck.

A man of God, to be sure.

BC meets him at the private gate the port directory said the Paladin IV would be docked at. As BC approaches, Longeux reaches out for and eagerly shakes BC's hand.

"It's an honor to meet you, Father! It's not everyday I get orders from the Vatican! I've been practically bursting at the seams, not being able to tell anyone and all. Imagine that, best commission of my life, and I can't tell anybody! And you," Longeux laughs, "you already know, so I'm not telling you anything!" He laughs again, "You ready to go?"

"Yes, yes I am, Mr. Longeux. It's nice to meet you as well."

I like his laugh. A little over friendly, but what the heck. Could be worse.

"They couldn't tell me anything about this trip, said you'd fill me in on the details."

"Yes. I'll do that once we set out. Can we board now?"

"Sure!" Longeux turns and cycles the hatch behind him open. "Right this way, Father."

Longeux reaches for BC's cases, but BC stops him.

"Thanks, Mr. Longeux, but I'm fine to carry these myself. You've got a whole ship to handle, don't worry about my luggage."

"Well, we're pretty much all set, really. I've got clearance for us to take off in about an hour. The Paladin's fueled and prepped for the flight. All we gotta do is get on board and go!"

Longeux motions BC ahead of him through the hatch, then steps through himself and closes the hatch behind him. They're in a small airlock, another hatch just ahead. Longeux reaches around BC and punches a code into the door panel in front of him.

The hatch opens on a passageway extending down to the ship. BC steps through into the passageway. It's square and accordion shaped on the sides to expand and contract in the distance between the outer wall of Luna Prime and the hull of the ship, with a central walkway and handholds running down either side.

Like being inside an accordion, complete with a handy walkway.

Longeux steps through behind BC, closes the hatch and punches another code into the door panel on this side. He motions to BC to continue down to the ship. BC feels the gravity let go as they walk down the passageway. His stomach protests, but he manages to keep his breakfast down. He fumbles a little in the low G, but Longeux reaches out and steadies him.

"It can be hard to adjust to the changing gravities, Father. I think you'll find it better once we're on the ship. She's a good ship, Father. The Paladin's been fueled, and I just had the air recycling system recharged, so it should be good and fresh. I don't have any cargo, nothing but yourself, like the Vatican asked. They paid me well. I'm not complaining, Father, don't get me wrong. Here we are, the Paladin IV!"

Longeux squeezes past BC to open the hatch to his ship, then steps aside to let BC enter. "Go ahead into the airlock, Father. Welcome aboard!"

BC passes through the airlock and into the Paladin IV. He enters a corridor open to both sides. The Paladin IV's colors appear to be green and gold. A green carpet lines the floor. Green and gold stripes run along about waist high on the gray wall in front of BC. And BC also notices there's definitely more gravity than there was just outside the ship. BC takes it all in as Longeux enters behind him, still talking.

"You know, Father, I go to mass a lot on the Moon and I don't remember ever seeing you there."

"I work more behind the scenes, Mr. Longeux."

"Well, I hope you don't mind me asking... if we're gonna be traveling past Sunday, I was hoping you might say a Mass for us, at least on Sunday. I know you're more casual than, say, the Cardinal. I like his masses. But even if you could just do the New United Reform Liturgy, even...

would you, Father?"

"Sure. If we travel past Sunday."

"That'd be great, father. Thank you! Are we gonna travel past Sunday?"

This should be interesting... never even been to a liturgy... suppose I can fake it. I've gotta wonder if the boys back home set me up with this guy on purpose. They're probably getting a good chuckle right now at the thought of me saying a Mass. Ha ha fucking ha. Wonder if the trip'll even take that long.

"I don't honestly know, Mr. Longeux

"I used to be a Roman Catholic, Father. You don't strike me as the Catholic type. I don't mean any offense, Father."

"No, that's okay, I wasn't. But, I'm the Pope's man now."

"Me too, Father. And we all follow Jesus, too."

What do I say to that...

"Amen, Mr. Longeux."

"Amen, Father. All right. I'm going to warm up the engines, so I'm heading this way," he nods to the right. "You head up that way," he nods to the left, "and you'll come to your stateroom. First door on the left. It says 'one' on the door, but it's actually the only one. Can't miss it." He turns and heads away from BC.

I hate it when they say, "Can't miss it." Usually means you will.

BC walks down the corridor until he comes to the hatch marked "one".

Hmmph. Couldn't miss it. Let's see what we've got for accommodations...

The stateroom is small but neat and well kept. It's a rectangular room, about ten feet deep and five feet across, with the ceiling almost seven feet high. The green and gold theme continues, with green carpet and green covers on the small, folded out bed. The walls are gray with gold and green piping along the borders of each wall. Opposite the bed there's a small table folded out from the wall, and a chair folded up from a square spot on the floor. BC also notices a seam along the four sides of the back wall of the room.

That wall's one big door. Probably opens on the cargo bay. And everything in here can be folded away, so this can become just another cargo space, looks like. A cargo space with nicely painted walls and carpet. Good use of space. I approve.

BC settles in, sitting down on the bed and collecting his thoughts as he listens to the thrum of the engines growing increasingly louder and higher pitched.

Amen. Yeah, right. And I can say a mass, too, sure. What was I thinking? I've never said a mass in my life! I only pray when my ass is on the line, anyway. Course, then again, prayer might be appropriate in this case...

Not much of a priest. This is what I get for once thinking it was an easy way to make some cash. It was, for a while. Good cover for the illegal import/export business. Didn't elaborate on that for Edwards, thank you very much. But then the reunification, getting sucked into the OPO, no choice, kill for Christ or else... Now it's off to kill someone in the name of Christ who is himself killing in the name of Christ. What a tangled fucking web...

The intercom buzzes, interrupting his reverie.

"Yeah?"

"Uh, Father, we're just about to leave. Thought you'd like to know we were getting underway. If you'd like some company, I could come get you and show you the way to the common area and the bridge?"

"Thanks, Mr. Longeux, but I think I'll stay in for now. I've been very busy, and I'm enjoying the quiet here."

"Fine, Father. Have it your way. But I'll need to get the details of our trip from you soon. I'll call you when we're clear of the Moon."

"Thanks."

BC hears the connection click off, and the sound of the engines changes again. The pitch drops, and the thrumming becomes low and bassy and vibrates the floor, the bed, the walls, everything.

They lurch slightly.

Must be pulling away from Reagan Station.

BC feels the floor shift as the ship sets out.

There are no windows in his stateroom, but in his mind's eye BC imagines them pulling up and away from the bunkers, buildings, domes and tunnels of Reagan Station.

Goodnight for now, Moon. Off to kill a killer. This one won't be easy, I know it already. I can just feel it. It feels wrong, weird, greasy and dark. Not that any of them are really easy, though, not really. I always think about them. Their faces all still come back to me. Not easy. Nothing's simple, even if you're doing "the Lord's work."

But it's what I do. And I'm good at it.

And the Pope, the fucking POPE tells me what to do, tells me I'm doing the Lord's work. He should know, right? He'd be the one guy who should know, who has the authority to say, "go, do this for God," right? Like M'Bekke said, best not to think about it too hard or examine it too closely.

I will take this guy out efficiently, as quietly as possible, and, hopefully, without a trace of evidence. Because it's what I do.

Mr. Longeux buzzes him again in about an hour.

"Hello, Father. We're out past the Moon's basic scanner range. I'll need you to fill me in on our trip. Reagan Station thinks we're going to the Wentworth Station. Where are we going?"

"I'll tell you on the bridge, if that's okay, Mr. Longeux."

"Sure, Father. I'll come get you. I made some dinner, so we can eat after we set the course."

Longeux is at the stateroom door in about a minute. He and BC head down the corridor to the right, towards the front of the ship. They pass through three different hatches, and wind their way through a twisting section past several different hatches. Longeux then leads them through one which opens onto a large living space.

A table with four chairs dominate the center of the room. The top of the table and the backs of the chairs are green, piped in gold.

"Oh look, all color coordinated!" Nice look, I guess. Better than red and gold! And there's enough gray on the walls and ceilings to remind you you're on a ship.

Gold and green stripes continue to run waist high around the four gray walls of the room. Also around the edges of the room are two exercise machines, a food prep station, and a small but gaudy shrine.

Wow, this guy's hardcore. I thought the conspicuous crucifix around the neck was a little much. Wouldya look at that shrine? I'm sure the Cardinal would approve

."Like my shrine, Father?"

"I was just thinking that the Cardinal would approve."

"Oh he does! He did, I mean. He's seen it. I asked him to come on board when I finished it, so he could bless it. He said he'd never seen a finer shrine on any ship, bigger or smaller, and he blessed it himself. I'm kind of proud of it. You don't think it's overdone, do you, Father?"

"The colors match your ship. The use of gold is quite striking."

"That crucifix used to hang over the altar of my town church back on Earth, back where I used to go to mass growing up. UIN terrorists bombed the church and our town about four years ago. The church burned down, but that crucifix was spared. It didn't melt, even in the middle of the fire. The priests said it was a miracle."

"Really."

"I was only visiting at the time. I used to work at the rectory as a kid, I was even an Altar boy, Father." Longeux laughs to himself as he remembers. "At any rate, I was visiting the priests when the first bomb went off. I helped them best I could. We got the fire put down. That crucifix was preserved. But then the group of terrorists came back. They had guns and molotov cocktails. The priests asked me to take the crucifix with me. They asked me to save it and escape on my ship as they delayed the terrorists.

"I could hear the shots as I ran to my ship. When I took off and saw the scene from above, it looked like half the town was on fire. There was no one left to give the crucifix back to, so I set up this shrine with it, in their honor.

"I hope it brings me good luck... So, how do you like the gravity?"

"Huh?"

"Most ships this size don't have artificial G. I rigged up this system myself. It cost me some cargo space but it's worth it. Must be all right if you didn't even notice!"

BC bounces on his heels."Nice job. Everything going smoothly?"

"Absolutely. Let's head up to the bridge and get going somewhere."

Longeux leads BC to a ladder in a recessed alcove across the room. There's a hatch in the seven-foot high ceiling in the alcove. Longeux climbs the ladder, pushes up the hatch and climbs up through. BC follows and finds himself in a small cockpit- style bridge, two flight chairs directly in front of him. There's barely enough room to walk between them. Longeux squeezes through first and sits on the left, motions BC in to the right chair. He too squeezes through and sits down.

An array of different switches and controls are spread out in front of him

I could probably figure this thing out. I betcha I could fly this baby. I've flown similar ones back on earth. The Santa Clara was a lot like this.

"We got off okay. Saw one of those flashers, but they stayed away, as usual."

"Flashers?"

"Yeah. They're these ships we've been seeing, that some of us have seen. They don't show up on any of our scanners. Nobody I've talked to who has seen one has been able to document it. They're always so fast, they're gone quick, like a flash in the corner of your eye. That's why we call them flashers, anyway."

"I've never heard about this. How long has this, how long have these ships, these, um, flashers, been around?"

"We've only seen them for about the last year or so. I've mostly heard about them from other freelance pilots. I've only seen them a couple of times myself. They were always gone before I could even try to get a reading on what they were. Same with the one earlier. Without documentation, we can't prove anything. If we filed reports we'd sound like liars or idiots or delusional, unfit to pilot. So we keep them to ourselves. You wouldn't have heard about them, I suppose."

"You saw one tonight? What do they look like?"

"Hard to say. They're really fast, you know?"

"Are they aliens?"

Longeux laughs, "What, are you egging me on, trying to make me sound like I'm crazy, Father? No, I don't think so. They look sort of normal, human-ish, I guess. They look like advanced military ships, but they don't have any markings. Another good reason not to pry too hard, I don't want anybody's military coming after me. I'm almost sorry I mentioned them."

"Don't be. I think I might have seen one of your 'flashers' myself, Mr. Longeux. Right near the surface of the Moon."

"Really? Right on the Moon itself?"

"Well, hovering just over the surface of the Moon, anyway. I was in an outlying building of the station, losing consciousness after an, um, an air leak, an accident, and the area I was in lost atmosphere. Just before I passed out, I saw a ship hovering outside that looked human made, but not like any ship that I'd ever seen. And it had no markings of any kind. Now, do I sound crazy?"

Longeux considers. "Nope. Sounds like a flasher, all right. Never heard of one getting that close to the Moon, though. They do move pretty fast, don't they, Father?"

"Yeah. Sort of hard to tell. I was passing out, but it looked like it disappeared pretty quickly."

"I've seen them around UIN ships, but they never

seem to be together. And I don't think they're UTZ because we would have heard something. Not officially, mind you, but through channels. We would of heard something."

"Have you, or anyone you've heard from ever seen them attack?"

"Nah, they just hover around the edges. Flashers. The name fits them."

"And you're sure they're not alien?"

"They're not alien. Don't talk nonsense, Father, not you, a man of the cloth..."

"You ever seen anything alien, Mr. Longeux?"

"Nope. I don't believe in them."

"Really? You don't believe in aliens? Even after seeing for yourself how vast space is?" BC looks out the window at the deep plush carpet of stars. "How can you deny that there are other beings out there somewhere? What about the ruins on Mars? The find on the Moon a hundred years ago the UN covered up?"

"Nothing ever came out of those, or came back for them, for that matter. Don't tell me you believe in aliens, Father?"

"I don't know for sure. But I don't think we can say with certainty they don't exist. How can you travel across the grand expanse of space and not feel that out there in the limitless void there must be others? I don't think God's creation is just limited to planet Earth, Mr. Longeux."

Laying it on a little thick... but it's his thing, he'll eat it up.

"I don't either, Father. But where are they? Why aren't they here now?"

"I don't know that, either. But I think they are out there. The evidence hasn't been strong, but there has been some evidence of something else out there. Maybe they're just waiting, watching us. How long will it be before they show up? What if they have already been here and gone? Are they peaceful or hostile..."

"Couldn't be much more hostile than we are ourselves, though, huh, Father?"

"No, I suppose not. Sometimes I wish aliens *would* show up and threaten us. Maybe the external threat from aliens, or even just their very 'otherness', would finally wake up humankind to our commonality, our unity, and bring us all together."

"That sounds like an awful lot to ask of aliens, if you ask me. Even Jesus couldn't do it. Or hasn't done it, yet, I should say."

"Well, we could use some help. Look at the mess we've made of things left to our own devices."

"We're pretty good at killing each other, aren't we, Father?"

"Yeah, we are at that, aren't we, Mr. Longeux."

The pilot changes the subject. "I need our destination details right away, Father. Where are we going?"

"Fortune Station. Do you know it?"

"Really? Fortune Station? No one goes out there anymore. The UTZ shut it down twenty years ago, gotta be. Too far up and out. It wasn't worth it. First launched as an old luxury station. I've never been there, but I know where it is. I'll get us there."

"Good. How long?"

"Let's see... ah, probably about three days, regular drive. It's pretty far from where we are now, but too close to use the transpace drive. I don't know if it's even available as a transit point for transpace, anyway, might be too old. There. Course laid in. We're set. I'll set proximity alarms, but otherwise we've got three days of quiet travel ahead, Father. Are you hungry?"

"Sure."

"I've got that dinner ready. Let's head back down and eat."

"Sure, Mr. Longeux, that sounds good!"

BC returns to his stateroom after dinner to digest both the passable lasagna Mr. Longeux served and the news about the "flashers."

They could be aliens, despite what Mr. Longeux and the other pilots think. They move so fast, how can you tell?

There were ruins on Mars and the Moon. Something is out there, or was out there. I wonder what they look like? How do they act? Are they hostile? Vastly superior to us? Or just like us? That's a sobering thought. More of the same might be the worst possible scenario. How will we treat them, I wonder? We'll probably be hostile to them no matter what they're like.

It would be nice if an alien presence unifies the Earth, shows us humans that we are all one. That's pretty close to what Jesus was looking for, I think I'm even on His side on this one.

Chapter Fourteen

Sunday is the third day of their trip. It's been quiet, no other traffic around, but BC wakes with a small bit of panic. He's got none of the books a real, proper priest should have to read the liturgy Longeux wants him to perform. He's got no clue. Longeux has left him to himself mostly, but he's expecting BC to perform this liturgy for him today.

It doesn't look like we're going to get there early. That was my only hope...

BC walks up to the common area. Longeux has thrown a white sheet over the table and pushed it over in front of his shrine. He's cleared the chairs away to the side.

"I thought you could use this as an altar. It's not consecrated or anything, but it's fine by me if you're okay with it."

"Sure, sure, no, that's fine. I'm a little embarrassed, though, Mr. Longeux. I've come to realize I haven't brought any of my liturgical books with me."

Longeux is surprised, but nonplused. "I've got the liturgy we need stored on the ship's computer. Hold on just a sec and I'll print it out for you to use." He walks over to a wall mounted screen, calls up the text, prints it out and brings it to BC. "Here you go, Father. New United Reform Liturgy. I keep a copy handy, sometimes say it for myself when I'm traveling on Sundays."

BC isn't even sure where to start. He takes the papers and stands behind the table in front of the shrine. He smoothes the papers out on the makeshift altar.

This should do... let's see now...

He raises his arms and a loud alarm sounds.

What the...

"Proximity alert, Father. Hold on, I'll be right back!"

Longeux runs to the ladder and disappears up into the bridge. BC follows, climbs up to see what's going on. Longeux looks back at him from the pilot's chair on the left, then looks back to the controls and shouts over his shoulder.

"We've got company, Father. It's a UIN scout. They aren't hailing us. We wouldn't know they were even there without the alarm being set off. That's not normal, usually they at least hail you. Not a good sign! Looks like they're charging weapons! Hold on!"

BC is thrown forward, feels his stomach leap up through his chest as Longeux attempts evasive maneuvers. He's on the deck in between the two flight chairs.

"Hold on, there, Father. We're only about four hours from Fortune Station. We're not on a direct route, so he probably doesn't know where we're going. They shouldn't care who we are or why we're here. But they're firing!"

BC is thrown sideways into the right side flight chair as he hears a boom and resounding clang at the same instant.

"We're hit!" Longeux yells, "Returning fire!"

BC pulls himself up and holds on to the back of the right flight chair, watching Longeux scramble to maneuver their ship around the UIN scout ship. Suddenly, the scout ship falls into view, large in the bridge viewport as Longeux brings his ship up behind it. Longeux flips switches and hits buttons on the console as missiles and bright laser fire flashes away from the Paladin IV towards the UIN scout. Bright orange blossoms flame up from the scout ship, blinding BC momentarily.

"We hit 'em! Hold on."

Longeux maneuvers the ship up and to the right of the scout. As the ship banks, BC is thrown back and down through the hatch, flailing and falling all the way down to the common room floor. He's all right, just shaken up. He gets up and dusts himself off, checking for broken bones.

Seems fine. Head hurts... there's a goose egg. Ouch!

BC climbs back up the ladder and through the hatch into the bridge, where Longeux is working furiously to keep his ship together and out of harm's way.

"They hit us again as we banked. We've lost some fuel. Father, why don't you get back down to the common area. There's a fixed seat you can strap yourself into in an access area just behind the shrine. There's a computer with a viewstation there, wired in to the bridge. We'll be able to talk but you'll be safer than you are flapping around up here. Seal the hatch as you go, huh? Go on!"

BC climbs back down and seals the hatch. He goes over to the shrine and finds an access handle behind the gilded crucifix. The shrine itself is mounted to the door, and moves aside with the door as BC opens the compartment.

Another muffled boom and BC suddenly finds himself on the ceiling of the small compartment.

The artificial G must have been hit! Shit. Which way is down? Damn... Oh, man, I don't want to be sick. Freefall, falling every which way all at once, love it...

BC pushes off from the ceiling and grabs the top of the chair as he floats down. He pulls himself down into the chair, straps himself in and activates the computer. It swings up into place in front of him. He hears Longeux firing again, sees flashes on the viewstation, hears Longeux from the speakers in front of him.

"We got 'em again, critical hit, looks like. They're going down! Shit, they've still got fire power..."

BC is surprised. He hasn't heard Longeux swear until now.

Wham!

The ship is rocked backwards, like a giant hand just reached out, stopped them, and pushed them back. The screen in front of him goes to static. The lights dim. Everything is strangely silent.

"Mr. Longeux?" BC tries the com unit in front of him. No response.

He unstraps himself from the chair. Moving slowly and cautiously in the zero G, he opens the access door and floats out into the main room.

The common area looks okay. Hard to tell in this dim emergency lighting. But we must have taken a big hit. I don't hear the engines. I hope that scout ship isn't coming around to finish the job! I gotta get back up to the bridge and check on Mr. Longeux.

BC works his way hand over hand around the walls of the room until he gets to the recessed alcove and the hatch to the bridge. He floats up the ladder to the hatch. It looks strange to BC.

It looks different. It's lower, bulging down. Shit indeed, Mr. Longeux.

The small screen next to the door clears up from static to a self test screen.

The ship's systems must have taken a jolt. Maybe they'll come back on-line now. Wonder if I can get this hatch open...

BC struggles with the hatch, trying to get the handle to budge, to get it to move. It's stuck. BC keeps trying to force it. He's thinking about going back to the stateroom for his handlaser when the screen next to the door beeps.

BC reads the screen: "Emergency: Door Sealed--Zero Atmosphere On Bridge."

Shit indeed, Mr. Longeux. At least there are no more booms, so far.   Hopefully, Longeux disabled the scout ship before they got him.

BC hears the Paladin IV's engines sputter back to life.

They don't sound good. And there's no way we're still going in the right direction... Can't get back on the bridge... I wonder if there's any other way to fly this thing.

BC floats down out of the alcove and hand over hands his way back around to the chair in the compartment behind the shrine. He straps himself back in and sees the computer's come back to life. He begins searching out how the ship's systems are controlled, trying to get control of the ship from the console he's on.

After about fifteen minutes, BC finds a way to transfer ship's controls to his terminal. He checks the engines, damaged but working. He checks the fuel.

Just about gone, that's bad.

He manages to set course corrections and points the ship toward Fortune Station. As more ship systems come back on, he tries to take a look around the ship. The main viewscreen cameras mounted front of the bridge are gone. He searches for other external viewers and finds one mounted on the top of the ship. He can see front and forward, but can't see any of the ship itself to see what external damage has been done. The engines are even beginning to sound normal again, but BC worries about how little fuel remains to feed them.

Got to save some fuel to maneuver in when I get to the station, so I can dock. Have to figure out how much to use for thrust. Shot in the dark... no scanners, can't visually see much of anything, either. Just gotta guess. Hope that's a good guess.

BC saves about a quarter of his remaining fuel for maneuvering when he gets to the station, then pours what's left into a long sustained burst, sending the ship in the general direction of Fortune Station.

With the ship's artificial gravity disabled, the force of the thrust pushes BC flat back in his seat. He hangs on and watches the screen in front of him.

.I don't think I'll be riding back to the Moon on this thing... just get me there, that's all I ask. I hope that scout ship didn't get to call any of his friends...

After almost four uneasy hours, Fortune Station finally looms in the console screen.

Hello, Fortune Station. Old looking. Man, this place looks primitive.

Fortune Station is about a mile long, made up of two fat ring sections each about a quarter mile across rotating in unison half a mile apart, connected to each other by four major walkways.

BC can't make out too many details. The station is mostly just a deep, unbroken, black silhouette against the stars.

Docking. How do I dock this thing? Wish there was an automatic "docking" button. I've got bring the ship in close and match the spin of the station, first. Place looks like a couple of donuts with four styli poked through them. Big fat old rusty donuts. Plain, no glaze. The far donut looks more lit up, so I'll line up on this closer, darker one. May be able to sneak in, we'll see.

BC fires thrusters and orients the ship, facing the darker "donut". He gets the ship spinning with the station, rotating slowly as they approach the donut "hole." There are two corridors crisscrossing the actual hole with a docking access in the middle. BC can see it on the screen in front of him as the ship approaches.

This camera is supposedly mounted above the docking hatch, so this is good. Ew... don't look at the stars, look at the station, not at the stars...

The station looks still in front of him, the stars spinning around them. Dizzying. The Paladin IV is almost next to the station when he sees in the view screen that the hatch he's been aiming for is blown.

Useless. Shit. If I remember the plans for this place there are hatches out toward the rim of the donut on this side, have to try to find one and dock. The rotation is gonna make that tricky.

He uses what little fuel he has left, firing maneuvering thrusters to line up with another hatch, still on this side of the donut, but down towards the edge, where there's a feeling of gravity created by the station's rotation. He starts to move the ship in towards the hatch, trying to keep "down" down as rotation induced gravity begins to exert its pull on the ship.

I better line the ship up right or I'll be walking across the walls or the ceiling...

Red lights suddenly come on. The ship's computer warns, "Collision Alert. Collision Alert. Collision Alert..."

"I know, I hear you, I know!"

BC gets the Paladin IV to stop just short of impact. He can see the station's hatch looming large. He fires directional rockets to bring the ship in slower, slower...

A loud, piercing, metal on metal screech echoes off the ship's walls.

Ouch! Not even close. Gotta back off, try again. Almost no fuel. How many tries do I get? Let's find out.

It takes two tries and a lot of scraping and bumping, but BC finally gets the Paladin IV to dock with Fortune Station.

Not the most graceful entrance. So much for sneaking in. Hope I didn't wake anybody up...

Chapter Fifteen

BC gathers his supplies together, some food supplements, his hand laser, the station plans, the wrist-worn dart launcher and the tranq darts. He straps on his weaponry, puts everything else into a small belt pack, and heads through the corridors of the Paladin IV for the airlock and Fortune Station. After figuring out the docking controls at the hatch, BC manages to get a docking collar in place to link the ship to the space station, creating an airlock. After the airlock pressurizes, he opens the hatch of the Paladin IV and gets into the airlock. He checks a screen built into the docking collar wall for atmospheric information on the other side of the door ahead. If all the electronics still work, he should be able to tell from here if there's air inside the station.

Be nice if there's air to breathe, huh?

All the controls look okay. He straps it on a breather mask.

Hello, Fortune Station. Let's open you up.

BC activates the outer door of Fortune Station and steps through into another airlock.

Doesn't look so old on the inside. Must be renovations done more recently. Still like forty years ago. Recently. Huh. Everything's relative.

He closes the outer door behind him, turns and reads one of the screens in the airlock wall to figure out how to open the inner door. After a few simple commands the door opens with a gasp. BC lifts up the breather to take his first breath of station air.

Yuck! Well, at least there is air... Eww. Smells like tombstones, cemeteries, death, old laundry, gym socks...

BC snaps the breather quickly back into place on his

face. He steps through the airlock door into the old station and seals the door shut behind him.

It's cold. He's in almost total darkness.

There is some faint light. Two frost and dust covered viewports in the same wall as the airlock let in a little light. It's the docking lights from Paladin IV, shining in from outside the station.

BC steps over to the viewports. Hoisting his shirt cuff over the heel of his hand he wipes off a viewport, wiping away frost and dust so he can look through to see the ship outside. He manages to clear away enough to see, soaking his shirt cuff with muddy, icy dust in the process.

What he sees is not good. The front of the Paladin IV on the upper left side, where Captain Longeux and the bridge used to be, is just gone.

Looks like someone took a big, burning bite out of it. Poor Mr. Longeux, chewed up by the black teeth of the UIN. Not fair at all, really, the whole life and death thing. He was a good, God-Fearing Catholic man, gone in an instant. Doesn't matter who you are or what you do, you can be gone in an instant.

Now me, I bring justice into the equation, really. Thanks to me, the evil ones really do feel the wrath of God. Maybe I balance it out... just a little. Maybe.

BC turns away from the window. He sets his handlaser on a broad, unfocussed dispersal beam and lights up his surroundings. This part of the station still looks abandoned. He's in a dusty corridor. There's a door just ahead on the right.

BC quietly slips through the door into what looks like a common area, with tables and chairs pushed off to one side and stacked on top of each other. There are worn and ripped tapestries on the walls, faded and worn carpet on the floor, a mix of dulled reds and golds and muted purples.

There's a control panel on the wall. BC tries it. Nothing happens.

Thought we might get some light, at least. No such luck.

BC turns off his light. He begins to quiet himself, slow his breathing, so he can listen for the sounds of the station, the hum of its inhabitants and its machines.

I may be able to hear them if I stay quiet, at least get some sense of where they are. Man, its pitch black dark... hope my eyes adjust. See if I can see any light leaking in from anywhere.

BC waits and listens, and lets his eyes adjust to the darkness. Even as his eyes adjust he doesn't see much of anything. But he does pick up on the sound of humming equipment, coming from somewhere on the other side of the common area he's in.

There is some sound, the hum of machines at work, some sign of life. No real light, though, not here.

He gives up and flips his hand laser back on, on the wide dispersal beam.

Guess they aren't using this area, yet. Looks like nobody's been in here for years. Well, they aren't fixing up what they aren't using, makes sense. Plenty of room here.

Well then, there's something I don't get. With room to expand, why do they kill off followers... that doesn't make sense! Scapegoats? Rebels among the faithful? Hope they aren't eating each other... Cannibalism would make this really ugly. Hope they're well supplied. I hadn't thought of that as a possible outcome. Taking eating the body of Christ a bit too literally...

BC makes his way across the room to where the humming is loudest. The twin metal doors in the wall there are sealed shut. BC puts his ear up to the doors.

Definitely where the humming's coming from. They must have gotten as far as the other side of these doors, then stopped and sealed off the rest of this side of the station. They've sealed off this side and beyond, for how far I can't tell. They might be using the area on the other side of these doors. Time to invite myself in.

BC adjusts the beam on the handlaser down, focusing it into a knife-length, high intensity cutting tool. He runs the beam along the seals on the door, burning his way through across the top, left to right, then down the right outside edge, along the bottom of the right door then up the center to the top. The edges of the door glow white as he cuts, cool to orange, then red, then finally dim and cool down.

He uses the handle on the door to pull it toward him. It's still warm as he leans it on him. He lowers it slowly, quietly to the floor. With the door open he can hear an alarm echoing in the distance on the other side.

Shit. Wonder if that's my welcome. Hope not. But it is. Gotta be.

BC inspects the door frame.

No sign of booby traps. Let's see...

BC finds a seat cushion and throws it through the door. Nothing. BC leans through the hatch and looks around.

There's light on this side, looks like old emergency lighting. Area looks just as deserted as where I just came from, but more cluttered. A lot of stuff piled up just in front of me here. Must be a storage area. That damned alarm is still going off.

BC checks his weapons, adjusts the beam of the hand laser so it will work as a blaster, and edges through the door. He can't get far. A pile of furniture is in his way.

He's at the end of a long, wide corridor that curves down and away from him, blocked by stacks of old beds, storage bins, lockers and shelves. The corridor extends past the point at which the ceiling seems to meet the floor of the corridor as it bends with the curve of the station down and out of BC's sight.

Betcha there are doors up beyond the curve. This is one of the main corridors for this ring section.

BC makes his way through the stacked and stored furniture. More ripped and faded tapestries hang on the walls. Worn and tattered carpet almost covers the floor.

The further down the corridor I go, there's less and less dust and more stored furniture. This area's seen people more recently than the common area. The emergency lights alone make it seem more inhabited, more used, but it's still obviously not a main part of their habitation here.

All this color and fabric... What a weird place. I guess if you're a sultan you can decorate the place however you please. Purple, red, gold, blue... interesting taste.

That alarm is still going off. That can't be good. Wonder how long until I get company?

BC moves beds, bureaus, shelves and storage bins and works his way down the corridor. The density of the storage items gets lighter the further he goes, the going easier.

This has to be the main corridor of this donut, this ring of the station. They can't use this donut much if they've loaded this main a corridor with old furniture and stuff.

What's that?

Not a sound but the absence of a sound. The alarm has stopped.

BC stops and ducks behind a stack of empty storage bins and waits. He doesn't have to wait long.

Two large, bearded men carrying metal pipes appear from down the corridor. One's a redhead, his long hair tied loosely back. The other's olive skinned with long black hair hanging limply straight down, vaguely Mediterranean. Both wear simple robes and sandals. They look around and approach BC's position.

Nice look... what's the style called, Retro-Jerusalem Rioter circa New Testament? This cult must be wacked. Looks like they take this back to the bible stuff a bit too literally. Sorry, guys. Gonna have to help ya meet your maker...

BC adjusts his handlaser. He sets the hair trigger. When he squeezes the trigger just slightly it'll shine a guide beam so he can aim.

Tight beam. Hot focus, pinpoint. Highly destructive on contact with, say, flesh and bone. I don't think they can see me. Looks like Red is going to pass me first. I'll let him get by, nail his little buddy with the beam, then hit him as he turns around.

The redhead turns back to his buddy. They stop.

"Are you sure it was this section?"

"Yeah. Most of the sensors on this side don't work, but something definitely hit the outside and attached. He says there's another one on board to kill Him."

They definitely use a capital "H" when they talk about Him... Gotta be "The Light."

"Quiet," Red shushes, then whispers, "If he's anywhere, he's up ahead in the unused area."

"I hate the unused area. Isn't it sealed off?"

"Would that stop a determined killer? Wouldn't stop me," Red says, chuckling under his breath.

C'mon, keep moving, guys...

"Let's keep going," Red says, and he walks past BC's hiding place.

BC whips up the handlaser, guide beam on. He pumps the trigger as the beam crosses the second man's left eye.

The man's head jerks back. His feet fly out from under him. His hands reach up to grab at his head as he falls flat on his back to the carpet. He hits hard, dead as he hits, parts of the back of his head, blood, and burnt bits of brain splattering out across the corridor floor behind him.

It takes all of about a second.

Red swings around as he hears his friend hit the floor. He can't see BC. As Red starts back to his fallen friend, he crosses BC's guide beam. BC pumps the trigger when the beam hits the center of Red's back. The superheated interior of Red's ribcage explodes out in front of him as he falls, seared muscle, bone and vital tissue spraying the wall, the floor and the body of the first kill.

He lands face down at the feet of his fallen friend.

Messy. Sorry, guys.

BC searches the bodies for some kind of i.d., some sort of signifier the cult might use for security. There's nothing on either man, not even a tattoo, at least as far as BC can see. All the men have on them are their robes, sandals and metal pipes.

How can you have a back to basics, back to the bible, retro cult on a space station, anyway? Seems kinda anachronistic to me. I'll have to find out the secret from this "Light" guy before I kill him.

BC makes his way past the men down the corridor and to the doors they came through. He ducks cautiously through the doors, handlaser at ready. No one's on the other side. The corridor continues on out of sight around the curve of the station.

Still looks deserted. Not as much furniture here. They're still not using much on this side of the station for anything but storage. They must live over on the other wheel.

There should be another set of doors I can't see yet, still beyond the curve, a sort of terminus for this corridor and one of the connecting corridors leading over to the other wheel. There are four of them I could see from the outside and on the plans. Nothing here is very well marked, though. I'm not quite sure where I am.

Those two back there must have friends around here somewhere, too.

They could be just around the curve, too.

And no more furniture means no more cover, unfortunately.

BC edges along the wall of the corridor until another set of doors does appear, heavier airlock doors at the end of the corridor. There's glass in the airlock doors, a sure sign of the sultan's wealth back in the early days of station construction.

Luxury! Guess the sultan liked to splurge. Shit!

There's a silhouette in the window. Another cult member. BC stops and watches.

He's not even looking in here. Hope that means he'll wait. I wanna erase some evidence back there.

BC scrambles back the way he came. He gets back to the bodies on the floor of the last corridor.

I want to drag them to an airlock, but all this furniture... well, it's not pretty but I know what I've got to do.

BC gets a small storage locker and sets it down next

to the bodies. He sets his hand laser on a broad swath slice setting. The laser's heat cauterizes as he uses the handlaser like a blade to cut through each man's torso and limbs.

Like a hot knife through butter, as mother used to say. Grim imagery, but quick work all the same. Easier to transport. Slice and dice, neat as you please. God help your humble servant...

BC spends five minutes cutting up the bodies. After he's done he starts tossing the pieces into the storage locker. He fills the locker and drags it through the common area back to the airlock where the Paladin is docked. He works as quickly as he can, trying not to think about what he's doing, trying not to get blood all over himself. He opens the airlock and piles in the pieces, then goes back with the locker again and gets what's left. It takes still a third trip to get all of the parts finally piled into the airlock. He keeps as quiet as he can as he commits this gruesome task, watching and listening for the men's silhouetted friend, waiting for him to come from down the corridor, to see him at his work. But he doesn't appear.

BC gets into the airlock with the gore and cycles the lock through. The outer door opens on the Paladin IV's docking collar. BC heaves the parts through into the collar, then sets the emergency explosive bolts on the docking collar.

I'll blow the bolts and cast off the Paladin IV. The men's body parts should float away with the ship. Some might cling to the side of the station, caught up in the spin, but most will hopefully float away. Rest in pieces... oh my God, I can't believe I just thought that. I'm turning into some kind of cheap horror movie freak. I'm just trying to hide evidence. Collateral damage, they used to call it, right. Self defense, too. They had pipes, your honor...

He rechecks the bolts. He goes back into the station through the airlock, and closes it behind him. The bolts fire just as the door clicks into place.

BC watches out the viewport as the Paladin and what's left of the men float away, then heads back towards the heavier hatches, back through the common room and down the corridor past the remnants of his two attacker/victims, to check on the cult member keeping watch. As he nears the heavy doors he sees the cultist looking through the window, right at him.

Shit! I hope he didn't see me! He had to...

BC presses himself up against the right wall next to the doors, just out of the window's line of sight. He waits. There's no sound. He wants to look, but doesn't want the other guy to be staring back, seeing him.

BC waits another minute and then risks a peek. The guy is gone.

Gone? Shit, what, gone for reinforcements? Not a good sign that he's gone.

There's noise on the other side of the hatches. The unmistakable sound of a cycling airlock. BC races back along the corridor and ducks into a hiding place. In seconds he hears voices getting louder. From his hiding place he can see down the corridor, sees five long-haired bearded men in robes carrying short lengths of metal pipe approaching.

Interesting. Weapon of choice here, I guess. Oh, fuck...

The cabinet BC's been leaning against collapses forward, falling into the corridor directly in front of the five. BC falls with it flat onto his face. He looks up just in time to see a length of metal pipe coming down, and then sees nothing else.

Chapter Sixteen

"Ah. It looks like our visitor is awakening. That was quite a blow you struck, Thomas."

Wha? Ow, ow, ow, ow, fuckin ow! My head hurts bad. Who's talking? Head feels swollen. I'd feel for a bump, but I think my hands and feet are tied. Hog-tied with rough cords, lying on the floor, somewhere on the station. Probably in the other wheel.

God, my head's been rung like a bell! Thank you, Thomas. Gonna try to pretend I'm still out, see if they buy it. Keep still, keep my eyes closed. Probably can't see anything with my face mashed against the floor like this, anyway.

"Do you know something, our uninvited guest? I know you. I know who you are. The last two they sent weren't known to me, but you, you I know! You've made quite the name for yourself in certain circles, Bernard Campion!" The voice stresses the syllables of his name. "You can open your eyes, now. I can see you're awake."

BC opens his eyes.

He's in front of a dais. Sitting on a large throne on the dais is an older man with long gray hair and a full mustache and beard, dressed in simple brown and beige robes. BC knows him from the photos in his package.

I see "The Light." Ouch! He's got the right look for this, I guess, very biblical. More old testament, though. Who was that guy... Moses. Yeah. More like Moses.

A man and a woman sit on small chairs on each side of the throne of The Light. The man at his right hand, the woman on the left. They're also dressed in robes, the man in brown, the woman in purple. They're both glaring at BC. BC can feel the eyes of other people in the room beyond his sight, a crowd watching behind his back.

The Light smiles down at BC from his throne.

"Hello, Campion," The Light says, disgust palpable in his voice, "I refuse to call you 'Father'. I know what kind of scum you really are." The smile disappears. "You first drew my attention years ago as a perfect example of everything going wrong with the church. Did you know that? I followed your so-called career, early on.

"You are the embodiment, the very incarnation, of everything that made me leave the church! Did you know that? I actually cited you, you by name, when I declared my intention to separate. You are heresy, Mr. Campion, in flesh and blood right here in front of me. Heresy! People like you are just a symptom of the greater rot at the heart of what's left of the church. It's all compromised. Now this," The Light spreads his arms out and looks around the room, "this is a true church you've wandered into, Campion. Men like you do not belong here. You're certainly not a priest in our eyes here. But then, you're no 'Father' at all, are you, Campion?"

Lecture over? Fine. I will say nothing.

"Trying for the strong, silent type, eh?"

Nothing.

"Brothers Joseph and Matthew went looking for you, Campion, and never returned. We can't find them now. We did find bloodstains, evidence of a struggle. And of course, we found you. But no sign of them. And no sign of your ship either. Did you put them on your ship and cast it off? Or did you just space them?

"What have you done with my brothers, Campion? Where are my lost sheep? You know I won't rest until I've found them. Or do you? Do you even know your scripture? Do you have any clue what I'm referring to, 'Father'?" The Light spits the word out.

BC remains silent. He keeps his eyes locked on The Light.

Fuck you. Maybe if I think it hard enough you'll hear it. Fuck You!

The Light starts losing his patience.

"You are Bernard Campion, are you not?" he yells at

BC. He springs up off the throne and descends the dais to walk around the bound BC.

"Of course you are! You are 'BC' aren't you?"

BC stares up at The Light as he paces around him, maintaining eye contact while The Light is in eyesight.

Let my eyes talk. They say Fuck you, too, you fucking nut. I will say nothing. Got to find a way out of this, but I won't give this guy a word of satisfaction. That's funny, using the Jesus defense on a guy with a messiah complex...

"I suppose you think you're being like our Lord, saying nothing. How dare you! God punishes false pride!"

BC gets chills.

That was weird... well, if you can read my mind, FUCK YOU!

"I don't like your attitude, Campion. I can read your face, your eyes. You communicate even though you don't say anything. You think you're better than we are, don't you? We're 'freaks', 'weirdoes', some strange cult! How dare you judge us! You're not better than we are. You kill people! I know! I know you're here to kill me, too. I knew that before I even knew it was you, as soon as a ship docked. Whoever had come had come uninvited. No one comes here to visit, except you assassins."

The Light stops walking in front of BC, locked eye to eye with him. He leans down close and whispers, "The other two before you tried to kill me, too, but they came to see the error of their ways. They came to understand the purity of our design. You could too, Campion. I didn't kill them. I haven't killed anyone. If they told you the same stories they told the others, and they told us, you've been lied to. No one's been killed here. No assassins, none of my followers, not even me. I aim to keep it that way. Although I never mind killing assassins, actually. That's just, well, justice."

The Light gets back up and addresses both BC and the rest of the room.

"This is the true church, Campion. We strive for real truth here. We actually follow the true teachings of Jesus Christ, not like the namby-pamby watered down pabulum that passes for 'Christianity' today! That supposed 'church' that employs such as you, Campion." He straightens up and speaks in a loud voice.

"You stand for everything we've left behind in today's so-called church. You are heresy incarnate! You have the nerve, the audacity to come here, to invade my home. You masquerade..."

The Light leans over him again and tears the priestly collar off his throat, " ...as a priest! Who do you think you are? Huh? Who do you think you are?"

BC doesn't answer. Not out loud, anyway.

Who am I? For you, for today? I am the vengeance of the Lord, come to bring you that much closer to the God you claim to worship. I'm your express trip to heaven, you arrogant fuck.

As if BC has spoken out loud, The Light glares angrily down at him.

"Get him out of my sight! He sickens me. Throw him in one of the empty rooms for now."

Two men grab BC by his arms and drag him out of the throne room. He's dragged down a long corridor to a small closet. They throw him on the floor, close and lock the door. He has just enough room to lie flat out on the floor. He lies there bound hand and foot in the dark.

Well, at least I'm not dead. Not yet.

BC tries to keep track of time, but it gets harder as the hours go by. At least 24 hours go by, as far as BC can figure, as he lies in the closet. When the door finally opens, The Light stands in the light in the door frame. A light comes on on the closet ceiling as The Light walks into the closet carrying a tray.

Nice trick of the light. Yuck, bad pun. Punishment. Too easy. Gotta be careful. I'm getting punchy.

"Campion, are you all right? I've come to ask your forgiveness." The Light's tone of voice and body language have completely changed. "I now understand you've been sent to me as a test, a challenge from God. And so far I have failed that challenge. 'If you love those who love you, what credit can you expect? Even sinners love those who love them. And if you do good to those who do good to you, what credit can you expect? For even sinners do that much... Instead, love your enemies and do good to them.' Luke six, thirty-two through thirty-five, mostly. In case you want to look it up later.

"Anyway, I've come to ask you to enjoy this food, to break bread with me. I've brought my Bible, too, if you're willing to pray with me. The New Jerusalem Bible, my favorite translation. Translated into English from the French. It's a poetic translation.

"Will you eat with me, Campion?"

I will not answer. This guy is way out there. He's unstable, clearly believes his own shit. That means he's capable of anything. Well so am I.

"Will you pray with me?"

Five minutes go by in silence. The Light sits and waits for BC to answer, then finally speaks himself.

"You test me. Fine. I love you, Campion, did you know that? As Jesus loves you, so do I. You are the most despicable creature I have ever encountered. Did you know that? Yes, I give you that distinction. The greatest test of unconditional love I have ever faced. But I accept the challenge."

Oh, this is so all about you...

"I will leave you be, for now. I leave you the food, the bread, and the book, my Bible. I'll leave the lights on. I will have one of my brothers come in and loose your bonds enough for you to eat and to read. They'll take you to the bathroom, too.

"I'd help you myself, but of course, then you could kill me. Jesus says I must love you, but I don't have to trust you blindly." The Light chuckles, "God respects intelligence."

The Light gives him a long look, as if trying to see inside him. He breaks his stare, turns, and walks quickly out the door, leaving the light on as the door clicks shut behind him.

Two of The Light's followers show up a short time

after he's gone. Without untying him, they lift him to his feet and shuffle him down the corridor to a small bathroom. They allow him to go in alone with his left hand free, his right still tied by a long rope to the binds around his ankle.

It's awkward, but BC makes it work. He can hardly turn around in the tiny bathroom space, but he manages and sits for some long anticipated relief.

After he's done they tie his left hand back with his right behind his back and lead him back to his closet. When he's back inside, one man stands guard at the door while the other unties both hands so he can eat and, presumably, read the Bible. They leave him alone and lock the door.

What incredible hospitality! And so many entertainment options!

BC picks up the Bible, looks at it for a few seconds, drops it back on the floor next to the tray. There is food on the tray, and BC hasn't eaten. He's hungry, so he eats; a chunk of bread, a slice of cheese, some sort of grain patty, and a water pack. It's filling enough.

After a while the two men return. They try to tie back his hands again, but BC resists. One of the men grabs the tray and raises it in the air above BC's head, threatening to strike. BC relents. They tie his hands, a little looser than they were before. Then they turn off the light and leave him alone again in the dark.

BC feels strange. Groggy.

Stomach's kinda queasy. They may have put something in the food. Damn, I should have known... all that talk about love and meanwhile they're... uh oh. Try to hold on... Drugging me up, that's consistent with cult brainwashing techniques. Wow, hard to focus... losing my grip, my senses merging together somehow, memory, smell, feeling, emotions, all cascading, crashing together, mental noise, no filters no way to separate all of ithappens all atonce...

When he comes back to his senses, BC can't be sure how much time has gone by. He's alone, on the floor, in the dark.

For how long? Probably six, seven hours... I don't know. Could be two days. More. No way to know when they start dosing you. Why don't they just kill me?

The men come back, walk him to the bathroom and feed him. Then they leave him alone in the little room. The light stays on. He's got nothing else to do, so he leafs through the Bible.

Blah blah blah. Irrelevant ancient mumbo jumbo. Wonder where I find the part about drugging your prisoners?
1   BC flips the pages of the massive book, waiting for... something. Anything out of the ordinary. Any sign that they've dosed him again.

Hmm. Nothing.

He falls asleep. His guards wake him up.

"Lunch!"

Lunch? Already? That doesn't seem right. Too soon.

They bring him to the bathroom again, and afterwards give him a tuna sandwich and some water. They leave him. He eats.

No psychedelic breakfast... let's see how electric lunch is. Hmm. Good tuna.

After about an hour, BC feels his stomach twitch.

Uh oh.

His gut clenches. His stomach feels like it's flipping over inside.

Oh no... can't stop...

"Huaugrlahun!" BC drops to his hands and knees, vomit erupting up out of him. There's no holding it in. "Huaurgurgh!" Puke spews from his mouth like a tuna smoothie splattering on the floor.

Oh my god, this does not feel right...

He senses more than sees the door open, and a bucket is thrown in front of him as he begins to throw up again. "Hunh!" BC heaves.

There's nothing left inside! Jesus!

BC tries to sit up on his knees. Another gut-wrenching heave rips through him and he coughs out bitter yellow bile into the bucket. When it feels like it's over, he sits back up on his knees again. Two guards are standing in the doorway. The one on the right has another bucket and a mop. The guard on the left steps toward him offering him a water packet.

I don't know if it'll stay down, but it's gotta taste better than this...

He drinks it down quickly.

Nope.

His stomach turns over. He hurls most of what he just drank back up into the bucket.

But it feels better than the bile...

"Bad tuna," the guard who gave him the water says. BC just looks at him.

Fuck you.

The other guard moves into the room and starts mopping up the vomit. The smell is pungent, almost overpowering, like a steaming pile of rotting fish and vinegar. BC feels his stomach clench, but it eases. He sits back up. The guard with the mop looks at him.

"C'mon!" He thrusts the mop handle into BC's hands. "Clean up your mess!"

Fuck you. Ah, what the fuck.

BC begins mopping up the floor.

I've gotta stay here, might as well.

He cleans up best he can. When he's done, the guard takes the mop back from him, and the other guard motions for BC to follow him out the door. BC complies, shuffling into the corridor. They lead him to the bathroom again, only this time the guard has a gun.

What, lead pipes now going out of fashion? Wait... Is that my gun?

"We're going to untie you, but I warn you, try anything and I will shoot you," the guard says, pointing the weapon at BC. He nods to the other guard, who bends down and begins untying BC.

Tempting, but no. Foolish.

The guard with the gun holds out a bundle, tossing it to BC when his hands are untied.

"Clean clothes. Go ahead inside the bathroom, get cleaned up and changed. You have ten minutes. Any longer, I come in after you, and I will shoot you. Go ahead."

Cool, my very own robe! Fuck. Might as well.

BC cleans up and changes, gets tied back up and escorted back to his closet. Someone's come while he was in the bathroom and finished cleaning the room. It's better than it was, but it still reeks of sour, rotten fish.

Did they do that to me on purpose? Hard to tell. Wonder if I'll be able to eat when dinner comes?

BC waits for dinner. And waits. It seems like hours go by.

How long has it been? I thought it'd be an hour or two at most.

He paces the length of the closet a few hundred times. Bored, BC picks up the Bible again.

I could read it, I suppose. Might help keep me sane, keep me focused.

BC finds he can't really focus on reading.

Ah, whatever. Can't concentrate. I'll try later.

He sits and waits.

This is ridiculous. I don't even feel nauseous anymore. Where are they?

After another couple of hours, a guard opens the door.

"Here's your dinner." He leaves a tray like the one the night before and leaves BC to contemplate whether or not it's dosed. And whether his time sense is off.

Was it really that long a time? If I was talking I'd have asked him what kept him! The guard acted normal enough, not as if he was late. Damn, I'm hungry, though. Gotta eat this crap even if it is laced with some kind of holy bug juice.

He waits again after eating to see if there is any strangeness.

Hmm. Nope. Nothing. I don't think so. I...

BC drifts off and sleeps soundly.

They serve him breakfast, lunch and dinner, over the next couple of days. Each time he eats he has to wonder if they dose him. They do dose him the second night, and BC finds it hard to focus the day after at all. He tries to clear his thoughts.

The intervals of time between my 'meals' don't seem regular. They lengthen and contract. They may be trying to fuck up my sense of time. Time is fluid, changing, unfixed and uncertain. How long have I been here, really?

They leave the light on in his closet and give him day, turn it off for night accordingly, but BC is growing sure the intervals aren't consistent.

Neither are the intervals between the times they wake him up, take him to the bathroom, and feed him. Sometimes it seems like only hours between his feedings and bathroom runs, sometimes it seems like a day or two.

It might be four days, I don't know. They're definitely fucking with my time sense. I don't think they're giving me real "nights" and "days." And the food. I've tripped out at least a couple times. However long it's been... I haven't seen The Light again.

Finally, The Light returns. It feels like a week later to BC, but he can't be sure.

"Mr. Campion! Will you talk to me yet? Hello?"

No.

BC says nothing. After five minutes of silence The Light proclaims, "Very well, then. I'm having you cleaned up and brought to dinner with us tonight, whether you'll speak to us or not. I've been failing my Lord with you. I haven't had you at my table! We'll see you there tonight."

Chapter Seventeen

BC finds himself cleaned up and sitting at dinner with The Light that night. He's strapped to his chair around the waste and around each leg, his left arm strapped down and his right left free so he can eat.

The warmest hospitality from my gracious hosts...

The food smells good. BC decides to eat. They share the same common serving dishes, so if he's getting anything funny in the food, they all are.

"Hope the food is good, Mr. Campion!" The Light says.

BC stops eating. He puts down his fork and just sits there, staring back at The Light.

"Don't stop on my account! Go ahead, enjoy it!"

BC remains still. The odors from the food in front of him, the baked fish and the summer squash, rise up and assault his senses, torturing him, testing his resolve, but he doesn't take another bite. He stares at The Light.

Fuck you.

BC doesn't move. The others continue their meal. BC endures the torture of the smell of the melting butter on the squash wafting over to him, the way the fish flakes off the plate onto the fork of the woman next to him, the way she smiles and closes her eyes after eating the fish, savoring its taste as she chews, chews, and swallows.

At the end of the meal he's led back to his closet, after The Light tells him, "maybe some day you'll eat with us, Campion. You just weren't ready. We'll have something brought to you later."

Later, as he eats alone in his closet, The Light's voice suddenly booms out from a hidden speaker.

"I'm glad to see you're finally eating, Mr. Campion. I

119

do not wish you harm. I wish you'd renounce your intent to kill me. If you pray for it, Mr. Campion, if you really mean it, God will grant you his forgiveness. You can confess and be healed and join us. Think about it, won't you Mr. Campion?"

BC freezes. He stops eating, backs away from the food and curls up in the corner.

The Light must be watching me on some hidden camera, talking to me on a speaker somewhere out of sight. I don't know where the camera is, but I will perform for no one. Fuck them for watching me. How long have they been watching me? No doubt this whole time. I should have known, I guess I assumed, but Fuck it! Fuck The Light! This bites. Why not just kill me now? Maybe I have to confess first. That could be it, or part of it. Confess so I can die pure, right? No thanks. But maybe I can use a confession angle to my advantage...

The Light speaks again, over the speaker, "Ah. I'm sorry Mr. Campion, I should not have disturbed you. Do not deprive yourself on my account."

BC doesn't move.

"I don't want to keep you as a prisoner if I don't have to, Mr. Campion. But you are here to kill me, and that really leaves me no choice. I will turn off the camera, now, though, and soon I'll stop talking and switch off the com to this room entirely. You'll have your privacy back. You will be free to do as you like. We will talk again soon, Mr. Campion."

BC sits in silence. After a while he decides to finish eating. The lights go out and he falls asleep. He dreams of being chased, of being chased, of being chased, again and again. He wakes up when the light come back on.

Morning? I just don't know. Less sure each time.

They bring him breakfast and a fresh robe. He eats, then changes, then sits and waits.

How much time has really passed? Is it really a week? Feels like it. Maybe. I'm trying to maintain my focus, but it's hard. I just don't know. These guys are experienced at brainwashing. I'm sure they teach that in Basic Cult 101, right? Lots of experience.

After a time, about "midday", a man BC hasn't seen before enters his closet. He's small, rounded, balding, robed like the others. He picks up The Light's Bible, and speaks after the door closes behind him.

"Hello, Mr. Campion. My name is Sylvester Kim. I am an assistant to The Light. As he remains your primary target, he's asked me to come here to hear your confession. Are you ready to confess?"

BC ignores him.

"I am here to take your confession, to offer you forgiveness and penance and absolution of your sins, should you so desire. To welcome you into our family, should you confess and be reborn with us in Jesus. You can be forgiven, Mr. Campion, if you'll only renounce before God your mission to kill The Light."

Why not? I'm stuck right now. This could be the way out. Then again, this could be just setting me up to be killed with a pure heart. It might be okay to help me on my way to heaven after my soul's been cleansed. I'll bet that's what they did to the other two before me.

"My... ahem, excuse me," BC clears his throat. He hasn't spoken for days. "My name is Bernard Campion. I am a priest, duly ordained by his holiness Pope Peter the Second, New catholic Church. I am an agent of the Pope, a member of the Office of Papal Operations, sent to investigate the man you call 'The Light,' for his holiness. I am then to report back on conditions here. I am not here to kill The Light. I entered covertly to try to observe the situation here without detection. In this I failed. I have nothing to confess. Plus, if I confess, you'll kill me, right? So, no. ."

"I see. So, then, you won't renounce all intent to kill The Light? Won't you ask the Lord to forgive you for conspiring to kill His Holy Servant on Earth?"

"I never planned to kill him. I never meant any harm. You misunderstand my mission here. If it makes you happy, sure, yes, I renounce all violence towards The Light. I never meant any."

I lie so well, so easily. Let's see if he believes...

"Do you confess these sins?"

"To you? Or to everybody listening in?"

"No one is listening in. We are in the private sanctity of your confessional."

This place is just about as roomy as those boxes, all right.

"Sure. I confess. Now, you kill me, right?"

"No, I have no wish to harm you, Mr. Campion. So, you confess to?"

"To having aimed to deceive, so sorry."

"Observe the forms, please."

"What forms?"

"You may not have these rules in your lax new church, but we do. We begin, 'Bless me, Father, for I have sinned. It has been, well, however long since my last confession and these are my sins.'"

"So, you're a Father, then?"

"Yes. The Light himself ordained me."

"But he's discredited. You're no priest."

"Under our rules, neither are you."

"So, then, are we even?"

"I don't think so."

"No?"

"I don't think you're ready to confess, either." Sylvester Kim turns and leaves the closet. BC is left alone again.

The hidden speaker crackles to life.

"Mr. Campion, Father Kim says you aren't really ready to confess your sins. I'm disappointed."

The Light. Hello fuckhead.

BC doesn't answer. After a moment of silence The Light speaks again.

"Very well. Stay silent, Mr. Campion.

"You have my Bible. Have you even looked at it? That copy has been in my family for years. I give it to you to read

122

and reflect on, Mr. Campion, so you may meditate on the Word of God. Let me recommend the first letter of John to you, for now. God is Love, Mr. Campion. If you do not know love, you do not know God. What God do you serve, Mr. Campion?"

Arrogant Bastard.

The Light does not speak again. They leave BC alone with the Bible for hours. No one comes with food. No one looks in on him, and the lights stay on.

I bet they're watching, though. I can almost feel it. Where is that camera?

Eventually, out of pure boredom, BC picks up the book.

At least it's something. Something to read.

He turns to the First Letter of John, Chapter Six, and reads,

"Anyone who says, 'I love God' and hates his brother is a liar, since whoever does not love the brother whom he can see cannot love God, whom he has not seen."

Nice words, anyway. Charming sentiment. Too bad no church seems to follow them. His specialness The Light doesn't seem to heed them either, since he's killed two men before me already. And how many of his own followers?

BC is left alone with the light on for a long time, so he keeps reading. It's something to do. He only used the Bible before to pass the "seminary" course he took to become a minister, so he could set up his own "nonprofit" church.

Didn't really read it then, just found the answers I needed and copied them out of it. Didn't really care what it had to say. It was a means to end. Well, nothing else to do...

BC reads. His days continue to pass in ragged fashion, with some meals dosed, and some days lasting God knows how long. But BC keeps reading, and begins to appreciate the Bible as a collection of writings. He has nothing else to do with his "days" as he sits in his box, prisoner of The Light and his followers, so he reads nonstop. Another week, maybe more, seems to go by. As the time passes, he finds himself reading all of the gospels, the

Acts of the Apostles and their letters and the letters of Paul.
Never actually sat down and read the thing like a book before. Funny. Most of what Jesus says, no one actually does, not anymore. This commune in space they have here might just be closer to what He was describing back then. Are they subtly brainwashing me here or what? Gotta remember, The Light is really a viscous fuck...

Chapter Eighteen

The Cardinal sighs. His afternoon nap has been interrupted by his secretary buzzing him with a priority call. Again.

The Cardinal has been receiving calls from Governor Marc Edwards. The calls started when Campion had been gone over two weeks. The governor asks each time if Campion has returned, and day after day the Cardinal's answer is the same:

"No, no, he's still away on the Pope's business, I'm afraid."

And each day the governor says something like, "it's getting to be a long time..."

The Cardinal's answer is usually something like, "There's really no telling how long it will take," to which Governor Edwards normally replies, "well, it's been two weeks," then it's "three weeks," then "four."

When Edwards says, "It's been over a month," and asks, as he often does, "aren't you worried?" the Cardinal finally admits, "well, yes... a little."

This surprises the governor, and worries him.

"You're finally worried, now?"

"Well, the Pope called asking me if he was back. That makes me start to worry."

"He made it sound like it was only going to be about a week when he left. He couldn't tell me what was up."

"Hmmph. You know more than I do."

"What can we do?"

"I don't know. I don't really think we can do much of anything, except wait, and pray for him."

"I'm not catholic, Cardinal."

"Then do whatever it is that you do do, Governor. I'll be praying for him. Good day."

Marc Edwards signs off. He doesn't like the Cardinal, never has, couldn't see why Governor McEntyre was chumming up to the guy back when. The Cardinal doesn't even get worried about Campion, one of his own men, until after a month goes by. Edwards wonders if BC is even still alive, wonders where he is out there as he looks out over the surface of the moon, past the rising Earth, into the deep carpet of stars.

BC is still alive in his closet, his cell, killing time by reading the Bible. They leave his bindings looser now, so he can exercise a little. He tries to keep some semblance of training going.

When he gets food, he eats.

He's decided he can't worry about what they're putting in the food. BC is sure they are drugging him, but not every meal. And he knows he needs to eat to keep up his health, his strength and his energy, so he eats what they give him and hopes his brain doesn't end up too freshly scrubbed.

Sometimes they turn off the light, so he sleeps. He can't really tell how long he sleeps when he does. He knows sometimes the lights are on for longer than a full day, sometimes shorter. He's not sure how much time has really passed. There are no clocks in his cell or along the route they walk him down to get to the bathrooms. There's no way to tell what time of day or night it is, or how many days have gone by.

Three weeks? Four, maybe? I don't know anymore. It's been a long time since I've been brought anywhere else but the bathroom. Even a long time since I've seen The Light.

BC sits in his cell and looks down at the Bible. He's read the book, knows it much better, now. It's helped him keep his wits as he's bided his time in the closet, given him something to do. He's had the chance to think a lot, to question... everything. His entire existence.

It's hard to maintain my vengeance of the Lord pose

after reading this stuff for real. It's not even in the New Testament. That's Old Testament. Seems to me the vengeance stuff is what Jesus was trying to eliminate, trying to change. Now it's all wrong. Goddammit, why did I let them get me thinking about this shit? I gotta get out of this place.

One night as he tries to fall asleep, BC feels the room peel away from him, the walls collapse. He sees a vast ocean spread out around him. He floats alone upon the sea.

God damned drugs. They've dosed me again. I feel clearer this time, though, but separate from myself, floating on the water. I am detached. Is this really some drug? This doesn't feel like the drugs they've been dosing me with. Hallucination from hunger, or isolation? It feels strangely good, right somehow.

Everything seems so simple. It's all so obvious from this height, laid out in front of me. Options, potentials, possible repercussions. It seems I can grasp each of them entirely, in all their complexity. If only each of us could see with such clarity. We'd all get along. It's so obvious! We just need to love. The more we love, the more we live after the body is left behind. That's what Jesus did, that's what I'm getting from all this reading. Everybody gets him wrong, everyone ignores the inconvenient parts of the book.

I see so much, yet my eyes are closed. This ocean is in my mind, this is only my cell, I'm on the floor curled in the fetal position with my eyes scrunched closed.

WELL, THEN, OPEN YOUR EYES.

What?

YOU HEARD ME. OPEN YOUR EYES.

Oh, this is great. Now I've got audible hallucinations happening. Must be good drugs they're feeding me. I'm not hearing anything. It's just inside my head.

MAYBE. MAYBE NOT. I CAN LIVE WITH THAT. OPEN YOUR EYES.

I'm not hearing anything! La la la la la...

C'MON, CUT IT OUT. OPEN YOUR EYES.

BC opens his eyes. There is a light around him. He is

in the center of the ocean, alone on the surface of the sea.

Yet somehow I can still see the lines of the cell, like two pictures superimposed, one over the other. And, wait, there's someone out there, on the water, walking this way. It looks like The Light!

YOU SEE ME AS HIM? NOT QUITE. THE OTHER IMAGERY WORKS, WALKING ON WATER AND ALL. THAT'S HAPPENED BEFORE. IT'S FUNNY HOW THE MIND WORKS, HOW IT PROCESSES THIS KIND OF EXTRASENSORY INPUT. IT'S ALL ABOUT FRAMES OF REFERENCE, REALLY. HOW DO YOU PERCEIVE THE UNPERCEIVABLE? BUT I AM NOT THAT MAN. SEE ME AS SOMEONE ELSE. HE IS FLAWED, AS ARE YOU. HE AT LEAST TRIES, THOUGH.

Man, I'm tripping hard.

THAT'S ONE WAY TO LOOK AT IT.

and you offer?

ANOTHER WAY. TO LOOK AT IT. YOU'VE OPENED A DOORWAY. YOU'VE LET ME IN. WHATEVER CHEMICALS ARE INVOLVED HAVE ONLY SERVED AS THE KEYS TO OPEN PASSAGEWAYS INSIDE YOU, TO OPEN YOU TO THE POSSIBILITIES, AND TO ME. YOU UNLOCKED THE DOOR. I MERELY WALKED THROUGH.

Okay, sure, whatever. I'm talking to myself.

THAT'S ONE WAY TO LOOK AT IT.

and now I'm repeating myself.

IT'S FOR EFFECT.

So, what, you're supposed to be who, Jesus?

IF THAT WORKS FOR YOU. IT'S A REASONABLE METAPHOR. YEAH, JESUS, BUT NOT AS PORTRAYED BY YOUR CHURCH, AS YOU'RE BEGINNING TO SEE. I DON'T RECOGNIZE THAT JESUS AT ALL.

Brainwashing is a wonderful thing. So, you're not really The Light, you're Jesus, and I'm not really tripping, I'm having some sort of visitation, right. Now you'll tell me the benefits of the cult's dental plan and why I should sign up after you've given my head a good scrubbing, right?

NO. I'M JUST HERE. YOU OPENED THE DOOR...

...yeah, I know, you just walked through it. I heard

you the first time.

MAYBE I'M YOUR CONSCIENCE? OF COURSE, YOU WOULDN'T RECOGNIZE ME THEN, EITHER, NOW, WOULD YOU?

Funny.

LET'S TALK ABOUT YOUR CONSCIENCE.

Why?

DO YOU HAVE ONE?

I don't know. I don't know if I do. Actually, I don't think too much about it at all, really. Do I? You tell me.

MAYBE AN UNDERDEVELOPED ONE. HARD FOR ME TO SAY.

I've been serving a cause; hell, I've been working for you if you're Jesus.

OH, HAVE YOU, NOW?

Well, yeah. I serve the Pope.

AND THAT HELPS ME HOW?

He's your guy, isn't he?

SAYS WHO?

Says him. He does everything in your name.

YES, HE DOES, AND I FIND IT QUITE ANNOYING. FROM HIM, AND FROM EVERYONE ELSE WHO KEEPS CLAIMING TO DO THINGS FOR ME, IN MY NAME. IF I'M GOD, DO YOU THINK I NEED PEOPLE DOING STUFF FOR ME? IF I'M GOD, 'THY WILL BE DONE,' YOU KNOW, IT'S DONE! NAH, HE'S JUST ONE MORE SHMUCK ABUSING MY NAME. I'M THINKING OF CHANGING MY NAME, YOU KNOW? MAYBE TO SOMETHING LIKE TED.

We beseech thee, Almighty Ted?

'JESUS' IS JUST WAY TOO USED AND ABUSED. SO MANY HAVE KILLED FOR SO LONG IN MY NAME. YOU DO THE SAME.

So sorry. Guess I'm apologizing to myself. The psychs would have a field day with this dream.

Well, then, what about The Light? Isn't he guilty, too?

SURE. WE'RE ALL GUILTY.

He's killed in your name as well.

HE'S KILLED MORE IN SELF DEFENSE THAN IN MY

NAME. YOU'VE GOT BAD INFORMATION.

Or at least I want myself to think I do.

THAT'S RIGHT, THIS IS JUST A HALLUCINATION. YOU'RE TALKING TO YOURSELF, TELLING YOURSELF WHAT YOU WANT TO HEAR. WHY DO YOU DENY ME?

Because you aren't real. You're me, a figment of my imagination enhanced and animated by whatever it is they've been spiking my food with.

ARE YOU SO SURE OF THAT? WHY AM I STILL HERE?

Go away, then. This will just be a fading memory in the morning.

YOU THINK SO? DO YOU BELIEVE, BC? WHAT DO YOU BELIEVE IN? DO YOU BELIEVE IN ME?

I believe in me. That's all I can believe in. I can't waste my time and energy believing in anyone else.

HOW SAD.

Sad? Not really. Practical. Realistic.

IT'S SAD. YOU DEPRIVE YOURSELF OF SO MUCH.

I'm not missing anything. Well, I miss <u>not</u> being in this place.

WHAT ABOUT LOVE?

Love? I've been in love. I've been with plenty of women. But whenever I trusted one, she usually fucked me over. If that's love, I'll pass.

THAT'S NOT WHAT I MEAN. YOU KNOW IT. THAT'S NOT LOVE.

Yeah, but, you see, I thought it was at the time, each time. At least, I think I thought I was in love. Another woman, one I didn't even know that well or even get to fuck, just fucked me over and left me for dead after trying to kill me. She was cute. I had seen her around, thought she was interested. She was, but not in a good way. Love? Forget about it.

I CAN'T. IT'S KINDA MY WHOLE DEAL, THE WHOLE LOVE THING. YOU HAVEN'T EVEN COME REMOTELY CLOSE TO LOVE, TO REAL LOVE, OR TO ME, FOR THAT MATTER. YOU USED MY NAME TO SMUGGLE AND

PROFITEER, THEN TO KILL. YOU KILL, YOU SAY, IN MY NAME, BUT MY NAME IS LOVE. YOU CAN'T DO THESE THINGS IN THE NAME OF LOVE.

Sorry. Didn't mean to piss you off.

YOU DIDN'T. YOU CAN'T, THOUGH SOME HAVE TRIED. I DON'T GET PISSED, I JUST GET DISAPPOINTED. AND SOME HAVE SORELY TRIED MY PATIENCE, MUCH AS YOU DO NOW. YOU DISAPPOINT ME, BC. YOU'RE A PUPPET WHO SERVES A PRETENDER. HE PULLS YOUR STRINGS. HOW DOES IT FEEL TO BE SUCH A GOOD PUPPET? OR ARE YOU A PUPPY? OBEYING YOUR ORDERS, OBEYING YOUR MASTER. HE HAS YOU WELL HOUSE TRAINED, WELL LEASHED, PUPPY.

If you're Jesus, I've done it for You.

NEITHER OF US BELIEVES THAT FOR A SECOND. YOU'VE DONE IT FOR YOU AND ONLY YOU, BC. SAD, AS I SAID. LOOK WHERE YOU ARE NOW, ALONE, DRUGGED, ON THE FLOOR OF A CELL ON A DESERTED SPACE STATION RUN BY A CULT, SUFFERING FROM SOME HOLY DELUSION OR VISION OR HALLUCINATION, ON THE EDGE OF INSANITY. NO ONE KNOWS OR CARES THAT YOU'RE MISSING. OH, SURE, YOUR EMPLOYERS WILL CARE IF YOU DON'T GET THE JOB DONE, IF YOU DON'T KILL THE LIGHT, BUT THEN THEY'LL DENY THEY KNEW YOU WERE HERE, AND SEND SOMEONE ELSE TO FINISH THE JOB. THEY DON'T CARE ABOUT YOU. YOU HAVE NO FRIENDS, NO FAMILY. NO ONE LOVES YOU. NO ONE MISSES YOU. SAD.

Harsh. Maybe even close to the truth. But I don't need anybody else, you see? I don't answer to anyone else but me. I don't want anyone to miss me, care about me, or to go and get themselves killed trying to help me. You're right. This is my situation, as it is. As I want it to be.

ARE YOU TRYING TO CONVINCE YOURSELF OR ME? AND YOU'VE ALMOST MADE A FRIEND OF GOVERNOR EDWARDS, HAVEN'T YOU?

Part of the job.

RIGHT. COLD. BUT IF ALL THAT'S TRUE, WHY HAVE YOU OPENED YOURSELF TO ME?

I didn't. You're just here. I don't know why.

YOU'VE BEEN READING MY WORDS. THE DRUGS OPEN YOU TO THE PLACE INSIDE YOURSELF WHERE TIME AND SPACE CEASE TO EXIST. YOU FOUND ME THERE. HERE, ON YOUR OCEAN. YOU CALLED TO ME ACROSS THE SURFACE OF YOUR SEA, AND I CAME TO YOU. I AM HERE BECAUSE I'M ALWAYS HERE. I'M YOU. I'M A PART OF A GREATER WHOLE, AND SO ARE YOU. I'M HERE BECAUSE I FOUND MY WAY HERE, HOW TO BE HERE, I ALWAYS DO. IT'S SIMPLE, REALLY. YOU JUST HAVE TO LOVE, WITHOUT RESERVATIONS, WITHOUT CONDITIONS.

That's not simple.

NOT FOR YOU. I KNOW. I'M SORRY FOR YOU. WHEN YOU LOVE THAT COMPLETELY, THAT WELL, YOU FIND YOURSELF IN TOUCH WITH THAT GREATER WHOLE, ALL THAT IS, ALL I AM, ALL YOU ARE AND CAN BE. AND WHEN YOUR BODY DIES, YOU FIND YOU CAN STILL LOVE AND EVEN FORGIVE THOSE WHO KILL YOU. FOR YOU DO NOT DIE, HAVING BECOME PART OF ALL THAT IS, PART OF THE GREATER WHOLE, BEFORE YOUR BODY PASSED AWAY. WHEN YOU'VE ALREADY GONE BEYOND THE BOUNDS OF TIME AND SPACE THROUGH COMPLETE LOVE, THOUGH YOUR FLESH HAS BEEN THE FOCUS FOR YOUR LIVING AND LOVING ENERGY, YOU'VE FOUND THE WAY TO REMAIN AS THE FLESH DECAYS.

So, because you loved so well yourself, your energy remains? You're immortal?

NOT SO MUCH IMMORTAL AS JUST ALWAYS. BECAUSE I LOVE, I AM. AS I AM WITH YOU NOW I ALSO WALK THE SHORES OF GALILEE, I VISIT SAUL, I AM ALWAYS, AT ONCE.

You rose from the dead?

PART OF ME NEVER DIED. I JUST BECAME... SOMETHING MORE. A DIFFERENT SORT OF PRESENCE. MY FIRST FOLLOWERS FELT IT WHEN THEY FINALLY BEGAN TO GATHER BACK TOGETHER AFTER I WAS KILLED, AND BEGAN TO REALIZE I WAS NOT GONE, BUT STILL WITH THEM. THEY PROCLAIMED, "DEATH CANNOT

CONTAIN HIM," AND THIS IS THE BEST DESCRIPTION OF IT. I AM NOT CONTAINED.

I'm surprised my brain can make all this shit up. It sounds almost plausible. Good drugs.

HAVE IT YOUR WAY, BC. BUT AT LEAST CONSIDER SERVING LOVE, NOT HATE. STOP KILLING. CAN YOU STOP?

No. If I stop, they kill me. No retirement except the final kind, I'm afraid. It's the rules. I didn't exactly choose this line of work, it chose me.

YOU STARTED DOWN THE PATH YOURSELF. YOU MADE THE RULES. YOU CAN CHANGE THE RULES. YOU HAVE THE SEED OF GREAT THINGS WITHIN YOU, BERNARD CAMPION. LOVE WILL HELP IT GROW.

The bright light dims, and BC is once again alone in the middle of his sea. He notices he can see the walls of his cell superimposed upon the image of the ocean. The lines of the room slowly become more distinct. BC blinks and the room comes sharply into focus as the lights flicker on and the door opens.

Damn! Slammed back into reality. If you can call this reality. What the fuck was that?

Two of his guards enter. They motion to BC, gesturing for him to follow them out and down the corridor. BC thinks over his dream as he shuffles down the hall.

That felt real in a way I can't put my finger on. I don't feel all groggy now. I don't feel all dosed. 'Course, there's probably so much in my system now I'm used to it. Ah, the bathroom.

They let him shower. He sees himself in the mirror and laughs. His hair and beard have grown out wildly.

Every inch the mad ancient prophet! Look at you! Just like them, now. Repent! The End is Near!

"Hey, hurry up. The Light is waiting for you."

Finally, his majesty is granting me an audience...

BC is led back to the throne room, his first time back there in at least a couple weeks. The Light sits in the throne, on the raised dais.

"Hello again, Mr. Campion. We've not spoken in some time. Then again, 'we' haven't spoken at all, really, have we? I've talked, and I know for the most part you've listened, but you've never said anything. That might be considered rude, Mr. Campion."

BC keeps silent.

"Very well, Mr. Campion. You did talk to Father Kim a while back, so we know you have a voice. You almost confessed. Why won't you talk to me?"

What the fuck...

"What..." BC has to clear his throat. He hasn't spoken in a long while now. "What about?"

"You're here to kill me. They've sent you to kill me, haven't they?"

"Why do you keep saying that?"

"I can see it in your eyes. The way you're looking at me, right now. The way you don't look at me. You're not as confident as you used to be, as you'd like to be. The truth bleeds out."

"If I didn't think you'd have me killed, I'd tell you to go fuck yourself, long and hard."

"Why so defensive, Mr. Campion? I must have hit a nerve. You pretend to be a priest, but such language..." The Light tsks tsks at him.

"I am a priest."

"Oh, really, and I suppose you do the Lord's work? You're just a humble missionary here to save us heretics, hmm?"

"I do the Lord's work, just as you do."

"What Lord? Who do you worship, Mr. Campion? No Lord I know! They probably tell you this," The Light makes a gun with his fingers and points it at his head, then jerks away from it as if he's being shot, "is the Lord's work... do they? Did they tell you God," The Light stood up, "would want me gone? Did they? Is it The Lord's Will that I be removed? You're just here to help me get closer to Him, then, aren't you? Aren't you!"

"Whatever. Whatever you say."

"Yes, it is whatever I say around here! This is my home, our home, Mr. Campion! We are a family, a community in the Lord! We are the body of Christ, Mr. Campion! You've been reading the Book, I know you have."

Damn. He has been watching me. Or having me watched. I'm a fucking lab rat.

The Light questions him, "Haven't you seen the hypocrisy of your so-called church for what it is now?"

"I see hypocrites everywhere I turn, your highness. Your majesty..."

"Don't call me that!"

"You're as bad as they are..."

"Am I? How dare you..."

"Why not? You've killed people in the name of God as a means to your ends. You've killed your own people and mine, too. You killed the two who came before me. Then lied to me about it."

"Self defense, I assure you."

"What, no turn the other cheek?"

"And have it blown off? Hard to turn the other cheek when your head's been blown off, isn't it? No, thank you."

"That's not in the Book. Some conviction you've got there. Impressive."

"Impudent. I liked you better silent."

BC shuts up. The Light waits. A long silence. Then, The Light speaks again.

"They did order you to kill me, didn't they?"

"Why do you keep saying that?"

"You arrive unannounced, you sneak in, you kill my brothers, you're armed to the teeth when we capture you trespassing..."

"...as we forgive those who trespass against us?" BC interjects.

"Shut up!" The Light yells. Then he gets quiet, intense. "I know who you are, I know you and your type, Campion. Someone like you takes life far too easily. And there's no other reason for you to come here but for you to take mine. I will defend myself against you, too. I must, you see. So many times the light has shone in this world, only to be brutally snuffed out by the fearful and the ignorant. So many great religious leaders lost. I'm trying not to let that happen to me." The Light is red in the face, flushed, and he starts coughing a dry, raspy cough. Kim, at The Light's right hand, leans in concerned, but The Light brushes him back with a sweep of his hand.

When The Light stops coughing, BC says, "So, you see yourself as another Martin Luther King, or Ghandi or maybe even Jesus, huh?"

The Light clears his throat. "Mock me at your peril, Campion. There are many here. They follow <u>my</u> word. They see <u>my</u> Light. 'Long as I am in this world, I am the Light of this world,' Mr. Campion. Do not mock me. It is not only my anger you stir up, but all of ours."

"So speaketh the Light?"

"Do not mock me! You do not yet know the pure righteous anger of God, Campion!"

"And you're the one to bring it down on my sorry ass, is that it?"

The Light just glares at him, stays silent. The Reverend Kim joins in on the stare as well. BC stares back at the both of them.

What the fuck.

"Why haven't you killed me already? Are you keeping me alive for your amusement?"

"No. You do not amuse me."

"Then why?"

"I can't kill you. Not outright. It's not my way."

"What is your way?"

"You must be confessed, given a chance to recant your ways."

"Oh. I see. And then you kill me, right?"

"No. If you truly confess, really change your ways, if you're honest and completely repentant, we'd accept you as one of us."

"You'd take me as a follower?"

"If I really believed you'd changed. You'd need to do

some serious convincing. But as I believe that Jesus is my savior and my Lord, so I also believe that no man is beyond redemption," The Light fixes his stare squarely on BC, "not even you, Campion. Even though I know you for the scum you are, I also know Jesus sat down at table with your kind. If He believed those as foul as you can still be redeemed, then so I, too, must believe. No man, no woman is beyond redemption in Jesus. You still have a chance to redeem yourself."

"You'd give me that chance? How do I redeem myself?"

Maybe this time I can work the confession. My only chance of ever getting out of this...

"Do you think you're capable of that degree of change, Campion? Do you really have it in you?"

"I don't know. But your offer surprises me. And I have been reading the Bible. What you say is true. Our church is flawed. We don't follow Jesus's teachings as we should. And maybe this is my chance to save myself, to save what's left of my soul, if you really mean what you're saying. I accept your offer."

"It's not really my offer..." The Light looks up to Heaven, "but, good, I'm glad I can surprise you. We do try to follow Christ's example. He was fond of second chances, even third and fourth. So, will you confess, then?"

"To what? To who? To you? Right here, now?"

"If you're ready. You can confess to us all, before the community, as they did back in the earliest days. Confess before the community, the body of Christ, and be absolved!" The Light draws up next to BC and places his hands on his head.

Here goes... Hope they buy this...

"Bless me, Father, for I have sinned. It has been too long since my last confession. These are my sins. I have plotted and tried to kill your servant. I have killed your sheep. Please, I beg your forgiveness, Oh Lord."

The crowd around them erupts in a rumble of murmurs and whispers. The Light's followers grow angry at hearing BC's blatant statement of offenses stated in so matter-of fact a fashion. Kim raises his arms, quiets the crowd, stills the murmuring.

The Light speaks, "The Lord hears your sins and forgives them. You are absolved of your sins..."

Phew...

"...and now you must serve your penance. Guards!"

Two of the robed and bearded men spring up at The Light's bark and grab BC by either arm. They begin dragging him out of the room.

"Hey! What are you doing? You said you wouldn't kill me!" BC yells. The men stop dragging him as The Light replies.

"You must atone for your sins, Mr. Campion! You can *say* you confess, you can start to free your soul from torment, but confession is not a get out of jail free card! You must show you are truly sorry for your sins by voluntarily taking on any penance we give to you.

"I give you your penance, Campion. Your penance is another week in your chamber. You shall read the New Testament and contemplate trying to become more Christ like. You may have already begun to save your soul tonight, Mr. Campion! You may have just saved your life as well. I was quite ready to have you killed as we began talking today, so consider this a vast improvement. Until next time! Goodnight," The Light says.

The guards again start to drag him out of the room. BC struggles to get his feet back under him, and half walks, half stumbles his way back to his cell between his two escorts. He "voluntarily" goes back inside, sits down, and listens as they close and lock the door once again. He picks up the Bible, flipping it open to the Gospel according to Mark, chapter one.

Penance! Shit. Well, I think he actually bought it. We'll see... I'm sure they'll be watching me to see how diligent my penance is. Better give them a good show.

138

Chapter Nineteen

BC is blinded by the light as the door to his closet opens. He's been awake, sitting cross-legged in the dark, serving his "penance", thinking of different ways of killing The Light. He squints, trying to see who it is, it's too short to be The Light.

"I don't believe you. I don't believe your confession."

Ah, Mr. Kim. Welcome...

"Why not, Father Kim? I've seen the error of my ways. I've spent this last month actually reading this damn thing," BC nods at the Bible, thinks again, "poor choice of words, sorry. But I did read it. The New Testament especially, just as He asked. We here really are closer to the ideals of the community as Jesus proposed it, as you read about it in Acts and in The Letters. I was wrong."

"You were full of shit, still are. I see right through you."

"You know, Mr. Kim..." BC gets up and stands looking down on Kim.

"Father. Please."

"*Father* Kim, sorry. You don't strike me as being too much like the rest here, either. You're full of a fair amount of shit yourself, aren't you? Aren't you!"

Kim has something in his right hand. BC sees him roll a finger over it and the door closes behind him. Kim holds up his hand to show BC a small black plastic cube.

"Room controls. Lights, speakers, mics, cameras, lock, all controlled by this nifty little device. One cube for each room in this section, the old sultan's little prison. Or maybe his bordello, hard to tell. At any rate, this is the one for this room. The sultan designed these controls to be both portable and personal, so he could carry them and use them as favors. If he gave you the cube he was giving you back your privacy. This cube controls everything in this room, and can shut off the mics, the cameras, the whole surveillance system. But just for this room.

"With the door closed and with this in my hand, we are alone. No one can listen in on us. And so I say again... I see right through you, Campion, even if He doesn't. I still see the murder in your eyes. You aren't hiding anything. You don't even know what day it is, do you?"

BC knows he doesn't.

Nope.

"You're nearly broken, Campion."

"Bullshit. And why should I believe you about that thing," BC says, pointing at the small black plastic room control cube. "You're just trying to set me up, trying to make it look like I don't regret my past offenses. You're trying to show them I really haven't confessed in my heart, so they'll kill me. Well it won't work!"

"Jesus, Campion, will you quit playing for the cameras? They're off, you can quit your act for the time being. This controls any access to this room, and it's all off. See?"

Kim tosses the cube at BC.

The writing is small, but legible. Controls for the camera, the mics, the light, the lock... just as Kim said. And all turned off.

"Here," Kim says, grabbing it back quickly. "I'm locking the door, that's all. I want to talk to you about something."

"What, do you have a hidden tape recorder? Is that it?"

"You are paranoid!"

"Well.." BC looks Kim in the eye, then looks around at the close walls of the room. "What'd you expect?"

"Look, Campion, calm down. Bottom line here is, I want your help."

"You want my help? How can I help you? And why the fuck should I?"

"You don't know, you've been in here this whole time. Those of us who spend our time with The Light, we've been seeing him... change. He's sometimes not himself. Not like He used to be. He's been sick. He has mood swings, sudden shifts in his attitudes and behavior. It's been happening a lot lately. Your arrival seems to have driven him over the edge.

"You've seen him, the way he's been with you. He was going to kill you after you first woke up today, that was his plan. Then he felt, I don't know, sorry or something, because he knows too well who you are. Do you know He's done nothing but talk about you this whole time you've been in here? He's spent hours watching you on the monitors, talking to us about your killings, the mockery of your rise to the priesthood. He's obsessed with you. He told me he wants to kill you but he can't," Kim says, disgusted. "God won't let Him, He says. He says you're a test. His test. I think He thinks you're his final test before He dies, and if He fails He won't end up at God's side."

"So, because He's not Himself, He may want to believe me... but you wish I was dead. What, you want me to kill myself? Is that how I can help you?"

"No. I want you to help me kill Him."

Holy Shit, indeed! Out of left fucking field!

"What?"

Kim can't speak. He looks like he can't believe he's just said what he just said. "I want you to help me remove Him. There. Now do you believe me?" Kim holds up the black cube, "I'd never say something like that unless I was sure no one could hear us."

"I can't believe you just said that. *You* want to kill Him?"

"I don't want to. I have to. You know what he said about religious leaders dying young? Maybe they have to. Maybe it stops working after a while. You do it for too long you begin to think of yourself as above everyone else, special, being tested personally by God, eh? Then you're no longer the great religious leader. See what I mean?"

"Not quite."

"Look, Campion, I'm so far the only one who sees The Light declining like this. If He can go out now in a blaze of Holy Glory, he'll be a martyr and his legend will be preserved, everything he built here will be preserved. But if I let His decline continue, let Him visibly deteriorate in front of everyone, we'll lose it all, the whole thing. The dream will die with Him, because He's too tied into it! We need to set Him free, to set the dream free from him, the way it was set free when Jesus died. He, too, shall rise, just as Christ did. We'll make sure of it."

"You keep saying 'we'..."

"I need your help."

"But why me? And how? My base of power ain't what it used to be."

"There's another reason you should help me. Do you feel clearer headed lately?"

"What do you mean?"

"I stopped the drugs they were feeding you about a week ago. They were keeping you pretty high. I need you clear headed and clean for this to work. And I thought you might appreciate it."

Now THAT'S interesting, considering that last hallucination... Is he lying? What is he up to? What is he setting me up for?"

BC asks, "For what to work? You're not being too clear."

"I have a plan."

God save me from the plans of short, overly ambitious, bald men.

"Of course. A plan. Wonderful."

"The Light has been speaking of you as his test from God, as I said. Now, He's speaking of you as a test He has passed. I'm here, officially, anyway, to ask you to eat with us tonight. You are His great conversion, you see. A brilliant accomplishment of the True Will of God and the Glory of His Son, Jesus Christ. And He seems to really believe this! I have... encouraged this. I know you still want Him dead, but I've said nothing of the kind to Him. To Him, I speak well of you. Very well. Extremely Well," Kim says, and almost chokes, "it disgusts me. "

"Why? I still don't know why you want my help. Or how I can help."

"You are the center of His universe right now. He stands at the center of our world, and so, then, do you, for now. This places you where I can use you."

"How?"

This should be good...

"What do you see when you look at me, Campion? I know. Short, bald, ambitious... am I right?"

That hits it just about right...

"Sure."

"What you don't see is a charismatic leader. I'm just not the type. Don't look it, can't act it. I know it, and I can live with that. But this place, this group needs a charismatic leader to keep it together. I think you could pull it off."

"What? I'm no celebrity. I've never even been big on public speaking... "

"I want you to be the leader I can't be, Campion. Don't misunderstand me, you won't really be in charge," Kim laughs, "Ha! You wouldn't want to be, trust me. You'll be the figurehead, while I run the place. As you may have guessed, I already run the place, while The Light's followers bask in His radiance. I can't let that Light sputter out. If He's quickly extinguished, legends can be born, but if he rots on the throne we are doomed. I must act to guarantee our very survival. When we take out The Light, someone has to step in and fill the void. That can be you."

"Not me. No way. Who'd believe it?"

"They will. We'll make them believe it. Trust me, The Light himself has already built you up into something larger than life: His nemesis, His test, His great new success!

"I'll help you get in even closer with The Light, close enough so He trusts you. If you can act the part of the newly converted fanatic, I can convince The Light you've come at the ordained time to follow him. I'll make you the son He never had in His eyes. We'll make your choice as His successor inevitable. Then, when the time is right, we'll make sure you're in a situation where no one can suspect you of anything, and I'll administer a poison I found among your things which I believe will kill Him as if from a heart attack. You'll then resist my attempts to elevate you, thereby ensuring your success as the rest demand you lead us."

"That's your plan? This is fucking crazy. You know that don't you?"

We don't have a fucking snowball's chance in hell of making this work.

"No, it really isn't. This will work. I have a few others who will support me as I support you. I've just been waiting for the right time, the right ally to make this work. You're it. There's only one problem."

"Here it comes. I knew it, there's always a prob..."

"We have to do this in the next two weeks."

"Two weeks? Two fucking weeks!"

Oh my God this guy really is fucking crazy. They all are here. Two weeks?

"Maybe two months, maybe, but two... You are crazy. No way. And why? Why would you do this, make me the boss?"

"Because I can't be, like I said. The others won't follow me. But they will follow you. And, on top of that, you have a life to go back to off this station.

"You see, Campion, I'm not asking you to stay here. Just the opposite. I'm asking you to go. Go back to your life. Leave us alone here. You'll be The Light in absentia, spreading the word to the rest of the world. So you'll need someone to run the station in your place while you're gone."

"You."

"Me. I can't be the 'leader' of this group. But I can lead them. I do now, really. I keep this place running, Campion. Do you think He has any idea how to maintain a space station?"

144

"I don't..."

"Not a clue, I assure you. He doesn't have to. He has me, why should He? With you, I'll have your reflected power and your stature as a figurehead to use as I see fit. If I need you to come back for some reason, I'll get in touch and you can return. I can't see you having to come back here too often. It will be a perfect arrangement.

"We had better be going. But think about this as we eat. Watch His behavior. You'll see what I mean. For all his anger and fear of you, Campion, He has a grudging admiration for you. He admires your scrappiness, He told me so, in private."

There is a pounding on the door. The Light yells on the other side.

"Kim! Are you okay?"

Kim turns around and opens the door.

"I'm fine, sir."

"The control for the room is missing!"

"I have it. Here," Kim gives it to Him. "I have it. I used it to turn on his lights."

"You locked the door, too. I thought Campion here might have gotten you, somehow. I want to believe you've changed, Mr. Campion, but I still have my doubts, it seems. Well, let's forget about it and head for the table, huh? It's time to eat!"

Dinner is again at the big table he's sat at before, only this time he's not tied down. They even sit him down close to The Light at the table, at The Light's request. Another plentiful meal is spread out before him.

"I can't believe the food! It's so good."

"The Lord provides, Campion. We have hydroponic gardens that Father Kim manages to keep running. We get a lot of our vegetables that way. And there's a supply ship that comes each quarter. We still have friends on Earth. They make sure we stay fed, keep us alive up here. You just missed the last ship, came just before you arrived. Next one comes in about two weeks."

Ah... that explains Kim's deadline. But, shit! I've been

here almost four months! They had to have kept me doped up for a while. They've seriously fucked with my time sense. Well, I'm on that ship when it leaves here. That's my plan. But first I eat!

This time at The Light's table, BC lets himself enjoy the meal, even overindulging a bit. Stuffed to the gills on his first full meal in weeks, he's almost falling asleep when The Light begins to talk to him after dinner.

"Kim tells me you want to remain in that tiny room even after your penance."

I do? He does? Sure...

"Yeah. I figure it reminds me of where I've been, where I come from, and what I need to aspire to. I'm used to it, too, I guess."

"You don't have to stay there, but I admire your ethic, Campion. You surprise me. You have more discipline than I thought." The Light laughs. "Maybe there's hope for you yet!"

"Um, thanks."

"You've come a long way already, Mr. Campion. And you've still got a spine."

"What?"

"I can see it. You've still got backbone, Campion. So many of these sheep are just that. Sheep! They can't think for themselves anymore. Followers. They always will be. You're not like them, are you?"

"I'm not? I'd like to think I'm not... but I was following the Pope's orders..."

"Yes, but you've stopped. You did not do what was obviously wrong, you've confessed, recanted, seen the error of your ways, as they say. There is steel in you, Campion. I've decided something, right here and now. I think you could be one of my priests."

Where'd that come from? One of Kim's seeds springing to life?

"I can see you're surprised. Good! Father Kim pointed out how far you've progressed, and how much more priestly you are now than when you arrived pretending to BE a* priest! Just your attitude about your room reminds me of a monk and his cell. You could be a priest, Campion."

"I thought I was one."

"Ah, but now, you can be a real one. One of mine! Do you want to be?"

"Yes, I'd like that. If you'll have me."

Kim must have been working on Him. This is too easy. It could all be a setup. But The Light seems to be for real in His unreality.

"We shall have you ordained next Sunday! I know it's soon, but I see no reason to delay. Never know how much time we have left, do we, any of us, eh? You'll have some studying to do first, but we'll grant that your former status in the NcC gives you a leg up, how's that?"

"That's fine. Thank you, sir."

"Yes, you're coming along just fine, Campion. Just fine. Father Kim will instruct you this week in what you'll need for Sunday. Yes, let's do that. This test... Hmm, well, excuse me. I forgot... I'm, uh, I'm going to bed now. It's been quite a day! Sleep well, Campion. Welcome to The Body of Christ!" The Light says, spreading his arms as He stands, encompassing the table, the people, the entire room with his gesture. Then He turns and leaves.

Grand exit. Guy likes his drama. Glad I can play a role. Didn't know I was gonna be one of the stars, though....

Kim comes to his room early the next day.

"You'll have to come with me for breakfast. Now that you're no longer a prisoner you no longer get room service, either."

"I'll take the trade off, thank you very much. So, where do we go for breakfast?"

"Follow me."

Over the course of his first free week, Kim shows BC around the station. They are only using this toroid, as Kim calls it. The other toroid is for current storage and future expansion. BC learns where the galley is, the throne room, The Light's quarters, the main dining room, and everything's relation to his room and the bathrooms. He learns his way around.

His daily sessions with Kim prep him to say the right things to The Light at dinner each night, strengthening the growing bond The Light feels toward BC. Father Kim also coaches him on what to say on Sunday. His ordination.

I've never really been ordained. Not like this. My first ordination came in the mail! My second was a sort of ecumenical group thing. Maybe third time's the charm. Or maybe I'll finally be damned for good. How much of this crap can I pretend to really believe? At least there's not much chance of lightning striking me down on a space station...

The rest of the week and Sunday go by in a blur. The ordination itself is a ritualistic, kneel, stand, sit, lie prone, chant sort of blur as BC recites his lines, plays his part, and accepts a sash around his neck symbolizing the Church as The Light declares, "Welcome to The Body of Christ, Father Bernard Campion!"

The rest of His followers crowd in around BC, laying their hands on him, welcoming him.

This is so fucked up. I hope you know what you're doing, Kim.

After the ceremony comes another lavish dinner. The meal is sumptuous, even though BC heard Kim complain earlier that their supplies were dwindling and the supply ship couldn't come soon enough. Throughout dinner BC keeps up his happy front, while inside feeling hollow and phony.

Something has changed. I used to be able to play these kind of games without feeling anything. Why should I feel bad about deceiving these people now?

When he gets up from the table after dinner, one of the younger women approaches him. She has long brown hair, and eastern, almost elfin features; large almond eyes, petit nose, a small, red blossom of lips. When she speaks her voice sounds warm and fluid, flowing and kind.

"Father?"

"Yes?"

"Do you have anyone to share your bed with you?"

"Ah, no. No I don't."

"I could join you, to help you celebrate your new oneness with us, if you'd like."

"I'd like, but I can't. Not tonight. I need to meditate on today, my sister. Thank you for your love offering, my dear."

The woman smiles wisely at him, "Perhaps some other time, Father."

"Perhaps. Goodnight... what was your name, sister?"

"Ruth, Father. Goodnight." She turns and walks away, turned down but not rejected. She looks back at him once before she leaves the room entirely.

So that's how it is here. Membership has its privileges! I could get used to this. Maybe I won't leave. But then Kim would probably kill me himself!

The Light approaches from across the room.

"Father, I'm surprised you pass up Ruth's charms!" The Light upbraids him with a laugh, "I should tell you, she doesn't offer them up often or to just anyone. You're a lucky man! One shouldn't refuse one of God's gifts when it is so freely offered..."

"I need to think tonight, to take this all in. I'm sort of overwhelmed right now."

"I see. Well, have it your way, Campion. *Father* Campion! Goodnight."

"Goodnight, sir."

"Oh, and one more thing," The Light says, reaching into his pocket, "here!" He hands BC the little black plastic control cube for his room. "It might even change your decision about Ruth. No one will be watching you now. That's yours. Sleep well."

BC looks at the cube. "Thank you."

The Light smiles at him, then he turns and leaves the room, leaving BC by himself in the dining room. BC pockets the cube, leaves the dining hall, and finds his way back to his room.

My closet. Home Sweet Home. Kim must have gotten The Light to give me that cube. That's why he wanted me to stay in this closet. So he and I could meet and talk without anyone eavesdropping. Stuck in this cell. Just another week or so. Three months! Wonder if anyone misses me?

"Governor Edwards?"

"Yes, Cardinal?"

"Yes, governor, well, the, um, The Pope has asked me to convey his regrets, but he can't..."

"Look, Cardinal, no offense, but the man is ducking my calls! I've gone through the proper channels, made the proper requests... It's been over a month since I made the request! I'm the head of Luna Free State, Goddammit! Sorry, Cardinal."

"Apology accepted. Governor Edwards, you've got to understand, His Holy Father is a very busy man..."

"Good-bye, Cardinal. You tell his royal holiness to look me up when he gets a free moment or two, won't you?"

Edwards slaps off the com, scowling.

"Betcha they've already written BC off," he says to himself. "Maybe I should, too."

BC wakes with his arms around Ruth.

Oh yeah.

She'd been persistent. After her third night asking, BC gave in. She was wonderful.!

BC stares at her. Brown hair down the middle of her back. Almond eyes, sharp and penetrating. She smells of cinnamon and vanilla. He breathes her scent in as they lie entangled. His reverie is shattered by pounding on his door. Kim opens the door and stands there, eyes wide.

"Father," Ruth says.

"Daughter," Kim replies.

"Daughter? What, for real, daughter?" BC stammers. Kim nods. Ruth kisses him on the cheek, wraps herself in her clothes and runs out past Kim. He comes in closing the door behind him.

"It is done."

"Done?"

"I did not think you'd refuse my daughter so many

times. She is a good daughter."

"Ruth is your daughter? You didn't tell me that. What is done?"

"The Light. While my daughter gave you your alibi, I did the deed. He is dead. Come, quickly, we've got to join the others." Kim opened the door and spoke in a deliberately loud voice. "Mary found him this morning. It looks like His heart."

Kim leads BC to the throne room. When BC enters, he sees the throne has been removed. In its place is the dinner table, cleared, draped with a black cloth, the body of The Light lying in state upon it. Followers are spread around the body, lying face down on the floor, crying, lamenting the loss of The Light.

My job is done! Remote killing. I can't believe Kim did it!

Kim gestures for him to approach the body. BC does, kneeling down before the table.

Suddenly, The Light sits up! Bolt upright, eyes wide open. His mouth opens, but no sound comes out. He moves his mouth, as if to try to speak, but still there's no sound. He falls back upon the table, his arms fall to the sides and his right hand hits BC full in the face as he pulls back away from the table. BC falls to the side, trying to catch himself as he crashes from his kneeling position to the floor.

The room is full of gasps and murmurs. Father Kim gets up from beside BC and looks down at him in feigned amazement.

"A sign! The Light's last breath and he blesses Father Campion! What could it mean?"

BC looks up in true amazement at Kim. The crowd is already pointing at him, talking about him, as he gets back up on his knees.

"The Light blessed him!"

"Blessed by the light!"

"Father Campion is chosen by The Light!"

That was Ruth.

Daddy's little girl does her work well. She didn't seem

to be doing it for Daddy last night, though. At least, I thought it was all for real. Never trust a woman, BC, you know better than that!

She sees him looking at her and smiles.

Well, that's real. Sweet girl. I like her. Won't trust her. Not too sure about the family...

Kim is addressing the crowd. "I believe we have just seen something miraculous! The Light was already gone, his body lying dead upon the table, when suddenly he rises as Father Campion approached him! He has anointed for us a New Light!"

Oh, man, he's reaching! This is too much, too soon...

Gasps and murmurs again fill the crowd. It's clear not all are buying what Father Kim is selling.

"He's not one of us!" somebody shouts.

Kim turns to the voice. "The Light himself accepted him, heard his confession, took him in and anointed him priest! What more does he need to do to become one of us? Will you turn away from The Light so soon after He's left us. This is fortuitous! The Light must have known something! He didn't kill Father Campion, but took him in. He took him on as a test, a project. He groomed him! Father Campion's arrival, conversion and his joining us as The Light leaves us is God's Will at work!"

BC knows what he has to do.

"Father Kim, I'm sorry, this is very flattering, but I can't accept what you're saying. There's no way I'm a New Light. These people need someone like you to lead them."

Kim rests a hand on his shoulder. "The Lord puts us all in the right place at the right time, Father. Who are we to question His plan? You are here, now, because we need you to be here! You are The New Light!"

"I don't know, Father Kim, this is all so sudden, so overwhelming. I can't think the Lord means for me to be the New Light..."

"I can help you, Father Campion. The signs are clear to me. Does anyone else see what I see?"

"I see!"

There are more answers from the people.

"Yes, Father Kim, I see. He is blessed by The Light!"

"There are signs. He is the New Light!"

"The Light Blessed him from beyond the grave."

"I see. He is the New Light!"

This is too bizarre...

BC gets to his feet on the dais, in front of the table on which lies the body of The Light. He looks out over the crowd. Kim is on his left, egging on the followers, "The New Light!" Kim proclaims, opening his arms to BC, presenting him. "The New Light!" Ruth says, as she looks up at him from the crowd, a smirk curling up the corners of her mouth.

I like that mouth. Maybe I'll just look at those lips for a while. Need to focus on something right now. This is surreal. What am I supposed to do now?

Ruth nudges two women, one on each side of her, and the three approach BC. They kneel at his feet. More of the congregation rise to join him on the dais. Hands begin to reach out for him, to touch him. He feels Ruth's arm snake around him, and the arm of one of her friends on the other side, as they kneel beside him. More of the crowd gets up, gathering around him, touching him. Kim is smiling at him. Finally, he smiles back at Kim.

You bastard. Memo to self: remind me never to fuck with him. His daughter, yes, him, no. Yeah, I'm The Light, all right. Let's see...

"I will try to serve you well, my bothers and sisters. I don't know that I can be what you want me to be."

"You already are," someone he doesn't know says. He can feel their love like a palpable thing as it pours off them.

I feel dirty. Could you have picked someone more unworthy? This is nice, but so wrong...

Even his jagged, hardened cynicism begins to melt as they continue to gaze at him with full attention.

What can I say?

"I can't tell you all how much I love all of you, right now. You're all incredible!"

Not lies. Just not the truth they think they heard.

"It doesn't matter what you'll have me do. I can't thank you enough for even just letting me be a part of you. Thank you."

One of the women looking up at him smiles and says,

"You do shine brightly, Father Campion. You do, whether you know it or not."

Chapter Twenty

BC manages to disentangle himself from the middle of the love-in and looks around for Kim, who has somehow managed to disappear. BC sees Kim's bald dome flash around a corner in front of him over towards Kim's rooms. He follows and knocks on the door to Kim's room when he get there.

"Come in, Campion."

The door opens. BC enters. Father Kim is inside taking off his outer robe. BC waits until the door closes behind him to speak.

"You poured it on pretty thick back there, didn't you?"

"You weren't helping your cause much. Your protests weren't even all that convincing! I wouldn't have believed you, 'oh, no, don't pick me.' I had to provide the drama. These people are used to it!"

"How'd you get the body to sit up like that? And his hand to hit me? Felt more like a slap than a blessing, though."

"I didn't do anything. That just happened. I thought I'd use it, improvise."

BC gets a serious chill and shakes it off.

"Spooky, isn't it, Campion?"

"That was weird. I felt better when I thought you had done it."

"I thought he was long dead. I used the dropdead so it would look like a heart attack. He was already cold."

"Wow. That's even freakier... So. What now, then?"

"The supply ship arrives in two days, we got their confirmation this morning. They're en route. They'll take you back to the Moon when they return, and I'll take care of things here, as we agreed."

"Trying to get rid of me so soon? Don't you want to bask in the New Light?"

"Look, we agreed. I help you, you help me. I can run this place a lot more effectively with you as an absentee Holy Father."

"I'm glad I fit your plan. Mine wasn't working so well."

"You were the right man at the right time, Father. Most of what I said was true, just *enhanced*," Kim says. "The two before you were slower, not as sharp. I couldn't use them. Look, there's one more thing you have to do.. You have to officiate at The Light's funeral before you leave. Do you have any clue what to do?"

"No."

"More lessons, then. We'll hold the Funeral Mass at 10 am tomorrow. That gives us plenty of time to teach you the Catholic Funeral Mass."

"Can't wait."

BC feels as filled in and informed as he can be when he prepares to say the mass the next morning. Kim has been grilling him on what to do when, what comes first, next, last. They studied just what BC had to do into the early morning hours.

"You have to win them over with this. There are still many doubts, despite my assurances and the love you felt last night. Your sermon is of vital importance. Do not falter," Kim tells him as they prepare for the service the next morning.

"Gotcha."

The mass goes as it should, smoothly, up to the sermon. BC gets his chance to address the congregation. He walks across the dais to the podium, clears his throat, looks out across The Light's followers, then begins.

"I came among you as an outsider, and still, you took me in. I came among you as a sinner, and still, you took me in. I came among you as a killer, and still, you took me in. Where I sowed hatred, you reaped love. How did you do it?

How did you save a wretched soul like mine? I can only say, I have seen The Light! The Light," BC gestures at the open casket before him, "showed me so much, showed me the error of my ways, showed me the infinite patience, and the infinite love..." BC pauses for effect "...of God Himself, of our Lord Jesus. He taught me what it was to truly follow our Lord."

If I had a shovel, I'd shovel in the morning...

"My only regret is that I could not spend more time with Him! If I had only seen my error, the fault in my ways, sooner! He had so much yet to teach. I have so much yet to learn. We all are left now without The Light to shine and lead the way, and we could get lost. I know Father Kim thinks I'm The New Light, but I don't know... I'll try to shine. I tell you there is light within each of us, the Light of Christ, and it's there for each of us to find. We need to shine for each other. We need to shine for ourselves. We need to see that the Light is not dead, no! The Light is alive, inside of each and every one of us! We just gotta let it shine. We need to help each other shine now, especially, for it will seem dark now that we have lost The Light.

"I spent deep prayerful time with The Light, time almost out of time. I can almost be there with Him again right now, if I allow myself. His love is still there, I can still feel it, real and strong. He loved so deeply, and so well, that His love continues to be with us, even though His body has ceased to breathe.

"God is love, and this The Light has shown us. This is what He illuminated. He showed us the sheer power of love in our lives is unlimited, for it is the power of God. How purely can you love? How well, how strongly? This was His challenge. He often quoted to me the First Letter of John, 'God is Love, Campion!' trying to teach me what truly following what Jesus taught really meant. The words of First John offer us a powerful challenge. We must love each other here and now, in this life, or we are not living as Jesus intended. We find our eternal life in this love! This is the essence of the message. The Light loved us all so well, so purely, so truly, that he is with us still whenever we think of Him in love! Think of The Light! Remember His Love! Can you feel it? Do you feel Him? He is with us still, I assure you, with us now! And We must not forget Him!"

BC bows his head, looking down at the body in the casket.

"Father Kim has called me The New Light, but, truly, none can replace Him. If I have been chosen to follow Him, I can only hope it is The Light himself choosing our next step, our further path. For I feel called to a different path. I feel called to spread the news, the love of The Light, to the rest of the world! The Light came to you, to us, to draw us together, to make us the strong mustard seed, the kernel about to explode into abundant life! I must now take the message back into the world.

"I will not be staying among you, but shining the Light unto the world to bring the message of The Light to those who still labor on in error as I did, those who still exist in darkness!"

The crowd is shocked, surprised. Murmurs and gasps are followed by whispering. BC can hear and sense their unease.

Alrighty, Kim, let's hope this works...

"Father Kim will lead in my stead while I am not here. We all know he can keep us together, even as I am apart from you. I will not be able to come back often, I fear, for I fear to draw attention to us here, to the true cradle of our faith, until we are sure the world is ready for us. Make no mistake, my brothers and sisters, this is our Eden. We have not left the garden! And yet, The Light leads me on to the greater path. I just dare not lead those who would ruin this place back here to hurt you, my new family, this body of Christ! This community built by The Light! We will continue to shine in His never-ending love!

"We will miss you, our Light, but we can see You shine on."

BC beams at the crowd. Father Kim looks pleased. The crowd sounds uplifted, happy.

I think they like me. Now for the rest of this mass thing.

The rest of the funeral mass cruises by for BC. The tough part is over. He's glad to finally get it done and get the whole thing over when it ends.

Glad to get off that altar. it's still not my element.

Father Kim comes up, "You handled yourself well. Those were true words you spoke, whether you spoke them in truth or not."

"Thanks, I think."

BC walks among the people and around Fortune Station after the mass, killing time before the supply ship arrives. The ship only docks for an hour, so once it's here he's on his way home. He looks at his cell one last time, traces his path to the bathroom, walks one full circle around the donut.

Kim finds him in his wanderings when the ship arrives.

"I'll walk you to the dock. Come on. You'll be back on the Moon in about two days, probably," Kim looks at the ground, then up at BC.

"You've changed, haven't you? You're different than when you arrived. I can see it. We really did get to you in spite of yourself, didn't we?"

"Do you think so?"

Let him have his illusions. He did my job for me, after all.

"Yes, I do. I can see it in your eyes. Or maybe I've become too much like you," Kim says, pausing, "Now that I've killed, you don't seem so evil. We all do what we have to do."

"Is that so?"

"Here's the dock."

The ship is already unloading. BC sees the captain directing the cargo off loading and walks up. Kim introduces him to Captain Engaway.

"You're going back with us, then, eh?" Engaway says to BC as he shakes hi hand.

"That's the plan."

"We leave in a half hour, no later. I recommend getting on board now. There is a cabin ready for you."

"Thanks, I will."

"Through the hatch on the left side, then right as you get inside. Find a crewman and ask for the guest stateroom. They'll tell you where to go."

"Thanks."

My departure's a lot less eventful than my arrival, that's for sure.

"Good bye, Father Kim. I leave the place in your capable hands, right where it's always been."

"Thanks, Campion. Shine on brightly. Check in now and then to help keep it legit, okay?"

"Sure. See ya,"

BC ducks in through the hatch and airlock into a nicer ship than the Paladin was. The guest stateroom is roomy, and complete with a bed, desk and night stand, with an attached refresher. There's even a viewport. BC sits and watches their departure out his stateroom window. He sees the dark silhouette of Fortune Station melt into the blanket of stars as they pull away.

This ship is faster than the Paladin, and Kim said they'll take a more direct route to Luna. Two days! Two days and I'll be home. Funny to think of the moon as home. Used to be Rome. Before that Boston, for a little while. And the Finch station. Luna Prime feels more like home than any of them did. I don't know why.

BC asks to use the radio, but he's informed they're traveling silent. Got to keep Fortune Station off the proverbial radar. He lies down in his stateroom and thinks about the last three months.

I might not be a great "Light" for these people, but despite what I said to them, their last one wasn't that great anyway either. So much hatred masquerading as love, pretending to be religion.

BC gets up and finds his way to the ship's common area to get something to eat. The Captain is sitting at a table playing solitaire. BC sits down at the table and asks the Captain how soon they'll reach the Moon. He laughs.

"The Moon? We aren't going to the Moon. We always take off and land from Earth. Who told you we were going to the Moon? We land in Panama, at the spaceport, in two days."

Kim! That bastard.

After they land in Panama, BC catches a quick connector to Vatican City. He's been trying to contact the home office since the captain began allowing communication the day before, but they won't authorize or receive his transmissions.

Not a good sign.

BC checks out the news on his connecting flight. He's been gone for three months. The war hasn't intensified any more than it already had. From what he can gather from the reports, no real territorial shifts have come about. Everyone still has their same holdings and principalities.

When he gets into Vatican City his ID only gets him in to a point. His appearance is an issue. With his wild hair and beard they don't recognize him at first, but his ID does check out, and they finally usher him into the inner sanctum of Pope Peter's Vatican to see the Big Guy.

Peter stands in informal robes in a small private sitting room in the Papal residence. He looks BC up and down as BC stands in front of him, looking like something out of the New Testament.

"You flew over from Panama looking like that? Well, I don't suppose anyone would recognize you. And you decided you had to grace us with a personal appearance, how nice, BC." Peter switches from false appreciation to a scathing condemnation, "I thought I told you not to come here?!"

"Good to see you too," BC mumbles.

"It's still good to see you, my boy. we have been worried about you, BC! You know we couldn't send anybody after you, of course. We hoped you'd find your way out again. You were gone a long time this time."

"Comforting."

"Still. You shouldn't have come here. You know we have to be extra careful in your case, BC. You've been off the radar, but we still have those same worries, about you, about your vulnerabilities, your cover. You could be blackmailed. They know you now, who you are, what you've done. You've become our weak link, BC."

"Have I? Have I really?"

How much does he really believe this? How much do I believe it? If that woman really blew my cover, then why hasn't it been blown? I mean, like, wide open? C'mon...

"Well, you do seem to be. Many would look at you as such. Though, now, to look at you, hmmph, well, doubt if they'd even recognize you."

"If you'd accepted my communication I wouldn't have had to come here in the first place. Look, I know you have your concerns. We all know what happened on the moon, and I know you think I'm now a liability to the organization. Let me show you otherwise. Look at the facts. The UIN has tried to tie us to McEntyre's assassination. They have failed! They have nothing on me. They've mentioned nothing! I've come through the crisis! I've done more than that. I've laid the foundation for a productive relationship for us with the new Luna Governor, Marc Edwards."

"Yes, I know about that. You know, he's been calling me about you. A very persistent man. We told him you were okay. Seems you have connected with him. Very good."

"I turned those cultists on that station around for us, too. The Light is dead and gone, and I," BC says with a flourish, "am The New Light! Those people worship me! I've proven my value, here, clearly!"

"You have, you have, BC. Fortune Station has been secured, eh? The Light, dead? Excellent. You are a valuable agent, an asset to the Vatican and a true soldier for Christ."

"So... what now?"

"You go back to the moon. Spend a couple weeks here first, recuperate, get a shave and a haircut, please... enjoy Italy for a while, but then go back. We don't know how secure your cover is. Keep cultivating the PR position and flack for the Cardinal. Cultivate your relationship with Edwards, get him solid on our side. Develop the situation. Most of all, maintain a low profile, and see what happens. Keep laying low for now. In the meantime, I'll try to think of ways we can strengthen your cover."

"Great."

Wonderful...

"Marino! Show Campion to some temporary quarters, would you? Good-bye for now, BC. We'll speak again before you go back to the moon. Thank you. And good work, again, on Fortune."

"Um, yeah. Thanks."

Chapter Twenty-One

I love Vatican City and St. Peter's Square in the morning. I never get over the way you can feel the history, the grandeur and great age of the buildings. History seems to resonate from the ancient architecture, the old stones, like you could reach out and touch it, maybe get transported back through time...

BC is sitting on the window sill of his borrowed apartment in the Vatican. From his perch he surveys the mishmash of ancient and modern that makes up Rome and Vatican City. As he looks out the window at the external world of Rome, he contemplates the nooks and crannies of the interior Vatican City grounds.

The Belvedere Gardens are beautiful, too, perfect place to sip an espresso and contemplate the day. Ya know, that sounds like a plan... Funny, used to seem like time stood still here. Guess that changed when the attacks started. Now time has caught up with a vengeance. The old police residence is badly damaged. There was some damage to St. Peter's and the square. Even the gardens suffered. Nothing's untouched. Everything seems more fragile now, somehow.

BC watches tourists pass by on the street below.

There are fewer pilgrims out here, I'm told, fewer every day since the attacks began hitting Vatican City.

At least they're rebuilding. Hoping it's not in vain, that it won't just get knocked down again by the UIN. They've done some repair work, but there are still so many places where the bombs hit, the lasers burned, still a lot of black marks on the landscape not yet healed. Ancient stones on top of each other for centuries have been knocked down leaving gaps in the old walls like missing teeth from a smile. Although I don't know why you'd be smiling if you were missing that many teeth...

I wonder what bothers the Curia more, the damage to the ancient buildings or the drop in cash flow from the tourist trade? They'll probably sell tickets to tour the ruins after things calm down to make some money back, cover their losses.

That's what I'd do, come to think of it.

BC wanders by the commissary and picks up an espresso, intending to make his way over to the Belvedere Gardens for his contemplated stroll. He brings the cup up to inhale the strong aroma of the coffee, feels the warmth of the glass on his fingers and palms as he breathes in the aroma.

Mmmm. Certainly one of this place's best features...

"Campion!"

Fuck.

BC throws back the espresso like a shot and turns to face...

...Marino. Must already be time. Shit, thought I had a while longer before the meeting. One last tongue lashing from the Big Guy.

Cardinal Marino stands with his hands folded in front of him on the white bib of his traditional crimson robes, staring at BC. "He'll see you now. Please hurry, he's in a mood."

Wonderful.

"Righto."

"He's in the public meeting room, third floor."

"Thanks."

BC heads off to see The Pope. As he walks, his thoughts turn to the moon.

I can't wait to get back to the Moon. This place is oppressive and boring.

I used to love it here. This was my home base.

Now, it seems stuffy, dead and lifeless. Boring. At least on the Moon I have something to do. Not that they couldn't find busy work for me here, if I was going to be here longer than just these last three weeks.

There's so much authority represented here, it makes me itch. Not my kind of place, for sure. The food is great, and the espresso, but everything else... I don't know, I'd say it's too old, but that's not it, not entirely. Even in St. Peter's, even looking up at the ceiling of the Sistine, I don't feel the same sense of, I don't know, "holiness", I guess, that I felt on that stupid space station. Hmm. How much of that is drug-related? They dosed me with a lot of funky psychotropics. And made me their new messiah, kinda. Wild. And now, here I am, back in the Vatican.

I wonder how ol' Kim is doing a month into his Messiahship? Hope it's going smoothly for the guy. I'd check in, but there's no way for me to get through to him from here. I've tried. Communications office says it's a no go. Whatever that means. At least they let me talk to the Moon.

Marc Edwards seems to be doing well. Turns out he's a real friend, kept calling the Cardinal to ask where I was. Good to have a friend like that for a change.

BC is lost in thought as he walks. He nods as he passes random functionaries in the halls as he gets closer to the Pope's meeting room. Some shoot him disapproving, officious glances, some merely ignore his passing.

It's weird. Compared to Kim and even the crazy old Light himself, everyone here seems like a businessman, not a holy man. They may be drugged up and crazy on Fortune Station, but they seem, I don't know, more real, more authentic... yeah, more holy, I guess.

Holier than the Big Guy, anyway. Gotta brace myself for the bitch out.

BC walks into the antechamber of the Pontiff's meeting hall. The Pope's secretary, another priest, looks up and nods at BC.

"Father Campion? Go right ahead in, he's waiting for you."

He waves him by. BC opens the heavy wooden door in front of him and walks into the papal meeting room, where

Pope Peter the Second awaits.

He is seated in an ornately carved dark wooden throne. The stark white official robes of his office contrasts sharply with his ebony skin. Sharp, piercing brown eyes light up his face and size up BC.

"Bernard, good to see you!"

"And you, sir."

Peter stares at BC, not saying anything.

BC shifts his weight as he waits under the pontiff's gaze.

A minute? Five minutes? How long...

"I said we'd talk again before you leave. You have... questions?" the old man finally asks him.

"Some."

"You leave today, don't you?"

"I'm going back to the moon this afternoon."

"And you want to know what's up, no doubt. I can understand that, er," he pauses, his eyebrows arch up, "that is what your questions are about, aren't they?"

"Well, yeah. Am I in or out?"

"You wouldn't be here if you were out."

BC gulps, "I see."

Pope Peter looks him square in the eye, "Yes, I see you do. You're still in, for now." He shifts in his chair, smoothes his robes, and looks back up at BC. "For now."

"There haven't been any new revelations made by the UIN have there?" BC protests. "I found no evidence of any exposure in my own investigating over the last two weeks here. Nothing in the news, no new statements... was there something through secure channels?"

"No, nothing like that. They haven't said anything more than they did originally. But I believe they're holding on to the information," Peter says with a heavy sigh.

"If they have it..."

"Don't kid yourself, you know they've got something. She got you on camera calling in here, didn't she?"

"Yeah, I think so. She had it in front of her when I looked up."

"Your cover is blown, on some level, unless she didn't hit record or something foolish like that. Are you that lucky?"

"I'm still here..." BC grins sheepishly.

"Right. For now," Peter repeats. BC stops grinning.

Peter continues, "But know this. The knowledge they have of you, the evidence they have, is a weapon they can use against you. Against us. Against," Peter looks around at the room, and beyond, "all of us. The church, the UTZ, the Earth, the Moon. That's a powerful weapon. If I had a weapon like that, I wouldn't use it until the time was just right, when it would do the most damage. I imagine the UIN are probably thinking the same thing. They are being patient with their information 'bomb'. And if nothing else, the UIN has shown us throughout the years that they can be very, very patient."

"So, what, then, I'm a time bomb?"

Pope Peter laughs, "Yes, I guess you are, good analogy. Huh, well, bad analogy, too." He stops laughing and frowns.

"So... you want me to keep laying low? I can't get much lower than I just was."

"Yes, I know. That was good!" Peter smiles, looks BC in the eye. "You were off the radar entirely! And you did the job where others had failed. And you left there in charge of the place! That was very good!" Peter says.

BC tries to take the compliment.

"Well, kind of in charge," BC says. "There's one of them, a Father Kim, who's really in charge. I'm a figurehead. I will have to go back there from time to time, though, to keep up appearances, keep the place under our control."

"Right," Peter says. For a moment he seems distracted. "Oh, yes," he says, as if remembering something, "While you've been recuperating here these last two weeks, I've been thinking about what we can do with you. I've decided to assign someone to work with you."

No fucking way!

"Work with me? I work alone. Period. I don't want, I don't need a partner!" BC protests.

"Relax!" Peter admonishes him, "I don't mean a partner. But Cardinal Andersen tells me you're not much of a priest..."

What the... I don't need this shit again! Not from this guy!

BC starts to protest but Pope Peter just keeps talking.

"I'm assigning you a trainer, of sorts. A tutor, to work with you on your presentation," Peter says.

Pope Peter draws close. BC can smell sour garlic on his breath as he leans in.

"Your cover has to be complete, impenetrable," he whispers. "You snicker. You shouldn't. You need to be convincing as a priest or you fail." He almost spits out the last word. He looks around, as if looking for spies in the shadowy corners of the room. "Your cover won't hold up for a second. You need to work on plausibly presenting yourself as a priest!" Peter declares. He draws back away from BC, looks down at his desk. "I've got someone in mind who'll be perfect. I've already assigned her. She'll join you on the Moon in a couple of days."

This is not good.

"I don't know, sir..."

"Yes, you do know. You know you'd better follow my orders. And this is an order. Just in case there was some confusion on your part. This is part of your job, Campion. She'll be reporting back to my offices, too, so don't think you can blow this off once you're out of here. I believe you'll find the Reverend Swan to be quite... well, persistent. Yes, quite persistent," he chuckles," she'll have you whipped into shape in no time."

"Wonderful."

Can my life get any more annoying?

"You can go now. Remember, keep your profile as low as possible. Be a quiet little priestly PR person for now, in the Cardinal's shadow. Keep him out in front for us up there. And say a mass once in a while, for Christ's sake,"

Peter chuckles again, "for Christ's sake, heh. Love the pun," he mumbles.

BC can feel Marino enter the room and move up behind him. He bows to Pope Peter. Peter extends his right hand, ring thrust forward.

Aw, Jesus, this sucks.

BC leans forward and kisses the ring on the pope's finger. Marino clears his throat as BC straightens.

"Your holiness," BC says, and nods to Peter. He turns and is face to face with Marino.

"I can't go anywhere with this one in my way," BC says in a loud voice.

"First, let him go, we're through here," Peter says. Marino, the First, keeps his eyes locked on BC's as he steps out of BC's way. BC smiles his best fake smile.

"Thanks ever so much," he says to Marino, words dripping with sarcasm. Without glancing back at Pope Peter he brushes past Marino, walks across the room, out the door, and down the hall.

No looking back.

Well, that was plain. Fuck up and you won't be here anymore. I certainly took "here" to mean "alive" here. Lovely people I'm messed up with.

"Campion! Where are you stomping off to?"

M'Bekke! Didn't even see him. Lost in thought. Haven't seen him since I've been back.

"M'Bekke! How are you?"

"I am well, BC. I heard you did well on Fortune Station. Good job. Kept a low profile and took out the objective. I must have taught you well."

"Well, well, well. Well, I wouldn't take any credit for my performance of late if I were you, M'Bekke. My star ain't exactly rising around here right now."

"Your situation is precarious. I pray for you, BC."

"You're kidding, right?"

"No. There are some things I take seriously. Despite appearances otherwise. You'd do well to remember that. And also remember I am your friend, as you have proven to be mine in the past."

"Thanks, M'Bekke." BC notices an awkward silence as he doesn't say anything else, neither does M'Bekke, but neither of them moves. Until M'Bekke speaks.

"The new governor on the Moon appears to be your friend as well. He was rather persistent in his calls after you."

"He's a good man, Governor Edwards. Not really a politician at all."

"Is he gay?"

What a question.

"I don't think so, M'Bekke. Besides, you know I'm not."

"Yes, more's the pity. That Edwards is quite handsome."

"He is single, M'Bekke. I don't know if he's gay. If it ever comes up in conversation I'll let him know you're interested."

"I only said he was persistent. I thought it was cute how he worried about you."

"I don't know if he's your type," BC shrugs.

"Too bad, it's been a long time... Well, off with you then," M'Bekke gestures with his hands. "Don't you have a plane to catch?"

"Your concern is touching, M'Bekke. My ship leaves soon."

"It was good seeing you, BC. Remember, keep..."

"I know, a low profile. Gotcha! Later, M'Bekke." BC laughs and heads back to his apartments. He's got about an hour before he leaves for the flight to the spaceport.

So much for the Belvedere Gardens, no time for quiet contemplation. Arrivederci, Roma... Course, I don't have much to pack. It'll be good to get outta here.

Chapter Twenty Two

BC takes a short-hopper from Rome to Panama. In Panama he discovers his shuttle leaves for Luna Prime in just over an hour.

Let's see if I can board the ship now, early. Be nice to settle in for the trip ahead.

His collar and credentials provide him with quick and easy access to the ship well ahead of the other passengers. He boards almost immediately. The passenger cabin is empty. Most of the attendants aren't even aboard yet. BC finds his way to his seat, puts his carry ons away, and stretches out to grab some sleep before takeoff.

Nice. Sometimes I feel like someone really is looking out for me...

BC lies back on the reclining acceleration couch with his eyes closed, hovering on the edge of sleep.

The passenger cabin is mine alone for the next half an hour. Ahhh, the gift of blissful silence...

BC is jarred awake as someone bounces into him. The passenger cabin is full of people stowing luggage, squeezing past each other in the aisle, and one of them has just plopped into the seat next to his, bumping into and waking him up in the process.

Wonderful. Company.

A sickly sweet floral smell assaults his nose.

What is that? Roses dying in the sun? Is that perfume? My God! I'm gonna gag.

"Hi there! I guess we're seat mates! I'm Sharlena, Sharlena Swan. Reverend Swan, actually. I'm with the church. Oh look, you are, too! Well, hello there Father!"

BC closes his eyes. He opens them back up. And focuses. Tall black woman, sky blue shirt with a clerical collar, leaning forward, trying to push carry on luggage into a space too small for it under the seat in front of her.

She's still there. Damn. I'd hoped I was hallucinating. That's her, though, isn't it? The one assigned to "whip me into shape." Thought she was supposed to come up in a couple days? Better be nice...

"Hi. I was, um, I was sleeping. Sorry."

"Oh, don't be sorry. Sorry I woke you up! I'm just really excited! I've never been to the Moon before; I could just die! I've never even been in space at all. Is this your first time?" the words spill out in a rush.

"No."

"Oh, good, so you're a veteran! You can tell me all about it when we're on our way there, Father... ?" She fishes for his name.

"Actually, if you'll forgive me, I was hoping to get some sleep."

She shuts up at this rebuke. BC closes his eyes, but he can feel her energy shift from excited to agitated as she quietly continues to try to shove her bag beneath the seat in front of her and ready herself for takeoff. Her nonverbal grunts and grrs as she strains get louder, until she lets out an exasperated, "oof." BC opens his eyes again. One of the attendants is standing in the aisle next to Reverend Swan.

"Reverend? Ma'am? We can stow that for you in back. It's really too large for that space."

"But it's my bag!"

"It won't be safe there during the trip, ma'am. Please?"

"All right. Here," she says, and hands the tote up to the attendant. The attendant struggles to lift and hold the bag, then turns and manages it back down the aisle.

"Sorry," Swan says when she sees he's awake again. "So, you're going to the Moon, too?"

"Be pretty foolish of me to be on this ship if I wasn't, huh?" BC shifts in his seat.

"So you're a wise guy, too, huh? I betcha I know who you are. You're Father Bernard Campion, aren't you?" She asks, looking him in the eye with an air of certainty and triumph.

"Who? No, sorry." BC closes his eyes. Swan keeps talking.

"Really? I thought you might be. It'd be a huge coincidence, but it could happen. I'm supposed to work with another priest who's traveling up to the Moon, too. I wasn't even supposed to be on this flight, but when I found out I could go early I jumped at the chance. Are you sure you're not him?"

BC doesn't open his eyes. "I'm sure."

"You wouldn't lie to another priest, would you, Father?"

BC mumbles a negative and pretends to fall back asleep. A sharp pain lances through his temples. He sits up involuntarily.

"Are you okay?" She asks.

She sounds so far away... Woah, I don't think so...

When BC comes to he's being smothered by Swan's sickly sweet perfume as she tries to prop him up. The attendant arrives with a hot towel for his forehead.

"You okay, Father? You blacked out, started to slide down to the floor," Swan asks with concern.

"Yeah, I'm fine. I'm okay now. I... I get migraines," BC says, pulling away from her ministrations.

"Yeah, looks like you got a whopper," she says as she settles back in her seat.

"I just need to sleep," BC says, closing his eyes again. The towel feels good on his forehead.

"Oh. Oh, sorry, Father. I didn't mean to bother you. I'll try to be quieter, so you can sleep."

Was that a hint of sarcasm in the reverend's voice? I wonder.

BC sleeps and the shuttle lifts off, carrying them to Luna Prime. BC doesn't wake up until they are just minutes from landing. The Reverend Swan, as good as her word, has been silent during the entire eight hour flight.

At least she didn't say anything to me that I could hear. What a dead sleep! I must really have been tired.

BC leans over to look out the viewport at the

approaching moonscape. Reagan Station. Luna Prime.

Almost looks like home. Been gone a while. Four months, plus.

BC watches the buildings, domes, passageways and bunkers of Reagan station grow closer. Then something catches the corner of his eye.

Flash!

It's there for all of two seconds, but it's there.

Was that a flasher? A flasher! Another one! Same type of ship. It didn't look alien. But it didn't look like any human ship I've ever seen, either.

Damn!

BC feels his head split with sharp pain, like an ice pick through his skull. He has to close his eyes, feels his consciousness swim then disappear. He only comes to when the Reverend Swan shakes him awake.

"Father! We're here! We're on the Moon! Wake up! Head still bugging you? Maybe it's the cabin pressure. I'm sure I'll see you again Father, probably in church, huh? I'm going now."

"Goodbye," BC says, groggily. Swan gives him a puzzled look, then turns to make her way down the aisle.

Got to get my shit together. Wonder if I did see that ship. Damn headaches. Where'd they come from? Where'd that ship come from? Contrary to the testimony of the late Captain Longeux, that one was awfully close to the Moon. What if they're actually locals? Got to be based somewhere. It looks like a transpace ship, though, so it could be based anywhere between here and Mars. Maybe in orbit. The Moon is a big place, too, though. Makes me wonder.

"Sir? Father? Are you all right?"

"What?" BC looks up. The attendant is standing in the aisle next to his row.

"You're the last one on board. It's time to get off."

"Right. Thanks."

Woah. Feeling kind of out of it. Got to wake the fuck up!

BC gets up, gets off the ship, makes his way through

the Luna Prime spaceport and heads back to his rooms in the Vatican Mission.

Luna Prime is bustling, people everywhere rushing to work, back home, on errands, social calls. Normal life continues for most people. BC does notice a couple of businesses are closed, shut up and dark.

If I remember right, those were Moslem owned businesses. They've no doubt left, since their government is attacking us. Looks like there have been even more attacks. There's construction everywhere. Maybe our section again, too. We've gotta do something to better defend ourselves here. They're gunning for us. You know, I really hope it's not my fault...

BC turns off the main concourse and walks down the smaller corridor that leads to the Vatican Mission on the Moon. Everything's shiny and bright, well lit.

Everything looks normal, but, I don't know, it feels different, somehow. Probably just me. I'm different. I felt all right when I was at the Vatican, back on Earth. It's just since I got on that ship this morning... Maybe I did get these headaches back at The Vatican but just don't remember? Is that possible?

What did they do to me out there on that crazy station? How many of those drugs they laced my food with are still in my system? They checked me out back in Rome, but what if there's shit they missed? Too many questions. I don't like it.

There are too many messages waiting for him back in his rooms. BC checks the most recent, then stores the others away for the future. The two most recent messages are from the Cardinal and Marc Edwards.

"Hello, Campion," The Cardinal's message begins. The Cardinal sounds more somber than usual. "Welcome back. I'll check in with you later today. There's... there's something I want to discuss with you."

He doesn't sound like his usual bubbly self. Wonder what's up?

Edward's message is next. "BC! I hear you're back today! Glad you're alive and well. I thought you were gonna be gone a couple'a weeks, not almost half a year! Hope you're okay and all. Call me when you've settled in. See you then."

Thanks for caring, Marc.

BC's conversation with M'Bekke comes back to mind.

Nah. I don't think he's gay... Does he have a girlfriend? Man, I need a girlfriend. A little female companionship would be nice, and I'm not talking about the quality time I'm going to have to spend with the Reverend Swan.

BC looks around.

Funny, this place really does feel like home. Rome was okay. And I sure don't miss my little closet on Fortune Station. It's nice to come back here. I'll return my messages later...

He sinks down on his bed and falls fast asleep.

BC dreams no dreams. Just a deep, long night's sleep. He still wakes up feeling hungover.

Did I go on a bender last night? I don't remember...

He checks his new messages. 34!

Thirty four messages? Man, I just got back, who's calling me like this? Wait a sec, what's this?

The most current message is dated four days after the date he got back.

I've been out cold for four days?

The Reverend Swan has been most persistent. At least ten of the messages are from her, both voice and text.

Seems I missed a meeting yesterday. So sorry, Swan.

The Cardinal and Edwards left several each as well. Edwards's most recent is from yesterday, early. He actually sent a med tech to BC's room to check on his health.

"He went in on my orders, found you sleeping. He said you're fine, but deep asleep," Edwards says in the message. "He said to let you rest, you must need it! I'll talk to you when you get up. Later."

I should feel better for having slept so long. Maybe I should see a doctor. If I get a spare minute. Got some mad catching up to do.

BC's head begins to clear as he gets up, showers, cleans up and dresses for the day. By the time he's shaved he feels fine. He looks at himself in the mirror.

I look okay, I guess. My eyes look clear, not bloodshot, pupils normal, responsive... Just my usual ugly self. Maybe older. I think the cult experience has aged me. No gray yet, that's good. Maybe I just needed to catch up with myself. Process all the shit I've been through. Hope there's no permanent damage.

BC's room com goes off. Edwards is on the line.

"Hey, BC how are you? I was worried about you, man!"

"Yeah, guess I needed some rest, huh? I've been through a lot in these last couple months. I'm okay, now."

"Good, good. When you've got some time to spare in the next day or two look me up, okay? It'll be good to catch up with you. Plus, I've got a couple of things I want to ask you about, get your opinion on. Give me a call, all right?"

"Sure, Marc, I will. Gotta find out what the Cardinal needs from me first, but once I do I'll call you. Thanks for being a friend, Marc."

Edwards sounds a little embarrassed, "Hey, BC, I don't have a lot of friends, so I try to take care of the ones I do have, you know? Later."

"Campion?" The Cardinal's com cuts in as Edwards signs off. "Father Campion, are you there?"

"Yes, Cardinal, I'm here."

"You feeling better?"

"Yes, sir, I am, thanks for asking."

"Good. Come see me at once."

"Sure, I will sir, be right there."

He sounds weird. Bossy for him, too. Tense and nervous.

BC get dressed in basic blacks, checks his collar in the mirror, then sets off to see the Cardinal.

The Cardinal's secretary waves him in, "Go ahead, Father, he's expecting you."

The Cardinal rises behind his desk. "Ah, Father

Campion, good to see you're still in one piece. Come in, sit down." He sits back down. BC sits down across from the Cardinal in a chair in front of the desk.

He sounds more normal than he did on the com. That's good.

Silence ensues. BC and the Cardinal sit across from each other. Neither says a word. The Cardinal looks down at his empty desktop, as if studying something BC can't see. BC just waits.

Preoccupied by something... He isn't even looking at me! What is up with this?

After a long few minutes, the Cardinal looks up, looks BC in the eyes.

"I've just recently found out about your last 'mission', the one that kept you away so long."

"What?"

"You're surprised, I know. I'm not supposed to know these things," the Cardinal laughs nervously. "Usually I don't want to. But this time I do. And I hear you, what, I don't know, what do you call it in your line of work? What? Eliminated? Neutralized? Fixed? Took care of.. whatever. I hear you've killed the one who called himself The Light."

Wow. Entirely unexpected!

"I can see you're surprised I know this. Well, I have my reasons for knowing. But is it true? Was it you? Did you kill him? Was that your mission?"

"I really don't know what to tell you, Cardinal..."

"Hmm. Guess you can't say, eh? Top secret or something like that?"

"Something like that."

"Is he dead?"

"Look, Cardinal, I really can't..."

"He is dead, isn't he? I can see it in your eyes, Campion."

What can I say?

"Did you know he was an old friend of mine? 'The Light'?" The Cardinal asks. He doesn't wait for an answer, just goes on. "We were in seminary together, all those ages ago. Seems like another life, another world ago, now."

"Really?"

This I didn't know. Small world. Small fucking universe.

"He was once a good man, Campion. A true man of God. He truly believed."

"He believed until the end, Cardinal."

The Cardinal snaps to full attention, eyes on fire at BC's tacit admission.

"So you did kill him!"

Whoa! Back, boy!

"No! I did not kill him! But he is dead. I'm sorry you've lost your friend."

The Cardinal calms down. "I lost him a long time ago, Campion. But you did go there, to his station? To kill him?"

What the hell...

"Yes, I did. Under orders. But I failed. They captured me, dosed me with God knows what drugs, and tried to brainwash me. It was torture; they made me read the Bible all the time," BC chuckles, trying to lighten the mood.

"I don't see the humor in any of this, Campion," The Cardinal says darkly.

"No, I see that." *Jeesh.* "Look, he meant well. But in the end, one of his own people killed him, because *they* felt he had lost his way. They used me to help them, and then they let me go. And set me up as an absentee leader, a figurehead for them to work behind."

"So... did you get to know him before the end?"

"Pardon?"

"Did you get to know The Light?"

"Sort of."

"Did you think he was a good man?"

"Honestly?"

"Honestly."

"No." BC shakes his head. "I don't think anyone who sets himself up as a god, or God's sole representative, is a good man. I think he was delusional. He might have meant well, started out good, but he couldn't see his own faults, see where he was going, what he was doing. Plus, he had them starve me, drug me, keep me in the dark for extended periods, mess with my head... those aren't the tactics of a good man, Cardinal."

"Yet you have changed. And I think, maybe, for the better. I can see that in your eyes, Father. Maybe not brainwashed, but... he got to you, didn't he?"

"Maybe. In some way." BC admits grudgingly. "But I never bought his philosophies. I did what I had to, to get out of there, but I'm not born again or anything like that."

"Well, he was never into the old 'born again' thing..." The Cardinal protests.

"You know what I mean. Born into his whole 'back to the future' deal, wearing robes on a space station, getting back to the first century from a mile high in orbit. Somehow, I never could see the early Christians living like astronauts. Still, I did learn a lot. I actually read the Bible. There is some validity to The Light's arguments that the church isn't what it was originally intended to be, what Jesus wanted it to be."

"He still taught that, eh? And they wear robes?" The Cardinal begins to relax a little. "You have been changed, Campion. Maybe more than you know. And I trust you when you say you didn't kill him. You didn't, right?"

"No, sir. I did not. I give you my word, for what it's worth. It was one of his own."

"Thank you, Campion."

BC feels like the meeting is over, and gets up to leave.

I guess the Cardinal heard what he needed to hear... but how the hell did he know all that? He had to know someone either on the station or somehow affiliated with them.

"Campion?"

BC stops, answers the Cardinal. "Yes?"

"Will things get back to, well, more 'normal' now?" He looks up at BC with pain in his eyes. BC feels the need to reassure him.

"Depending on how you define normal, Cardinal,

yeah, I think so. It's really up to the UIN, when you think about it."

"Warmongers! They hate us, you know that don't you, Campion? It's them you should be 'fixing'!" The Cardinal spits out.

"Of course."   *Didn't mean to set him off...* "I'll check back with you later, Cardinal. I've got to go see the governor."

"Very well, then, Campion." The Cardinal looks back down at his desk, again as if studying something BC cannot see.

"Thank you, sir," BC says, and turns to go. He leaves the Cardinal's study and heads back towards his rooms.

Glad that's over with! How could I know The Light and The Cardinal were old buds? And **how** *did he know what I was up to? Maybe my cover* **is** *blown...*

BC turns the corner onto the corridor leading down to his rooms and groans. The Reverend Sharlena Swan is standing directly in front of the doorway to his quarters. He tries to turn around before she spots him, but she's sees him all the same.

She shouts after him, "Father Campion!"

As he casually walks away, she runs up after him.

"Oh no, Father, you're not getting away from me again! I know who you are now!"

She passes him and stands directly in front of him. A tall woman, she glares at him eye to eye. "You know, it's not nice to lie to a fellow priest, Father Bernard Campion!"

"Sorry about that. I try to travel incognito, part of the job. You should've known that." BC keeps up a brave face.

"Mysterious BS from BC, how apropos. How OPO!" Swan laughs at her own wordplay.

"Do you mind?!" BC says in a loud whisper, giving Swan a sharp look.

We're in a fucking public corridor, shut up about the OPO...

"Sorry, secret agent man," she says, undeterred. "I've been assigned to you by the Pope himself, and I have the

Cardinal's blessing to take up your time for training, *and* you've already lied to me and avoided me. You haven't returned any of my messages..."

"I've been out of it for the last couple days. Literally. Blacked out for four days straight, you can check the medical records if you want."

"Those headaches, like on the shuttle? That was no act, I could tell. You were in pain. I felt bad for you... until I found out who you were and how you'd lied to me!"

"Jeesh, all right, already. Yeah, I'm a little worse for wear after my last assignment. I needed some down time to recuperate. But I'll work with you. The Pope told me I had to."

"Yeah, he told me to make you, 'more priest, less PR man'," she laughs.

Did he now? The Bastard!

"Look, Father. I'm not a hard person to get along with. This doesn't have to be a painful process. I teach priests and seminarians all the time, and no one has been killed or even maimed," she looks down her nose at him, "up until now. So let's get started!"

"What, started maiming?" BC shakes his head when she just glares back at him. "A joke? C'mon! Fine, we'll get started. Only not right now."

"You sound like Augustine." She shakes her head, "Why not right now? No time like the present!"

"Sure. Right. But, look, I've got an appointment with the governor *right now*, okay? I've got important business, church business, to attend to."

"I'm talking about important church business of yours, too.

Persistent.

"Yes, you are. Fine. Later on, we'll start. For now, you'll have to excuse me."

BC turns and walks back to the door to his quarters. Swan follows behind him.

"Don't think you've escaped me, Father," she says. "I have it on the highest authority. Your holy ass is mine, at least three hours a day!"

Damn, is that smoke coming out of her ears?

"I'll see you this afternoon at three!" she tells him. She turns and storms off down the corridor.

Oh, I can see this is gonna be fun.

BC opens the doors to his quarters, ducks inside and closes and locks them behind him.

Free at last...

He walks without stopping through his living room to his bedroom. He sits down on the bed and rubs his face with both hands. A lingering flicker of a headache is lurking just beyond his attention, glimmering like mirrors on the periphery of his sight, and somehow behind his eyes at the same time.

Trying not to pay it any attention. Hoping it goes away. Swan didn't help it any, that's for sure.

It's almost a little like vertigo. Or the remains of a bad hangover. It could be. A bad drug hangover, from the psychedelic cocktails they fed me on Fortune Station. It could be. Even a month later, though? I don't know. Well, gotta call Marc.

"Get me Governor Edwards," BC calls out to the com. After a short pause, the com dings him back to let him know Edwards is on the line.

"Edwards here."

"Hey Marc. It's BC. Still want to do some lunch?"

"Had we scheduled lunch?" Edwards is confused.

"You were my excuse to get out of a couple meetings, so I was hoping..."

Edwards laughs, "That's fine, it can be my excuse to get out of a couple things here, too. You wanna meet me here in about a half hour?"

"Sure, that sounds good. Half an hour."

"See you then."

The com clicks off and BC sits in the silence, rubbing his eyes, his temples, thinking.

Silence is bliss. Damn Peter for sicking Swan on me. She's a piece of fucking work. Can't stand her already. She seems more like the Cardinal's type of priest than Pope Peter's. I'm tempted to call and complain, but it'd do no good. No good at all.

I'd like to believe that maybe it's just massive stress causing these headaches. But deep down I know it's not 'just stress'. Its not like a concussion or a hangover, it's more... what? Echoey, I guess. Things echo. And things shine, too, like the flicker and glimmer of mirrors in the corners of my eyes. The echo and the shine, just all too much all at once. And all I want to do is make it stop. Make it stop!

BC feels the shimmering ease. The echoing stops. He drops his hands, opens his eyes again. He blinks.

There. I think I'm okay. For now. Wish that worked every time.

Chapter Twenty Three

An hour and a half later, BC and Marc Edwards are finishing lunch at one of the burger joints off the main dome. BC feels really good for the first time in months.

Happy, almost. Don't want to think that too hard, might jinx it.

"You were right about the California Burger. The guacamole was really rich."

"We just had a good avocado harvest from hydro. Report crossed my desk yesterday. Sometimes being the governor can be an asset in ways you'd never imagine," Edwards says with a little chuckle. He finishes his own burger off with a final bite and a smile as he chews. BC feels someone approach from behind.

"Hello! Father Campion! What a coincidence!"

Swan! So much for happiness. Maybe I did jinx myself...

She walks around and smiles down at the governor and BC as she stands between them tableside.

"Reverend Swan, how good to see you again. I'm having lunch."

"Looks like you *had* lunch, Father. Was it good?"

Edwards clears his throat, "BC, are you going to introduce me?"

BC grudgingly remembers his manners, "Sorry, Marc. Governor Marc Edwards, may I introduce the Reverend Sharlena Swan."

Edwards stands and shakes her hand, "Reverend."

"Governor. Nice to meet you. You have a nice city here."

"Thank you."

"I love this dome! I'm checking out the stores and restaurants. I have some time to kill before I meet with the Father here at three."

BC groans. Edwards and Swan both look at him.

BC laughs a nervous laugh, "Did I say that out loud?"

Swan shakes her head. "Well, as I was saying before I was, um, interrupted, I'm enjoying exploring your city, governor. I'll be on my way, now." She looks at BC, "It's good to see everything here is just as I was told it would be," She turns back to Edwards, "I was told Luna Prime's main dome is beautiful, and it is." She nods, "Governor Edwards. Father. See you shortly." She turns and walks away.

"She seems nice," Edwards says. "I don't see why you don't like her. You know," he lowers his voice, "you could have been nicer."

BC explodes, "Nicer! She was checking up on me!"

"What?"

"She was checking up on me! Checking up to see that I was actually having lunch with you, with the governor! You heard her," BC imitates her voice, adding some bitchiness, "'just making sure everything here is just as I was told it would be!'"

"She was complementing the dome! And, anyway, why would she be checking up on you in the first place? Is she your new boss?" Marc asks him.

"Ha! Far from it! But she was assigned by the Pope to train me in some of my 'priestly shortcomings', so she has something on me. I have to spend three hours a day with her for the next couple months, learning what I'm supposed to already know. She's supposed to teach me to be a better priest."

"So why check up on you?"

"Like I told you when I called you for lunch, you were my excuse."

"To get away from her?"

1   "Her and the Cardinal."

Edwards smiles. "You're funny sometime, BC. Why wouldn't she believe you were having lunch with the governor? Is it that farfetched?"

"No. I don't think so. But I lied to her before."

"When was that?"

"When I first met her. On the shuttle trip back here. She sat next to me. She asked me if I was Father Bernard Campion. I said I wasn't so she'd leave me alone."

"So... you got off to a real good start with her, huh?" Edwards says sarcastically.

"Uh, yeah."

"Still, she seems okay, BC." Edwards says sympathetically.

"You just don't know her yet," BC insists, shaking his head.

"What do you call a female priest, anyway?" Edwards asks innocently.

BC jumps at the opening, "'Reverend' is acceptable, but I prefer 'pain in the ass'."

"So, 'Reverend' Swan is going to teach you to be a priest, huh?"

"Not if I can help it."

"You sound like a kid trying to ditch school, BC," Edwards laughs. "How many 'lessons' have you had so far?"

"None yet. I've been out cold the last four days, you know that. But I don't think she believes that entirely, either. Whoa..."

There's the head thing again... sharp pain. Almost a noise...

"BC? You all right, BC?" Marc asks.

"Man, I don't know. I've been getting these headaches. Like I told you over lunch, they drugged me up pretty good a few times on that station. I think these headaches may be like the aftershock, the aftereffects of the drugs.This really sucks." BC pinches the bridge of his nose and tries to think the pain away again.

"Your eyes just rolled back in your head. Like you were possessed or something. Not a pretty sight."

"So sorry." BC winces. "But I think I'm going to have to excuse myself, Marc, and go lie down for a little while."

"Another headache coming on, huh? You should go to the infirmary, get checked up on."

"The doctors down at the Vatican poked and prodded me pretty thoroughly and found absolutely nothing wrong with me. I'm really not that thrilled at the thought of going through it all over again."

"Our doctors might find something they missed," Edwards offers.

"Maybe," BC says as he stands, a little wobbly.

Just not right...

"I'll see you later, Marc. I gotta go."

BC walks off, trying hard not to stumble as he goes.

Feel like I might throw up.

He manages to keep it together and keep his California burger down all the way back to his quarters. The headache keeps trying to come on, insistent, refusing to yield. When he finally sits down on his bed, his stomach calms. The throbbing in his head eases somewhat.

Hope I didn't look drunk walking back here. Swan would love to hear that, probably go right into one of her reports to Pope Peter. Damn, I'm tired. I can't believe after sleeping for four days that I'm tired again already. What the fuck is wrong with me? What did they do to me?

BC lies down on his bed. He sees the message light blinking, but ignores it and drifts off into dreamless sleep.

Chapter Twenty Four

BC wakes up with his door alarm ringing repeatedly. RINGRINGRINGRINGRINGRINGRINGRINGRING...

My headache is gone but now there's a whole new one starting. Who the hell is so annoying? I swear, if it's Swan I'm gonna kill her!

"Who is it!" BC calls out to the com.

A woman's voice comes back over the com, "BC, it's a blast from the past, man, it's me, Fiza! Let me in!"

Fiza?

"C'mon BC, you gotta remember me! It's Fiza!" she whines.

Fiza! What the... Where the fuck did she come from? What rock...

"Let me in, man, c'mon!" She's getting loud.

"Fiza? Is that really you? After all these years?"

God save me from old girlfriends... especially her!

"Surprised? Yeah, it's me! Hey, c'mon, fucking let me in already, you shit!"

Forgot about the mouth. Good thing it's as lovely as it is foul... least it used to be. And she was quite skilled with it as I recall, too. Might as well let her in before the whole embassy hears her.

"Come in, Fiza, come in and have a seat. I'll be right out."

BC hears the door open in the next room. Fiza calls out.

"BC?"

"I'll be right out," he says, getting up and smoothing his clothes.

How long did I sleep that time? Only a couple hours. Past three, though. I'll hear it from Swan.

He walks out into the living room and Fiza is sitting

on the table.

Kept her figure. Damn, she still looks good. Looks like trouble, as always. Forgot how short she was. Wearing her hair short and dark these days. Last time it was long and strawberry blonde, for a little while, anyway. I liked that, took me hook line and sinker, whatever that means.

"Hello, Fiza."

"Holy Shit! Look at you, a fucking priest! No fucking way!"

"It's been a long time."

"You've really got them fooled, huh? You big liar! A *priest*. Nice costume! Good scam! You know, where I've been, they'd shoot you on sight dressed like that."

"Okay, I'll bite, where have you been?"

Fiza smirks, "yeah, I remember, 'you bite.' I like that," she laughs. "A priest! Huh. No priests on Mars."

"Mars! You've been on Mars," BC says with disbelief.

"On Mars. With the Moslems. Not my scene at all! It sucked, completely."

"You. You were on Mars? You expect me to believe this?"

"You don't forgive or forget, do you BC? Yes, I was on Mars. That's why my hair is dark. I had to dye it to hide there, blend in. What?"

"You always lied so easily, Fiza. I forgive you, but I won't forget all the fucked up shit you did to me back then. I promised myself a long time ago I would never believe you again. The only thing about you I can trust is that I can trust you to lie."

"Ouch. Forgive me for I have sinned, Oh ye of little faith," Fiza says, "Get it? Faith?" She laughs at her own joke.

"Shut up," BC says. He rubs his eyes and forehead with his right hand.

"You know, all of a sudden you don't look so good, BC. You all right?"

"I was until you showed up. Why are you here, anyway, Fiza? What do you want this time?"

"Do I have to want something? Maybe I'm just visiting an old friend."

"You always want something."

"Oh, can priests fuck these days?" Fiza asks with a wicked grin.

"That wasn't what I meant."

She keeps grinning at him. "Oh no? Too bad. You see, it's late, and I do need a place to crash, just for tonight..."

The mind is strong, but the body is weak... I should be going to see Swan...

Fiza gets up off the table and walks over to BC. She tugs at his collar.

"Does this come off? Oh lookie here, it does indeed." She pulls the collar off and unsnaps the button behind it, then wraps her arms up around his neck, looking up in his eyes as she draws in close. "How's about we get reacquainted, huh?"

She starts kissing him. BC can't stop kissing her back. All her betrayals melt away for now, all the bad memories, the time she left him for dead, the guys she slept around on him with, the fall she let him take when their grift went south... a lot to melt away, but the mind can easily go blank when a beautiful woman is wrapped around you.

The body is weak... well, that's hard enough. Oh yeah, she does like it when I bite like this...

BC wakes up early the next morning, feels Fiza still sleeping beside him. He mentally berates himself for forgetting all his Fiza rules. Rule number one had to be 'do not sleep with Fiza'.

WHAT THE FUCK WERE YOU THINKING!! You let her in again, all these years later! Don't you learn fucking anything? What the fuck were you thinking! She's fucking poison!

Fiza stirs, turns over, and kisses his cheek. "Morning, handsome. You still got it, you know that honey? That priest collar didn't fool Fiza, hon. Bless me Father for I have sinned!"

"Shut up."

Remember how much she always fucked up everything in the past? Let's not repeat the same mistakes again and again, okay? Good, I'm talking to myself. She really does bring out the best in me.

"So, this whole priest thing," she says. "What is it, some con gone out of control?"

"You could say that," BC says.

"I did." She smiles a fake smile and bats her eyes at him.

He ignores her and goes on, "I figured religion would be a good cover for my import export scam I was running on Linderstern Finch. You remember that station, don't you? That's where you left me the last time you fucked me over, remember? Remember leaving me for dead? The good old days!?" BC says, his voice slick with sarcasm, "God, what was that, ten years ago? Forgive me if I'm not nostalgic."

"Harsh. You got any drugs here?" Fiza starts rummaging around.

I'd grab her to stop her, but I know what will happen then. Not again. She turns anything physical into, well, sex. She's very good at that sort of manipulation. And very good at that.

"No. Trust me, after what I've been through the last couple months I don't need anything else in my system."

She looks at him, a little puzzled, but plows ahead. "Yeah, BC, you know I remember Linderstern Finch. But I don't want to dredge that all up and rehash it over and over again, okay?" She's getting louder. "We both made mistakes. Were we young and stupid, and let's leave it at that, okay?" Her face is red. She suddenly seems aware she is almost shouting. She regains her composure, and asks BC in her softer voice, "What did you do after Linderstern Finch?"

"It's a long story..." BC shakes his head.

She can change emotions on a dime. That's fucked up.

"How about you tell it over breakfast?" she says.

"It's so sad, the way you have to work everybody, get

something out of them."

Fiza jumps up off the bed with the sheets wrapped around her and yells down at BC. "Jesus fucking Christ! Will you give me a fucking break! Get over yourself! I just asked for some breakfast, not the fucking Moon! I fucked your brains out last night, didn't I? I'm not the only one who wants something!"

"All right, calm down, Fiza, calm down. Jesus, look, I don't know what to think."

Fiza calms a little, "I think you should make us some breakfast while I freshen up." She ducks into the bathroom and closes the door. BC gets up and walks into the living room to muster up some breakfast.

Hmm. Headache's gone, anyway. One of them. The other's in the shower...

His message light is still blinking. Six messages from Swan.

Delete.

BC throws together some muffins for breakfast. After the refresher, Fiza walks into the living room wearing only a sheet wrapped around her.

"Breakfast?" she asks, looking down at the muffins on the table.

"Best I could do on short notice. Coffee?"

"Please. There's no coffee on Mars, did you know that?"

"So, you're sticking with that story, huh?"

"I'll tell you all about it sometime. But, come on, you told me you were gonna tell me how you became a fucking priest!"

"They made all the different denominations minister's priests in the Great reunification, five years ago."

"Yeah, but how did you get to that point? Come on, juicy details!"

"Don't talk with your mouth full! Nice. Don't play with your food like that. Yeah, I get it, muffin and muffin, funny."

"Why don't you eat them both?"

The body is weak... the mind is pretty weak, too, when

you get right down to it. Speaking of getting right down to it...

BC is in the refresher a half hour later, beating himself up again.

I cannot keep doing this! Gotta be pheromones or something. Undeniable attraction. Carnal desire, whatever you want to call it. Lets her wrap me right around her little fucking finger. And I'm not 19 anymore. I should be over this sort of shit by now.

"Can I come in?" Fiza yells from outside.

BC opens the door, steps into the bedroom. "I'm just coming out."

"Do you mind if I use it again?" she asks.

"Nah, go ahead."

"Don't think you got out of telling me your story," Fiza says, before she closes the refresher door behind her.

BC gets dressed while she freshens up. He calls the Cardinal.

"Good morning, Campion."

"Good morning, Cardinal."

"You missed your time with the Reverend Swan yesterday, Father Campion. She's quite upset with you."

"I know, and I'm sorry. I had every intention of being there, but I'm afraid I'm still getting these terrible headaches. I took sick again just after lunch yesterday, and I'm afraid I won't be able to work today, either. I'm sorry, Cardinal."

"Well, if you're sick, you're sick. I'll tell Reverend Swan. But you best get well soon, Father. The Pope himself sent her up here just for you, my boy. Just for you."

"I know. Bye."

"Good-bye."

"Who was that?" Fiza asks as she walks, nude, out of the refresher and across the room.

"The Cardinal. I was calling in sick."

"For me? How sweet!"

"Not just for you. For me, too. They want me to work with this woman priest. She's supposed to train me to be a better priest, since I became a priest by such dubious means." BC says the last three words with mock gravity.

"Did someone say doobies?" Fiza says and laughs.

"Dubious. And no, no doobies. I told you, no drugs. I'm trying to get normal again."

"You're not normal now?"

Can't tell her what really went on...

"I've been sick, and on some medication. I'm better now, but there's still some residual effects, some headaches I get from time to time. I'm trying to let the remnants of those drugs pass out of my system before pouring any new ones in."

"I see. Sick, huh?" Her brow furrows and her mood suddenly darkens. "Nothing fucking contagious, better not be or I'll fucking..."

"Relax, nothing like that, you're fine, don't worry."

"So let's get back in bed."

"Fine, but I don't think I can..."

"Shhh," she says, putting her finger to his lips. She taps his nose. "Tell me how you got into this mess. How did my favorite young con man get conned into a priest's collar?"

They get back in under the covers and spoon up close to each other.

I don't know why I'm letting myself fall into this again. Into her. So she wants to know?

"Fine. Well, then, despite the fact you brought the UTZ goons down on us on Linderstern Finch..."

"Sorry, okay? Get over it! Go on..."

"... I found a way to escape their notice, stay alive and on the station, and keep the smuggling operation going. I answered a classified ad from the Holy Redemption Church of Jesus. I remember the ad's headline caught me, 'Get Nontaxable Status!' Anyway, they sent me ordination papers and tax forms and for just fifty dollars I officially became Brother Bernard Campion of the Holy Redemption Church of Jesus!

"I recruited a bunch of my friends as my church members, my congregation. I even got some members of my family to join. Since my congregation was growing, The Holy Redemption Church of Jesus raised me to Reverend status."

"Hallelujah!" Fiza says, and nudges her head into his shoulder.

"I used our nontax status to cover my import/export deals. You're gonna like this part. With the Reverend status I could easily arrange for travel visas for myself, so I began to act as a courier for several 'nontraditional' business interests operating on Luna and Earth."

"Organized crime?"

"More disorganized than anything. But they paid well. And the money I made running for them paid my way after I got kicked off of Linderstern Finch." BC shakes his head just thinking about it. "That happened a year after my 'ordination'. I lost my station job because they didn't like the stuff I had going on on the side. But it was the stuff on the side that was making me the real money."

"Ain't that always the fucking way," Fiza says with a little laugh. "Where did you go after you got kicked off the station? Were you homeless?"

"Not at all. I had places set up on Luna, in orbit, and on Earth. The job on the station had almost become unnecessary. But it helped explain my travel activity. After I lost the station job I couldn't make the same runs anymore. But I could still travel between my residences as the Reverend Campion of The Holy Redemption Church of Jesus."

"Do I hear an amen?"

"Amen. Eventually, even the Holy Redemption Church of Jesus got swept up in the Great Reunification of 2104. We were absorbed into the New catholic Church, and I was granted priestly status. They welcomed me into the greater church and even assigned me to a rectory on Earth, in Boston."

"They had no idea what you were all about?"

"No idea at all. At least not at first. Things were pretty chaotic in the church back in those first couple years right after the reunification."

"Yeah, I remember that. Didn't a lot of popes die, like, right in a fucking row?"

BC laughs. "Yeah, until Pope Peter got in. Peter the Second. Took a lot of balls to take that name."

"That was a pretty big deal too. First black pope, right?"

"Yeah. And the first pope to come from a church other than the old Catholic Church. It was bound to happen. The new church was too huge. It was a mess. They had people like me in it! Peter, old Leo, well, he's a lot like me, like I was. It was easy for him to rise to the top. When chaos reigns, those who will do anything in order to gain power gain that power pretty easily. There are no checks, no balances to stop them. Leo Benford is ruthless. He rose really quickly. And I did okay, too."

"This is the pope you're talking about?"

"Yup. He came up from the streets of LA. Brought in his own 'security force' after he was raised to the papacy. They were all gangsters."

"The what-acy?"

"Papacy. It's what being the pope is called."

"Oh."

"His security force got a new name right after they joined him at the Vatican. He renamed them the Office of Papal Operations."

"The OPO? Oh my God, you're OPO!" She starts jumping up and down on the bed, as if BC were some music star. She almost squeals when she says, "I knew it! Holy shit! Do you kill people? When did you become OPO?" She drops back down and snuggles back up close. BC feels her trembling in excitement.

Cat's out of the proverbial bag. Might as well...

"I was recruited into the OPO three years ago, in 2106. The OPO began digging up the dirt on the priests who came into the New catholic Church from fringe denominations like mine. Whenever they found someone like me with a checkered past they'd use that to 'encourage' us to join the OPO. It was join or be brought up on all your old charges, for most of us. And then, you don't leave the OPO. Once you're in, you're in. You're either in, or your dead, plain as that."

"Rough job. That collar chafe, then?"

"A little."

"So, what do you do for them? You kill people? Are you an assassin? How many people have you killed?" Her breath is hot on the back of his ear.

She can barely contain herself. She's almost turned on by this shit...

"I can't say. The OPO is supposed to be involved in public relations," BC says in mock seriousness.

"Yeah, like anyone believes that. Everyone knows the OPO is like the pope's secret police."

"Not me. I'm a simple spin doctor."

"Right. Last time I checked, they didn't have to keep spin doctors on the job with death threats. You're as much a spin doctor as you are a priest. It's funny, though, I never thought of you as an assassin or a spy."

"Why not?"

"You're too much of an old school con man. Assassin, spy, that's too respectable. But, then, look at you. You, a fucking priest! Good thing they don't have that nasty ol' celibacy thing anymore..." Fiza disappears beneath the sheets and BC decides his storytelling is done as his mind goes elsewhere.

Later, Fiza talks BC into going out for lunch.

"If anyone sees us, tell them I'm an old friend who's in visiting and I made you come out to lunch even though you're sick. It's all true, isn't it?"

"Sure."

BC mulls their conversations over as they walk through the main dome.

I've already told her way too much. I could just kill her. But there's no holy justification for that, though, no holy orders. I could justify it as necessary for covering my tracks, but then they might kill me for getting sloppy. Maybe I am.

Getting sloppy.

Fiza looks around as they walk, making a show of taking in the surroundings. "Look at those pine trees! They look like fucking green toilet brushes!"

"Nice. Maybe watch your language out in public with a priest?" BC asks.

"Right," she agrees, ignoring him. "You know what I mean, the way they're so straight up like that?" Her attention shifts, "Let's cross the pond!" she shouts. She starts to run towards the central pool and the nearest walkway. BC has to quicken his step to catch up.

"I didn't think I'd find a place like this here. So wet, and lush. So much nicer than Mars."

"Still sticking to that story? I think it's your turn to tell some truth. I won't believe most of what you tell me. Safer that way. But I'd love to hear your story so far."

"Why won't you believe me."

"Because you lie. And there haven't been any non Moslems on Mars in the last two years because the UIN killed them all!"

"Let's go sit down somewhere. I'll tell you all about it over lunch."

"Fine. How about that place, the French one?"

"Nah, I hate French. Polynesian?"

"Sure."

They make their way to a little Hawaiian themed Cafe just off the atrium. They sit and look at menus. After they order, Fiza defends herself. "It wasn't easy being on Mars. I had to hide. I dyed my hair. I had to wear a veil!"

I could almost believe her.

"Right."

Their food arrives. They drop the discussion and dive in to their lunch, both of them hungry. Their silent feast continues until a familiar voice calls from the atrium.

"BC!"

Edwards!

"Marc! How are you?" BC asks, standing up to shake Edwards's hand as he walks over to their table.

"How are you, BC? They said at your office that you were out sick today." He looks Fiza up and down and begins to grin.

"I'm feeling a little better. And I have an old friend visiting. She demanded I come out to lunch. Fiza, this is Marc, Marc Edwards. He's in charge of this place."

"What, the restaurant? You know this pineapple is..."

"No, Fiza, the Moon. Marc is the governor of Luna Prime!" BC laughs.

"Oh, fucking ay, I am so fucking embarrassed, I'm sorry, governor. It's nice, I mean, it's an honor to meet you," she says, shaking Edwards's extended hand in between both of hers.

"It's an honor to meet you too, Miss Fiza. Any friend of BC's is a friend of mine." He eases his hand out of hers.

Edwards catches BC's eye and winks.

Oh great.

"Well, hey, I can't stay. I'll let you two get back to catching up. BC, give me a call when you get a chance, okay? See you guys later!" Edwards turns and walks quickly away.

"He knows you're getting laid," Fiza says with a knowing leer.

"What?" BC almost

"He's happy for you! You can see it in his eyes, he knows."

"Please. Could you please keep your voice down?"

"What, worried about upholding your image?"

"Never mind. Tell me more about Mars."

"It sucked. Dirt and sand. That's fuckin' Mars. Dirt and fuckin' sand, red sand, everywhere, always in your hair, in your makeup, in your cra..."

"Hey, we're in public, huh?"

"You started it! You asked me!"

"Right. Eat your lunch."

"Make up your mind."

"Okay. Eat your lunch."

"Fine," Fiza huffs. She digs into the Polynesian

delight on her plate and shovels it down in silence. Every so often she looks ups from eating to glare at BC until he looks up, meets her glare, and goes back to eating. She holds her glares for a short time longer, then goes back to eating, too.

"Why were you on Mars?" BC asks when she finishes. Fiza just glares at him. He presses his point. "I find it awful hard to believe you've been on Mar..."

"I was hiding. That's it. Like I told you."

"Who were you hiding from?"

"It was, I was just, I was hiding, okay? Look, can we drop this?"

"Drop what?" The Reverend Swan has suddenly appeared table side between BC and Fiza.

Can this get any better?

"Reverend Swan. Hello," BC says with little enthusiasm.

"Hello, Father Campion. Glad to see you're feeling better. Who's your little friend here, Father?"

"This is an old friend of mine, Reverend. She demanded that I come out to lunch even though I told her how sick I am with these headaches I've been getting. Anyway. Fiza, meet The Reverend Swan. Reverend Swan, may I introduce you to my old friend, Fiza."

"Nice to meet you," Fiza says.

"And you likewise, I'm sure," says Swan, dismissively.

Fiza and Swan warily size each other up as they extend hands and shake. Swan turns from Fiza to address BC.

"Father, we have to start working on your rites and rituals training! Your lessons await!"

"You mean you came looking for me? I'm eating! I'm ill! I have a visitor! Excuse me!"

"Looks to me like you're almost done. Anyway, I've arranged with the Cardinal to free you up from some of your public relations duties while you work with me. Hmm. I was told you were sick today, but you look fine to me. So guess what? We'll begin in a half an hour. I'll expect to see you in my office then. Nice to meet you, Ms. Fiza."

Swan turns and walks briskly away.

"Looks like you should be hiding, too, maybe, huh?" Fiza says with a little laugh.

"We'll talk more about your hiding on Mars later," BC says, "Let's head back to my rooms for now. You can wait for me there."

"Wait for you there?! Why? I wanna see this place! I'll play tourist while you play priest."

"I thought you were in hiding?"

"Not here! At least, not yet, anyway!" she laughs.

Half an hour later BC sits in front of Reverend Swan as she revs up her lecture.

"...things are looser now, true, and you are in the loosest branch of the NcC, but really, Father, some decorum, please." She finishes and glares at him from behind her desk.

"What?" BC asks?

"That little number you were brunching with earlier... not exactly discreet, Father Campion." She actually "tsk, tsks," at him.

"Now, look here, you're criticizing my friends, now?"

Who the fuck do you think you are, bitch?

"You have an image to uphold, Father, whether you like it or not. And a post coital brunch with some little floozy you've just boffed, both of you sitting there all glowing... not the image you should be projecting, if you get my drift."

I'd like to set you adrift in space right about now...

"Look, Swan, let's get this straight. I may have to follow along with you on church stuff, but you can keep your opinions of my private life to yourself, okay?" BC says quietly, trying to keep his temper checked.

Swan continues her attack, "I'm supposed to teach you to be a better priest. That's exactly what I'm trying to do. Being a priest means more than saying some words at Sunday Mass. It's a whole lifestyle."

"That's fine, but you weren't assigned by Pope Peter to train me into a new lifestyle. You're here to simply help me brush up on some of the finer points of the rites and rituals, stuff I'm rusty on. That's it. I'll let you do that. But I'm not going to let you judge me!" BC almost shouts.

Damn, don't need to get heated, she has no real power over me... Got to maintain control...

Swan tries to assert herself, "What I'm to teach you is for me to decide as your teacher. Our interpretations of my assignment seem to differ. You are..."

"Shut up, Swan." BC says levelly. "Stick to your mass lessons, leave my private life alone, and we'll get along fine. Stick your nose where it doesn't belong and you'll be gone faster than you can say, 'return ticket to Earth, please'."

Swan just stares at him, mouth drawn tightly closed, eyes full of fury.

Is that steam coming out of her ears?

BC stares back at her. She remains silent, so BC says, "You've been brought in to teach me, Reverend Swan, but make no mistake, I outrank you. And although you were brought in at the request of my superiors, if I give the word, those same superiors will send you back where you came from, real fast. It's up to you, Swan, really. You can make it easy or hard on both of us. Your choice. What's it gonna be?"

Swan stares at him, considering.

Considering how to dissect me, by the look of it. You know, though, her eyes have quieted a little. And her face seems a little more relaxed. We'll see...

BC stares back. Their eyes stay locked until Swan breaks the contact and looks down at her desk.

Eyes still lowered, she says, "Very well. Have it your way. But I will teach you how to be a better priest. In my own way. You're just going to have to deal with that, Father Campion. Shall we begin over?"

BC relaxes. "Fine. Go ahead."

Swan looks up at him, says, "Okay, Father. We'll start by finding out what you do know. Tell me what you know about the Sunday New United Reform Liturgy."

Better.

"Let's see. It's new, united and reformed, and it's said on Sundays, right?"

Attempted humor.

Swan scoffs, "Yeah, right. Here, take this," she says, and hands him a red leather book about an inch thick.

"What's this?" BC asks.

"That," Swan says, the glare back in her eyes, "is the book we use for the New United Reform Sunday Liturgy. It has all the liturgies we use in it, actually. Are you telling me you've never seen this book before?"

"Um, well, not that one, no," BC stammers out.

"I can see we have a lot to work on," Swan says, "if you don't even recognize the book..."

"See, Swan, plenty of work for you to do without your prying into areas you don't belong in. We'll do fine."

Swan ignores the comment. "Turn to page 25," she instructs BC.

Three hours later and BC feels like his head is going to explode.

"That's all for today, Father," Swan finally says. "Thanks for your time. We'll see you here at ten tomorrow morning for our next session."

"Right. Tomorrow at Ten. See you then, Reverend Swan," BC says and almost leaps up and runs out of her office.

Too much information!

He rubs his temples as he walks back to his rooms. No headache actually appears. It gives BC some time to think.

A lot of what Swan was just hammering into my skull was kinda familiar. A lot of the rites we read through today are similar to what The Light's people use. Funny, though, Most of the NcC stuff seems simplified, dumbed down.

'Course, I don't want Swan to know I know any of it. Keeps her out of my business if she figures she's got to cover everything.

I kept thinking about Kim's lessons. I liked him as a teacher better than Swan, that's for sure. Taught me just what I needed to know, not all this extra BS Swan seems to think is important.

BC opens the door to his rooms to see Fiza sitting inside on the sofa.

"I thought you were going out exploring?" BC asks.

"I did. I thought you might want something to eat. They said you'd be done around now."

"They? Who said that?"

"The Cardinal and his secretary. What?"

"Shit, Fiza, you've got to be more, I don't know, discreet, less in people's faces!"

"Why BC, are you ashamed of me?" Fiza asks playfully, batting her eyelashes.

BC looks at her without answering.

Maybe I am. Can't tell her that. Won't go over well.

"No, that's not it. It's just... my position right now is a little dicey. They want me to become a better priest, The Cardinal wants me to study with Swan because he thinks I'm lazy, The Pope figures Swan will help me strengthen my cover, which he thinks is already blown! They're looking to me to be more, I don't know, priestly, I guess. And, unfortunately, you don't quite fit that image."

Fiza pouts.

"Aw, c'mon, don't... look, you've worked scams with me in the past. Granted, that was a long time ago, but this is the same thing, Fiza! Work with me here!"

Still pouting, she asks, "What do you want me to do?"

"Just lay low for now, okay? And don't talk to any church people!"

"Okay, okay, I can do that, just calm down, all right?" She goes from a pout to a glare in a split second.

"I am calm!"

"Yeah, right. And I'm a nun." She glares at BC, shakes her head. "Okay. Tell you what. You can go out on your own and get something to eat by yourself, okay? I don't like you much right now, so I'm gonna go my own way for now, okay. I'm outta here." She gathers herself together to get ready to leave.

BC doesn't try to stop her. "All right. Be that way. Do you want to do dinner later?"

"Maybe. Maybe not. I don't know right now. Bye," she says, and heads out the door.

If the door swung shut instead of sliding, she'd have slammed it. But it wouldn't kill me if she disappeared again for good. How did I get tangled up with her again so quickly? I guess you forget all the bad shit over time. Maybe I've got that forgive and forget thing going for me. Probably get me screwed, usually does, right?

Fiza doesn't show up for dinner. She doesn't return at all that night. BC has mixed emotions when he wakes up alone the next morning.

I can't be sure if I'm happy or sad. Funny. Wonder where she is?

Chapter Twenty Five

BC gets up and into his day without a sign of Fiza. When he gets out of another excruciatingly painful three hours with the Reverend Swan, he heads back to his rooms to find his com unit waiting with a message from Edwards. He calls him back.

Maybe he wants to do a late lunch. Almost one-thirty...

"Hey, BC! Thanks for calling me back," Edwards answers.

"Hi Marc. What's up?"

"That friend of yours, Fiza?"

Uh oh.

"Yeah?"

"She's in some big trouble, BC. How good a friend is she?"

"Huh. I ask myself that same question a lot, Marc. Anytime she shows up. What's she done now? I haven't seen her since this time yesterday."

"Probably because she's been in LSC custody."

"Oh."

"She didn't do anything here on Luna Prime. But the UTZ has a boatload of old warrants out against her. Some of them on really serious charges. We're talking extortion, grand larceny and even murder, here, BC."

"Really? She's not a murderer. The other stuff, maybe. Even probably. But Fiza's no murderer. And since when does the LSC do UTZ security work?"

"She was shopping around the atrium. Her ID must have set off some alarms somewhere in the UTZ and so they asked us to intervene on their behalf. We have some mutual cooperation and extradition treaties with the UTZ, BC, always have. We enforce nonpolitical laws... like larceny and murder."

"So what happens to her now?"

Edwards rubs his forehead. "That's what I've gotta figure out. That's why I called you. I've kept her off the UTZ radar since we picked her up. They think we're still looking for her. I can't keep up the stall tactics too long, though. We've either got to turn her in or get her out of here. She dropped your name when the LSC picked her up, so I found out and intervened, but it could get messy, know what I mean?"

With her its always messy

"What was that?"

Did I say that out loud?

"Nothing. Just thinking out loud. She's really good at making messes out of things."

Edwards chuckles, "Good friend, huh? Or do you just sleep together?"

"It's that obvious?"

"Sure. You were both glowing when I saw you yesterday. I'm not stupid. Hey, I was happy for ya, figured it'd been a while."

"Oh, thanks," BC says sarcastically.

She was right. But this shit. It all starts all over again, never fails.

"Hey, she's cute, I'll give you that. Hard to resist, I'd guess," Edwards offers his sympathy.

They both laugh.

Edwards get serious again. "I can release her into your custody, BC, but you've got to get her off the Moon. Understand?"

"I get it. I'll make arrangements."

"Good. I'll have her brought to my office. You can meet her here and then spirit her away. Can you be ready to go in, say, three hours?"

"Yeah, I'll use my magic powers," BC cracks. "No, really, that should be enough time. I'll be there. And Marc?"

"What?"

"Thanks for looking out for her. She's not a bad woman. No matter what they say, I can't believe she's a murderer. She's just... misguided. But, thanks, all the same."

"Sure, BC, no problem. See you here soon." Edwards clicks off.

She kept a low profile, all right. Well, at least I know now why she was hiding. Extortion, larceny AND murder!? Good job, Fiza. I might even hide on Mars if I had to get away from all that shit.

BC sighs.

At least I have some friends in high places, as well as the low...

BC sees Fiza curled up on the corner of the couch in Edward's reception area when he enters the governor's offices three hours later. She looks small, legs folded up against her, her arms encircling them around her ankles, holding herself together in a tight little ball.

She can sometimes look so vulnerable.

She looks up when BC walks in.

"Hello Fiza."

"Don't say anything, okay, BC?" she says in her quiet voice.

"I only said hello. Hey, Marc."

"Hey, BC. Well, here she is. I told her what I told you. She can't stay here. I can say we never found her. If they find out we did, I'll insist she was released in a case of mistaken identity, but either way UTZ investigators will be in my face about it before too long. You've got to get her off the Moon," Edwards says. He turns to Fiza, "I'm sorry you can't stay here. Is there anyplace else you can go?"

"Not back to Mars, that's for sure," she says. Edwards is clearly surprised. But she keeps going, "I jut barely escaped with my life from there this last time." She doesn't bother to explain, although she sees the confusion on Edwards's face. "There might be one possibility," she offers.

"What's that," both BC and Edwards ask almost simultaneously.

"I can go to one of the old orbiting stations. It used to be in my family, ages ago. It's owned by a UTZ CEO, but my family has an ancestral claim and right of sanctuary there. It's not ideal, but it's something."

She is so full of shit! We'll talk about this.

Edwards is relieved. "Good!"

BC shakes his head, "I don't know. You know, I haven't been able to arrange for a private ship yet. Nothing's available right now."

Edwards has an idea. "Since it's an orbiting station, I can line up a small commercial transport for you myself, no questions asked. BC, why don't you take her there? We'll keep you under the UTZ radar... but I got to tell you, going to the station of a UTZ CEO sounds like walking right into the arms of the enemy. You'd better hope he honors your familial claims."

"It's all I've got," Fiza says, shrugging.

"All right, then. BC, she's yours. Your custody. Why don't you go back to your place for now, BC. I'll have someone get in touch with you shortly about the ship. Which station?" he asks Fiza.

"Huh?" she says.

"Which station are you going to?"

"Oh. Wentworth Station."

Edwards is again surprised. "Richard Wentworth's Station? You sure?"

Fiza nods, "Yeah."

"Okay, then. We'll get that taken care of in a few minutes. I'll see you later, BC. Good-bye, Miss Fiza."

BC thanks his friend, "Thanks again, Marc. For everything."

Fiza chimes in, "Yeah, thank you, Marc, you're okay."

Edwards nods. "Thanks."

BC and Fiza head back to BC's rooms. Neither says a thing. Once they're back inside the rooms, BC turns on her.

"Okay. Time for some truth. Talk to me. Why does the UTZ want you for murder? Extortion, larceny, those I can see, but murder?"

"I didn't kill anyone, BC, honest! They're all trumped up charges! I was running in some pretty high powered circles in the UTZ a couple years ago. I was a mistress to several different UTZ CEOs, until one decided he wanted me all to himself. I went and lived with him on his station for over a year. We were happy, although his friends and family frowned on our whole affair. He didn't have a wife anymore, so we weren't doing anything wrong. They just didn't like me. Said he was slumming, that I was trash."

"Nice people, huh?"

"Yeah. But he was good to me, BC. He was warm, and even funny in his own way. He was into kinky sex, but you know me, I'm flexible. I made him happy. We had a lot of fun. Until one time, in the middle of... of everything, he has a heart attack and dies, right there in bed. Well, as you can probably imagine, his family rushed me out of there and off the station before he was even cold. All my credit, everything he gave me, they wiped away as soon as he was dead. They sent me away on the first ship they could."

"I see."

"No, you don't. Not yet. Because, BC, he had promised to take care of me! He had it all drawn up legally, he showed me. He said he knew I'd outlive him, and he knew his family would try to keep me from his fortunes, so he had his lawyers draft documents that protected a small share for me. I saw it! I didn't want a lot, just enough to survive on. They tried to shut me out completely! Keep me from leaving with anything of his. I managed to grab a few things of sentimental value to me as they were giving me the bum's rush out of there. When his family found out about it, they filed the charges. They claimed I bilked him out of his money and then killed him. They started the UTZ's hunt for me. I never had a chance to defend myself. That's the whole truth of it, BC. I never killed anyone, you've got to believe me, and I didn't take anything that wasn't already coming to me!"

"I see."

I don't believe you, Fiza, but I'll play along. It's just easier. I hope you really do have an "in", a way to get on board this UTZ station, because it sounds to me like the last place you should be going.

"You 'see', huh? Does that mean you believe me?"

"It means I see."

"Cryptic."

"Fine."

Edwards finds them a ship that gets them off the Moon and off towards Wentworth Station later that night. BC has to promise the Cardinal he'll be back in a week, for Christmas.

The Cardinal even made a joke about it... "just be back in time. Christmas is one of those times in the church year when those who don't usually come to church actually attend. You should feel right at home!" A sense of humor. Who knew?

The small commercial freighter carries several passengers. BC and Fiza have a compact stateroom to themselves, a tiny space barely able to fit both of them lying down. Sitting up offers a little more room.

This has to be the smallest stateroom I've ever been in. Economy of space is one thing, but this is ridiculous.

"Three days, huh? No transpace point?" Fiza asks, as she fidgets in her folded up bed, now a chair.

"Nope," BC answers, "too close to Earth. Are you sure you want to go to this place?"

"I've got no choice. This is my last ditch effort."

"I might know one other place. Fortune Station. Ever hear of it?"

"No. Should I have?"

"Not necessarily. It's old, supposed to be abandoned, but there's this religious cult that lives there, and I'm their, um, leader."

"What the fuck? Get out! You are just full of surprises! Why didn't you tell me before!"

"I don't know. I didn't think of it. Not exactly your kind of people."

And I'm not sure I should inflict you on them...

"How so?"

"They're really religious. They believe in what they're

preaching, what they're living. You wouldn't like it. Probably too rigid."

Fiza doesn't say anything. After she thinks for a minute or two, she says, "I can fit in in a lot of places you might not think I could. Like Mars, huh?"

"True. I still don't believe you were there."

She punches him in the arm. "You fuck! What do I have to do! I was there! It sucked! What more do you want?"

"You want me to believe? Tell me more about it," BC prods.

She somehow glares and pouts at the same time.
Nearly irresistible...

"Come on, Fiza," he pleads.

She plays coy for another moment or so, then tells BC, "Not that you believe a word I say..." she pauses and glares at BC just a little harder, "but people live miserably there. I told you before about the sand, it gets in everything, fucks up all the airlocks and any other seals. They're always short on water, too, and most of what water is there goes into the terraforming project.

"They're trying to get the place to be more like Earth, but I don't think it's working. Most people there don't think it's working. The equipment is old, cobbled together from what's left of the old UTZ terraform factories and the busted up Japanese installations. And the terraform factories are hellholes, but most everyone has to work there at some time or another. The Ayatollah demands it! You see." She says the last in a mocking tone.

"Everything on Mars is old. Surplus and leftovers from the old Jap base and the ripped up UTZ outpost. They have recycling, water reclamation, that stuff, but none of it seems to work too well." She scrunches up her nose, as if she smells something foul. "It never seems to get entirely clean, either, it always seems kind of grungy, no matter where you are.

"And the people are depressing. They're all brainwashed into hating the UTZ, your church, and anyone else they feel has beat on them. All they talk about is coming back to Earth, back to their stolen Mecca, and how their hardships now will be rewarded by Allah in the end. Boring. But it keeps them in their place, keeps fueling the hate that drives the war. You can feel it," Fiza says, and shudders. "I could feel it." She pulls up into her fetal position, arms wrapped around her drawn up knees. "So, do you believe me, yet?"

"Sounds true, I'll give you that. Who'd you rip the story from?"

"Argh!" Fiza stands up. "If I could storm out and go somewhere I would! You are impossible!"

"And you, my dear, lie at will all too easily. I'll reserve judgment for now."

She sits back down and stews. BC stands, folds down his bed, and climbs on to catch some sleep.

"You should try to sleep some, too. Fiza," BC says as he lies down.

"What about the station you were telling me about?"

"Never mind. It was a lie," BC lies. "I made it up."

"Fuck you."

Fiza stands and tries to fold her chair back down into a bed, but with BC's bed already down, she has no room to maneuver. She opens the stateroom door and steps out into the hall outside.

"Fold my bed down!" she yells in to BC. He sits up on his bed, reaches over to her chair and folds it down into place as a bed. With both beds in place, there is no room to walk in the stateroom. Fiza climbs through the door and up over onto her bed. She reaches back, shuts the stateroom door, and finally flops down.

"Wanna fuck?" she asks.

"Why not? Nothing else to do," BC answers.

About all we have in common now anyway. And what she does best, I suppose. I wonder if her orgasms are lies, too? Know what? I don't care!

They kill a couple of days while the ship is enroute to Wentworth Station. They hear periodic announcements from the Captain over the PA system, but none that catch their attention until on the third day they hear, "Father Bernard Campion to the purser's office, please. Father Bernard Campion. To the purser's."

BC freshens up and dresses in his basic black and collar, and heads to the public section of the ship. A couple of queries later and BC finds himself at the purser's office. He knocks and enters.

"Hello?" BC asks an apparently empty office.

"Hold on, be right there," a voice calls from an adjoining cabin. Then a thin face capped by a short shock of red hair emerges from around a doorway. "Yes?"

"I was paged?"

"Father Campion?"

"Yes. Are you the Purser? Who am I supposed to... what's this about?"

"I'm the purser," the man says, coming in to the room. He's a slight man, small frame, perfect for ship crew. He's wearing the ship's uniform, pale blue jumpsuit with red pin stripes. "Your docking request at Wentworth Station has been refused," he tells BC. "Wentworth station is a private station. Without their okay, this ship can't dock there. They've refused. Said there is no such ancestral claim or right. Sorry."

"Did you ask them nicely?" BC asks, already knowing the answer.

"Look, Father, it's my job to..."

"Sorry. I was trying to make a joke, inject some humor into the situation. Can I ask them myself?"

"That's the next usual option, actually."

"How long do I have to persuade them?"

"We'll be in the station's range for about a day, maybe 20 hours. After that we won't be able to dock and keep our schedule."

"Okay, I'll be right back. I have to get somebody."

"Your lady friend?" the purser asks, then blushes.

"My what? How do you know..."

"From your, um, your docking request, you know?" The man sounds as sheepish as he looks.

What the fuck is up with this guy? Maybe saw Fiza and got the hots for her or something. Sure is acting weird.

"Yeah. Sure. Look, I'm going to get her and come back so we can ask again. Okay?"

The purser nods. BC storms back to the stateroom and confronts Fiza.

"They won't let us dock! So much for your family connections."

"What?"

"The purser's call. Wentworth Station said no. We can't dock there! No such ancestral claim and shit. What are you trying to pull here, Fiza? What have you gotten me into this time, huh? Your family had nothing to do with this place, did they?"

"Don't have a heart attack, BC. It's just a misunderstanding. I just need to talk to them myself," Fiza says, eyes wide.

"Good, because we get the chance to do that. That's why I'm back here so soon, I came to get you. Get dressed and let's go. Now."

"Okay, okay, don't get so pushy. You are so ugly when you get like this, you know?" she rants as she pulls on a one piece black dress.

"I don't like being lied to. Constantly. It's this thing I have about, I don't know, honesty. Interesting concept. You might try it some time."

"Jesus Christ, you must believe your own shit, 'cause now you're preaching, too. Just shut up, BC, and lead the way to wherever we gotta go to talk some sense into these fools," Fiza says, an extra dose of attitude thrown back at BC as she pushes past him out the door of the stateroom to wait outside in the corridor. BC passes her and they both head to the purser's.

"Okay, Red," BC says to the purser when they enter the office, "fire up the com unit, please."

The little redheaded man is sitting behind his desk. Two other crewmen flank him on either side. All three men stare at Fiza, looking her up and down, obviously checking her out.

I'm usually not the jealous type, but these guys are way overboard.

"Excuse me!" BC says, moving a little in front of Fiza. She moves sideways and steps up next to him. Their eyes snap to him. "Did you even hear what I said?"

The redhead nods, "Yes, Father." The two other men go back to ogling Fiza.

Too much.

"Wentworth Station," the com unit speaks. The screen stays dark, no video.

"Yes, Richard Wentworth, please," Fiza says before anyone else can speak.

"Fiza!" BC can't help blurting out.

"Who is calling?" the com asks.

"Please tell him it's Fiza calling?"

"A moment, please."

A moment appears to be about five minutes. Then a deep, rich, resonant voice comes out of the com.

"Fiza."

"Richard. Hello."

"They tell me you've come to visit. I find that hard to believe. Is it really you?"

"It's really me. Send video, okay?" Fiza asks the purser.

"Sending video signal," the purser says, touching a control on his desk.

"I'm surprised you're here," Wentworth says. His signal remains audio only.

"I have nowhere else to go."

"Yes. I could see where that could be true. You've burned every bridge you've ever crossed, haven't you? You've burned this one as well, I'm afraid. I wouldn't say you're exactly welcome here, either."

"I'd hate to have to sell my secrets to seek asylum somewhere else," Fiza says with a false air of regret.

"Are you trying to blackmail me, Fiza? I hope not. That would be dangerous. Even fatal. Be very careful what you say. Try to be more subtle, if you can comprehend the concept."

"Can we dock and talk about it?" Fiza asks Wentworth.

"Okay, you can stop here. But there is a price, and this time you'll have to pay up, my dear."

"Not the cops?" Fiza asks, alarmed.

"No," Wentworth laughs, "not the cops. My price, not theirs. But I will grant you my protection and asylum, for that price. Dock, and we'll talk about it, over dinner."

BC nudges Fiza.

"Can my friend come over, too? He wants to check the place out, make sure I'm okay on your station. He's escorting me here."

"That him? A priest? Not your usual crowd, Fiza."

The crewmen in the room start to snicker. Wentworth yells over the com, "You men! Why are you laughing?"

"Nothing, sir, it's just that what you said reminded us of something we were talking about earlier that gave us a good laugh," the little redheaded man says, leaning in towards the com.

"Really. Then share that with us now, won't you?" Wentworth's voice demands.

The crewmen are silent.

"Well, I'm waiting," Wentworth says over the com The silence continues.

"Well, if it's not that funny," Wentworth says, "shut the fuck up, okay? Where was I? Oh yes, bring your holy friend over for dinner as well. You'll be met at the ship dock when you arrive. Good-bye," Wentworth signs off.

Fiza turns to BC, excited. "See! We're in! I told you we would be."

"That price he mentioned sounded pretty steep, Fiza. Do you know what he meant by that?" BC asks, shaking his head.

I've got a bad feeling about this...

"Not really. I figure I'll have to work for him or something."

BC looks at the men, still undressing Fiza mentally.

I gotta say something.

"Do you guys mind?"

The crewmen look back and forth among themselves, until the purser looks at him and speaks.

"Sorry. She's sexy, huh?"

Fucking attitude, too. Little shit.

"You guys need some shore leave, or at least cold showers. Give it a rest, huh?"

Hear what I'm not saying: I don't want to have to kill you...

"Sorry, *Father*," the purser says, accenting "Father" in a strange way. "We'll dock in about an hour. We'll call you."

BC turns, grabs Fiza by the arm and propels them both out of the office.

"Someone jealous?" she says as they walk quickly back to their room.

"Hardly. But those guys were just rude. Shit, you just eat it up anyway, don't you?" BC accuses her.

"It's flattering. Sorry! Doesn't matter, we'll be off this ship soon. And on to Wentworth Station!"

"He didn't sound too excited to see you."

"No, he isn't. But I knew he still would, anyway," she says confidently.

"After you threatened him!" he protests. "Go ahead," BC lets her enter the stateroom ahead of him.

"Still a gentleman, huh? Thanks. Hey, stop worrying, we're in, man!"

"Right. We're in."

Whatever that means.

Chapter Twenty Six

BC and Fiza cross a spacious walkway from their ship to Wentworth Station. BC marvels at the opulence already apparent.

This walkway and the airlocks are larger than most I've seen. The transparent top panels let you see the whole station as you approach. Designed to stun and overwhelm, no doubt. Nice digs. Nicer than Fortune Station by a mile.

Fortune Station was one of the earliest built private orbital stations. Wentworth Station was started over fifty years ago, BC figures, because the main cylinder of the station still rotates to create gravity.

It had to have been built before artificial gravity was feasible. Course, the rest of it was built afterwards, clearly.

The airlock in front of them, their way into Wentworth Station, enters a stationary section of the structure. The facade of this boxy part is constructed to look like an office building back on earth, like one of the skyscrapers in New York City. The artificial gravity reinforces the effect. The rotating main cylinder sits on top of the boxy section.

"Looks like a big camera, I've always thought," Fiza says. "Or a big metal dick. Just like Richard himself. A big Dick," she starts giggling at her own joke. She looks at BC for a reaction but he ignores her. She stops laughing. "Fine. Be like that."

They reach the airlock doors. An armed guard stands on either side, dressed in a gold, red and black station uniform, a variation on the standard green uniforms of regular UTZ troops.. The one on the right motions them to head in through the airlock. BC notices the guards have UTZ insignia on their uniforms as well as Wentworth Station logos. After BC and Fiza walk past them, they each fall in behind BC and Fiza.

"No going back now, huh, BC?" Fiza asks, trying to lighten the mood.

"Just play nice, and let's try to get out of this alive, 'kay?" BC doesn't hide his growing anger over being played by Fiza yet again.

Can't hide this headache I'm feeling come on, either. Just hope it's not a bad one like before. Not now!

The airlock shushes shut behind their escorts. BC looks around the massive reception area.

Must be nice to be able to live like this, even out here. Place looks like a mansion in a movie. All business outside, all pleasure inside. Nice.

"If you can afford it."

"What?" Fiza says.

"Huh?" BC asks.

"I asked you first. What did you just say?"

Did I say that out loud?

"Nothing. I was just appreciating the lovely black marble floor."

"Only the finest for Richard Wentworth, baby," Fiza says with sarcasm.

"Correct, Fiza," says an older man entering the reception area. He's dressed in a red and gold smoking jacket and dark pressed pants. His slippers let him approach BC and Fiza without their hearing. His dark hair is gray at the temples, set off in stark contrast to his light caramel skin. His features have the sort of generic, too perfect look BC's always noticed among those wealthy enough to have themselves cosmetically enhanced.

Gotta be Richard Wentworth. One of the wealthiest and most powerful men in the UTZ, right there. Since the OPO works with the UTZ hierarchy, I gotta figure he knows something about our operation. Wonder if he's an ally?

"Hello Fiza. Hello, Father. Welcome to my home. Won't you come with me?" He asks, then turns and walks across the room and down a corridor on the left.

BC notices Wentworth never looks back to make sure BC and Fiza are coming.

Clearly a man who expects to be followed. Might as well...

They follow Wentworth along a series of turns and corridors, finally arriving at what looks like an elevator door. He presses a button in the wall to the right side of the doors and they open, revealing a small room with four chairs.

"Come, sit down, and strap yourselves in. We're going up to the main section. The elevator has independent artificial g, so we won't feel it as we rise, turn, and match the cylinder's rotation. Quite ingenious. My father's top engineers designed it ages ago, still works. Go ahead, sit down." Wentworth sits buckles himself in. "The straps are just a precaution. Just in case the g lets go or something else goes wrong. Here we go." Wentworth taps the controls built in to the arm of his chair. The doors close. The small room has no windows.

It feels like an elevator. A weird, big, sit down, strap in elevator. Can't be the only way up there, too cumbersome for workers and anybody with any real business to take care of. Just the luxurious way, I'd bet. And escorted by the man himself. Red carpet treatment!

The doors open again after a minute. A new corridor opens up in front of them, this one with a plush red carpet running down the middle of the black marble floor. Wentworth undoes his chair's straps and gets up first. BC and Fiza undo their seat belts and follow him out.

"You see? No sense of weirdness, vertigo or free fall! Just like an elevator ride! Now please wait here," he says.

As BC watches Richard Wentworth walks away down the corridor. BC notices again he never looks back.

Fiza says something under her breath that BC can't make out.

"What?"

"Nothing. Just those stupid androids of Richard's. They always creep me out."

"That was an android?"

"You thought that was him?" Fiza starts laughing at

BC. "Man, you do have delusions of grandeur, don't you? You think he'd come see us in like that himself? I thought you'd been places, Campion? Don't tell me you've never seen a mechanical manservant?" She laughs again.

"Never one that good, evidently. And I've never met the real Wentworth."

"You'll know it when you do. Trust me. He has a certain, I don't know, charisma, I guess," she says, losing herself in her own thoughts and memories as she trails off.

"Wonderful. Can't wait to meet the man."

"Here come his guards. Should be soon, now."

Two guards lead them down the long corridor to a large vaulted hall. A huge semicircular table dominates the center of the room, a giant "C" laid flat. The guards motion for BC and Fiza to enter the mouth of the "C" and they walk into the center.

Ten well dressed, evidently powerful people sit along the outside edge of the table. Each has attendants hovering behind them. It is apparently dinner time, as each of the ten has a plate of food in front of them. A personal guard stands directly behind each diner's chair to watch their backs. Servants bring food and drink to the table through the center of the "C", creating a continual flow of servers passing by BC and Fiza on both sides as they stand in the center of the circle. No one speaks to them at first.

Wow, hey, this is great, watching a bunch of rich fucks fill their faces. These folks dredge up all that hostility I thought I'd come to grips with. I hate 'em just looking at 'em. And I was doing so well at not judging...

BC sees the man who resembles the android sitting directly in front of them, at the center of the outside edge of the "C". He is busy eating some pinkish piece of meat, ripping chunks of it off the main slab on his plate and chomping them down.

He doesn't bother to notice them standing there until after the meat is gone and he's downed a glass of red wine. This takes about fifteen minutes. Then he looks up and speaks. His voice booms out, amplified by some hidden method not readily apparent to BC.

"Fiza. It really is you. You've got balls, girl. Sorry about the language, Father. If you really are a priest. You guys can fuck these days, huh?"

BC is caught off guard, no doubt Wentworth's intent. "What?"

"Purser on that ship you came on had a camera on your room. You guys were the porno hit of the voyage, evidently. Fiza doing what she does best, as always. But I don't know you, Father. If you are a priest."

"I am. You Wentworth?"

"What do you think? You two hungry?"

Before they can answer, Wentworth is motioning for two people seated at his left to move over. They give Wentworth briefly indignant looks, then slide their seats over. Wentworth motions to someone and chairs are brought for BC and Fiza.

"Come around, come around and sit down," Wentworth gestures magnanimously with his right arm. He nods. One of the servers escorts them over and they are seated next to Wentworth. BC is directly to Wentworth's left, Fiza next to him on his left. Clean plates are placed in front of each of them, and servers suddenly appear on the other side of the table with an assortment of dishes to choose from. BC picks a broccoli and cheese dish, while Fiza grabs her own pink slab of meat. BC then opts for a light white wine while Fiza sips a cabernet sauvignon.

This doesn't suck. Wonder if that meat is really beef? Broccoli must be grown on board. This is good! Haven't eaten like this since Rome. And look at the other guests! That news guy, what's his name, from the UTZ network news. His date. Or maybe she's with that other guy. I think he's a CEO, another board member. DeMar or something like that. That woman over next to Fiza is Sabine something or other. A Pop singer on Wentworth's recording label. Must be a lesbian, looks like that young little fawn next to her is her date. Too bad, the little one is yummy.

Should have known something was up when the

purser and his buddies acted so weird. How'd Wentworth know, though? Oh man, headache really coming on...

"So, Father, how do you know Fiza?" Wentworth is talking to him. BC tries to focus.

"We, um, we go back. A long way. I haven't seen her in years, until she showed up a few days ago." BC closes his eyes, trying to wish the headache away.

I do not need this headache shit right now...

"Are you all right, Father?" Wentworth asks.

BC opens his eyes. "I'm fine."

"You don't look well," Wentworth says with some hint of concern.

"I have a bad headache. That's all."

"And Fiza? How are you?" Wentworth smiles an unhealthy smile at Fiza.

That sounded almost sarcastic. He certainly didn't mean that at all. And she's not answering?

BC turns and looks at Fiza, whose head is lolling back and forth as if she's about to pass out.

"Wha?" she says, trying to open and keep open her eyes.

Too much wine? That's not like Fiza. What goes on here? Damn, my head!

"Whadyadotome?" Fiza slurs out. "Icantmovemyarms! I... unh," she passes out, chin dropping to her chest. The guard behind her chair pulls her back from the table. He waves a second guard over and they lift Fiza, one on each side, and drag her out between them.

Wentworth watches them then turns to BC. "Miss Fiza appears to be tired. We'll put her to bed. She'll be fine. We'll give her a job here when she wakes up, make her useful. You can leave on the next ship back to the Moon, Father. Your work here is done. Father?"

What the fuck is going on here?!

"What..." is all BC gets out before he passes out, too.

Chapter Twenty Seven

BC wakes up in the passenger/co-pilot seat of a small two seater transport ship cruising through space. He's strapped in. The pilot is about foot away, humming to himself as he runs through a maintenance check on the main screen in front of him.

"Who the... where are we? Who the hell are you? Where are we going? What the fuck is going on here!" BC explodes as he wakes up.

"So many questions... and such a mouth, Padre." The pilot is on the heavy side, crewcut hair, looks old military. He smiles at BC. "They said you weren't your normal priest. Horny. Heard you made quite a tape."

BC just stares at him.

I'd kill him but I don't know if I can fly this thing.

He keeps smiling at BC. "I work for Mr. Wentworth. He asked me to give you a ride home. That's who I am and where we're going. Couple of your questions, anyways."

"Why did he drug me and Fiza? Where is she?"

"From what they tell me, no one drugged you. You complained of a headache and dropped. Passed out right there at Mr. Wentworth's table! Not too polite, Padre," he chuckles. "Miss Fiza, she was sedated so she could get some rest before starting her new job for Mr. Wentworth. That's what I'm told, anyways."

"I want to talk to Wentworth!" BC demands.

"Sure, I'll call him. He said you'd probably want to talk to him when you woke up, said he'd take your call. You're lucky, Padre, he doesn't do that for most people. Doesn't always do it for me, anyways. Hold on, I'll call him." The pilot gets Wentworth on the com.

Wentworth appears on the video screen in front of BC.

227

"Father. Good to see you again. Glad you've recovered from your migraine. When you had your spell, I thought you'd want to return home as soon as possible. Drex was kind enough to do the honors." Wentworth smiles at BC over the com.

The pilot speaks up, "My pleasure, Mr. Wentworth."

BC interjects. "Was it a 'spell' or did you drug me?"

"You just passed out, Father. I had nothing to do with it."

"Like Fiza did? You going to try to tell me she just 'passed out' too?"

"No. She I had drugged. Guaranteed her cooperation. You I have no interest in whatsoever."

"Why did you drug Fiza? What has she done to you?" BC protests.

"Quite a lot, actually. Most of which I certainly wouldn't discuss with a priest. Unless I was on my death bed, perhaps. If you even are a priest. Still a question in my mind. Especially after seeing that tape. Never trust a Purser, Father! Hey Drex, when you were Purser on the Wentworth commercial liner, you ever secretly record people in their rooms having sex?"

The pilot laughs, "All the time, Mr. Wentworth, all the time. People make the funniest faces! Everybody records passengers, it's common practice. At least around the crews I've been on, anyways."

"Did you ever record me, then, Drex?"

"Oh, no sir, I know that would have gotten me killed, I bet. Or fired, anyways," he says, laughing.

Wentworth laughs, "Something to keep in mind in the future, eh, Father? So. Are you really a priest?"

"I'm really a priest. I work for the Vatican. You can ask the Pope himself."

"You think I can't? I can call your bluff right now, 'Father'. I've known Peter for years."

"So have I. I work for him personally." BC gives the last word more weight.

"You're one of his men? You? You mean OPO?"

"Don't know what you're talking about, sir," BC says with emphasis.

Not on an open com channel!

"I see."

"What about Fiza?"

"Why? Is she of interest to the O... to your people?" Wentworth corrects himself.

"She's not, no. It's more, um, personal."

"I'm sorry, then, Father. She'll be staying here, working for me. It would be best if you forgot all about her. She isn't a good person, Father. She screws over a lot of people, sometimes the wrong people. And she owes a lot of the wrong people a lot of money. She owes me a lot of money. I'm giving her the chance to work it off, all the while keeping anyone else from coming after her. She'll work for me to stay alive."

"What kind of work?" BC asks.

Wentworth lets out a low chuckle, "There really only one thing Fiza's any good at, as you well know, Father. We'll put those skills to work full time."

"She won't..."

"She will! Because she does it or she dies, it's very simple, Father. She'll be pumped full of drugs to keep her happy. Best she can hope for."

What a fucking slimeball.

"You're an evil man, Wentworth."

"Evil? I've been called worse. And 'evil' is such an outdated term, an outmoded notion, a quaint superstition from the past. Is self interest evil? Is pleasure evil? We all serve ourselves first, even you, *Father.*"

"Evil is entirely relative. It all depends on your perspective. The OPO perspective no doubt allows you to do things with a clear conscience that others would label evil. In fact, you have no basis for calling me evil given what I know you do!"

"Look, no talk of the O word. O-kay?!"

"Listen, you fool, this is a secure channel, I'm not stupid! I know a lot of you in the OPO are killers. I know. I've

229

given the orders. I know Peter, but I don't know you. Let me tell you, Campion, this is not getting off on the right foot for you, see? Because I'm gonna find out who you are. That could make things worse for you, if you continue to annoy me." A cruel edge has entered Wentworth's voice.

"Now look here, I..." BC tries to protest. Wentworth continues, cutting BC off sharply.

"You are going back to the moon. I'll find out who you are soon enough. After I do, you'll be no trouble to me. No trouble to me at all, understand. Anyone I know, I can keep tabs on. And I will. Don't worry about Fiza, Father. Don't cross me over her. She isn't worth it! She's a user, she uses people. She used me, she used you. Now I'll use her, and let several others in my employ use her as well. Why don't you just forget about her, Father? It'll be for the best. That's the last time I ask. This conversation is over. Good-bye, Father. Drex, switch to secure mode."

"Yes, sir." The pilot puts a headset on and switches off the main audio. BC's screen goes dark. BC listens as the pilot receives instructions. All he hears on this end are a lot of "uh huh"s and "yup"s.

Wonder if they're telling him to kill me. Pleasant thought.

"Right. Transport out." The pilot takes off the headset and turns main audio back on. "We have a slight problem, Padre," he says to BC.

Here it comes...

"The UIN is on the move, some kind of major ship movement. They have a handful of ships on this flight path, so I'm going to detour out and around them. It's going to take us longer to get there, but we'll get there alive, anyways."

"What about your orders to kill me and dump the body?" BC jokes.

"What? Oh, you're joking. But that's not funny. You'd be dead already. And I wouldn't be talking to you, not like this, like we are now. If I have to kill you I don't want to know you," Drex says, shaking his head.

"I know what you mean." BC says.

And I do. You are so right...

"Yeah, right. Sure you do. Thanks for your sympathy, Padre, anyways."

You'd be surprised, big guy.

The pilot keeps talking. "You don't trust Mr. Wentworth, and that's okay. I don't always trust him myself, but he pays me very well, so I do as he says. He says take you back to the Moon. So that's where we're going. Go back to sleep if you want. This is going to take a while." The pilot turns to his control panel and gets to work adjusting their course. BC stares out the window at the impossibly dense field of stars.

So many far away suns. Space isn't really black, it's all stars.

BC falls asleep, only to be jarred awake as if he'd fallen.

"Good Morning , Padre! We're under attack! UIN scout ships. I'm trying to fly us out of this," the pilot says. "You awake?"

"What?" BC tries to wake up fast.

"UIN scout ships, short range, firing at us. Probably means there's a cruiser nearby. At least one. I'm trying to go where they can't."

"Is this ship armed?" BC asks.

"Not really. It's supposed to be way too fast to need armament. There are defensive shields, countermeasures, that sort of thing. But no missles, no lasers. Woops, here they come again, hold on!"

The pilot hits something and the ship jumps up and out of the line of fire. BC is pressed down hard into his seat by the g force as they continue to leave the scout ships in the dust. The pilot hits the same control. Fast as it started, the transport decelerates, and BC can catch his breath again.

"Woah," BC manages.

"Yeah, wild ride, huh? Got us out of there, though. No sign of UIN cruisers either. Guess I picked the right direction."

"Good guess."

"Not good enough! Shit, here they come again. Hold on!"

The ship is pushed sideways hard.

Feels like some giant just backhanded the ship across the galaxy.

"They hit us," Drex says. He calls up specs and assesses damage on the screen in front of him. He also calls up navigational charts, switching back and forth as he figures out a course of action.

BC scans the stars outside. He can just barely make out the glint of metal among the stars where he knows the UIN ships are. Other flashes are laser fire, maybe missiles launching. Drex runs the calculations he needs for another speed burst.

"Hold on, here we go," the pilot says, and he punches the control switch. The small transport leaps away from the fighting, safe for the moment until the slower ships can catch up.

"We can't keep this up, Father. We can't take more hits or missile fire, either. We need to find someplace to hide. I've been looking at the charts, and there's an old abandoned station nearby where we might get some cover. I'm already heading for it."

Could it...

"What's the station's name?"

"I don't know. It's on the charts. Freedom or something."

"Fortune?"

No way.

"Nah, I don't think it's... no, wait a sec, here it is. Yeah, it is Fortune. You know it?"

"Yeah, pretty well. I spent some time there earlier this year. I know those people."

"People? What people? I thought it was abandoned?"

"It was. But a religious cult moved in and took it over a few years back."

"Oh. Then this is gonna be fun... Hey, that's strange." The pilot is drawn to his control screen.

"What?"

"I'm picking up UTZ ships, lots of them, all around Fortune station."

"UTZ ships?"

"Looks like they've seen us and the UIN scouts. I'm sending friend all the way, hope they... Yup, they've seen us and acknowledged friend. We're okay. They're sending a couple attack ships out to chase off the UIN scouts."

Two streaks flash by them.

"There they go."

The pilot relaxes, smiles over at BC.

"Looks like we're going to be okay, Padre. We did get hit, though. The ship needs some repairs, so let's dock and do what we have to to get going again, quick. I promised to get you to the moon. I keep my promises," he says, smiling at BC, "Or at least I try to, anyways."

"Sure," BC says, distracted. All he can do is stare. Fortune Station is surrounded by UTZ ships. Ten UTZ battle cruisers, several transpace transports. And the station is completely lit up.

Not a good sign. Funny, I told them I'd come back, and here I am. Couldn't stay away. But what the fuck is the UTZ doing here in force?

Chapter Twenty Eight

Drex brings their transport in to dock with Fortune Station, right next to a hulking UTZ battle cruiser. Just after BC hears the airlock bolts lock into place their ship starts shaking.

"The whole station's shaking!" the pilot yells. "Must have just gotten hit! Guess those UIN scouts are pretty feisty." A dull metallic thud rings through their ship and the shaking intensifies. "Another hit! They might have bigger friends nearby." Drex unbuckles his safety harness and begins to stand. " Let's head inside the station. Rather be in there than out here right now."

"Sounds good to me." BC gets up and heads for the lock behind the pilot.

He turns to BC. "You said you know these people?"

"Yeah," BC says, but he's no longer sure the people he knows will still be on the station. Or even still alive.

Drex steps aside and opens his arms, gesturing for BC to go ahead. "You go first, then, okay?"

Aw, jeesh, way to show some fuckin' spine, man.

"Why not," BC agrees. He cycles them through the airlock. They enter Fortune Station and are immediately flanked by two UTZ soldiers.

"Identify yourselves!"

This is all wrong.

"Hi, how are you? Can we come in? There's some bad guys shooting at us out there," BC says, syrupy and sweet.

I don't think these guys have a sense of humor. Don't think they liked the sarcasm...

"Who are you?" The soldier on BC's right demands.

"Actually, you know, this is funny, it really is, but,

234

technically? I'm in charge of this station. So I should ask, 'who are you?' and 'what are you doing on my station?' You could be in some trouble here, mister!" BC puffs himself up best he can.

This takes the grunt by surprise. It at least causes him to stop and think his way through the statement in an attempt at comprehension. He abandons the attempt and falls back to his defensive default setting and angry demands.

"We're with Commander Urdru, Fourth Fleet, Third Division. We've been here a month and I've never seen you before, Father." He talks past BC, "Commander!"

A UTZ Fleet Commander walks up from the left.

Commander Urdru, I presume.

"What? What's going on here? Who are these clowns?" he barks.

The soldier points at BC. "Sir, This priest says he's in charge here. Asked us what we were doing on *his* station. Lotta nerve, sir."

Urdru looks him up and down, assesses him. Then he does the same to the pilot. Finally, he looks BC in the eye.

"You really think this is YOUR station? What, are you this 'Light' we heard about? You?" he asks in a mocking tone.

This one knows about The Light. Is that good or bad? I'm thinking bad.

BC tries to answer. "Actually, I'm the *New* Light..."

Urdru cuts him off, "I don't care! What's your name? Both of you!"

"Drex." The pilot says.

"Bernard Campion," BC answers. Urdru smiles when he hears the name.

"Campion? I have heard of you!" Urdru says. "You helped secure this place! One of the Pope's men, am I right?" he asks.

Jesus! Isn't this jarhead familiar with the concept of confidential?

Urdru starts as he sees BC's glower and realizes his mistake. "Sorry, Father. I don't know what you do or who you do it for, but you did a good job here," he says, trying to patch over his first statement.

"I did?" BC asks. "Thanks, I guess. Where's Kim? Where's the people who were here?"

"You mean those nutty cultists? We cleared out those squatters just after you secured the place, sent them back to Earth. It was easy, we just moved in and took over. I remember they kept throwing your name at us, saying you promised them they'd be 'left alone'. They 'had your word!' they said. That was a good one! It's funny, I thought at first they were saying 'champion' until I found out what your name was, who you were."

Yeah, I'm obviously no champion... But fuck this asshole.

"Who gave you your orders?" BC demands of Urdru.

"The UTZ Council, who else? With Pope Peter's blessing. How could you not know?" Urdru is perplexed.

"Guess I'm out of the loop. I've been on vacation," BC quips. "So, the cultists are all gone?"

"Oh yeah, long gone. We've been using the station as a base for a couple of weeks. It's really old, though. Nothing works right. And so much of the place smells like incense. Makes me gag."

A dull metallic thud rings out and the station starts shaking again. Urdru gets distracted by someone yelling on the com in his ear.

"Sorry, Father. We got a whole bunch of UIN coming down on us. I think you guys brought them in on your tails! Thanks so much! I gotta run! We'll talk after things calm down." Urdru turns and runs back the way he came.

BC, Drex, and the two soldiers all look at each other. BC nods to the pilot, "Let's go." He heads off in the direction Urdru went. The pilot follows. BC walks confidently ahead until they walk through section doors that close behind them. Then he turns and tries to look through the glass to see if the soldiers are following. They're not. They're back at their post. He looks at the pilot and smiles. "Always look like you're going where you're supposed to be going, doing what you're supposed to be doing, and you can get away with almost anything," BC advises Drex, "especially in the military!" BC gestures for Drex to follow him. "I know my way around here a little. We probably want to go this way..."

BC leads them down a corridor to the right that opens on the cafeteria where The Light's altar once stood. It's gone now. The entire room has been turned into a military command center. Several technicians monitor equipment that lines the walls of the room. Urdru stands at a center console. Not wanting to deal with him again just yet, BC leaves the cafeteria for a side corridor. The pilot soon follows. BC stops, and stops Drex.

"I've got to check on something," BC tells him. "I'll be right back. You stay here. Ask around in there for help fixing your ship," BC says, nodding towards the cafeteria. BC starts to go, but the pilot stops him.

"Hold on a sec," he says, and a strong hand closes around BC's upper left arm before he can escape. Drex holds BC in place. "Where are you going?"

"I just have to check on something from before. I'll be right back, I promise. You're my ride home! Speaking of which, just go in there and ask them to help you with repairs. Throw around your bosses name. Maybe it's good for something."

"Not a bad idea. Okay, just be sure to come meet me back here," he says.

BC walks away.

"Don't you leave without me!" he shouts back to Drex. "I won't."

Why don't I believe he's sincere?

BC finds an old com station off the beaten path.

Just what I've been looking for. Got to see if there's any kind of message left for me from Kim or... there.

Kim's face appears, bruised and bloodied on the right side.

"Hello, Bernard. I'm about to be forced out of here at

gun point by your UTZ thugs. How nice. Why did you lie? To me, to all of us? Judas did no worse. You are not a light of any kind! But you've always known that. You're a sham. A sham I thought I used, but you used me all along. You used us all. I should have known. Betrayer! You serve no one but yourself, do you? That is so sad. Do you even know how to tell the truth? This is my fault, really."

The image goes dark. End of message.

Well, fuck me, Kim. I didn't know. I maybe should have known, should have expected they'd do this. What can I say? Sorry?

BOOM!

A blast hits outside, close by BC's position. He's rocked to the floor by the concussion, hears the hissing of escaping atmosphere.

Don't blow! Not yet! Explosive decompression? Where's the nearest sealable door? Back here...

BC find his way back towards the cafeteria, seals doors behind him as he goes. He finds the pilot of his transport standing idle in the room while soldiers scramble and Urdru barks out orders at them.

"No repairs until after the battle," the pilot tells BC. "Not even for Mr. Wentworth. Although they did compliment me on the use of a very impressive name."

"Did they now? Too bad. What now?" BC asks.

"Guess we'll have to ride it out," Drex says. "We won't get anywhere in my little ship while this is going on."

"Guess not," BC agrees, reluctantly.

Don't know if old Fortune Station can take much more of a beating. 'Riding it out' may not be an option...

A series of echoing metallic booms get louder and louder. The station shakes with each one. BOOM. BOOM. BA-BOOM.

Closer and closer. There's some real firepower coming in on us. Got to be more than scout ships at this point. And this place has no defenses! Unless these guys installed some since they've been here. Doubtful. Probably just relying on the UTZ cruisers outside. If they're getting past them, there's more out there than a couple UIN Scout ships.

Urdru calls over the com. BC hears him echoing on the station's com system and yelling in his ear at the same time.

"Okay, people, that's it. This place can't take any more! We're bugging out. Report to your ships, we're heading out!" Urdru shouts. "Let's go!"

BC and Drex are suddenly in the midst of a swirling sea of scrambling UTZ regulars.

"Not good," BC says. The pilot nods in agreement.

"We should find a ship to adopt," Drex says. "If we try to leave in that little transport under this kind of heavy fire, we're dead. It looks like staying here ain't an option anymore, either. Anyways. Better to get aboard a cruiser or a heavy transport if we can." The pilot looks at BC to see if he agrees with the idea.

BC looks around the cafeteria. The techs are packing up and carting off their equipment with surprising speed. The room is already almost empty. He spots two guards leaving through a door nearby.

"Let's follow them," he says, nodding at the two and stepping in behind them. Drex falls into step beside BC. They follow the two UTZ guards out of the cafeteria, down the main corridor, through a side corridor, and out an airlock into a troop transport ship. BC and Drex stop once they're inside the ship, and watch the guards continue on their way into the ship.

Drex looks at BC with new admiration, "Hey, that worked, that was good," he whispers to him as the ship's airlock cycles shut behind them.

"Thanks, I think," BC say, "but we're not out of this yet."

Chapter Twenty-Nine

What a stench! Never realized these troop transports smelled so bad! Seems over crowded. 'Course, we're over crowding ourselves. But at least we're off Fortune Station. Not so fortunate for the cult. I shoulda known Peter wouldn't honor my promises. You know, I swear I saw something about bearing false witness, somewhere...

BC and Drex are crammed in elbow to elbow with about thirty UTZ soldiers in the hold of the UTZ transport ship. They had to find somewhere on the ship to stay for the trip, and this hold seemed as good a place as any. They haven't heard any sounds of battle since leaving Fortune Station.

Guess no one's shooting at us, for now. Be nice if we're heading for the moon. Beggars can't be choosers, though, huh? Oh man, again?

BC keeps getting pushed into. He holds his ground, but a guy on his right keeps leaning back into him.

I hate this.

The trooper turns around, finally, and BC catches a hot blast of sour whiskey breath. He's got an almost empty bottle in his right hand,.

"Hey, sorry, man. Merry Fucking Christmas, huh? Fuckin' Moslems, no respect at all. Oh, wait, you a priest? Oh shit, sorry Father. Didn't mean to swear in front of a priest. My mom would tan my hide if she heard I did that, even at my age!" He laughs himself silly at his own drunken wit.

Christmas? Wow, almost forgot in all the craziness of the last few days. It's actually Christmas already. Geesh, the Cardinal will be pissed I'm not back there helping him.

240

Hey, I'm trying to get there. I suppose I better answer the drunk with the gun....

"They never forget, do they?" BC says. "They like to remind us by attacking on Christmas. Probably should have seen it coming, huh?"

The guy's a little confused.

"Huh?" he says.

"The Christmas Massacre?" BC prods him.

Drex leans over, "BC don't waste your..."

The drunk gets louder, interrupting. "Wait, I remember! Like in that movie, right? We starved 'em on Mars, back in the 70's. Then we came in and hit 'em hard, took back our UTZ stations on Mars. A great victory, right?"

"Don't think I saw that one." BC says.

Probably propaganda. Military training film for the UTZ.

"Might have been a victory for the UTZ," BC continues, "but for the Moslems it was the Christmas Massacre. They thought it was their food transports returning after a year of nothing. Anyone who could get a suit on went to see the landing. They were surrounding the ships. The UTZ commanders on board those food transports kept the ships closed up until a massive crowd had gathered. Then the doors opened and instead of food, the starving crowds found troops firing at them."

"Yup," the drunk soldier agrees, then makes a gun with his hand, "fsssshhh, fsssh," he slurs the sound of a laser. "Made quick work of 'em. Glorious victory with few casualties."

Pointless to argue with a drunk, especially one with a gun, let's remember. But I gotta say something... damn.

" Not too glorious, mowing down the starving and the weak, women and children some of them, huh?" BC says. "Few casualties on our side. But we killed ten thousand people in a matter of hours. Maybe five thousand in the first minutes. So they don't forget. All I was saying."

The drunk starts to get belligerent, "What the fuck, Father, you on their side? They're the ones shooting at us out there, case you forgot!"

BC has to laugh. "Not at all, calm down, son. I'm just a man of peace, is all."

Trying the paternal touch. Don't think I can sell it, though. Such BS, BC...

"Look, it's not funny," the guy says. Before he can say more an announcement blares out over the room's com.

"Attention. Attention. Bernard Campion to the bridge. Father Bernard Campion, report to the bridge at once," a humorless monotone intones.

BC turns to go.

"Hey, that's you? You special or something?" the guy asks, reaching for BC's departing shoulder. BC turns back and grabs the guy's arm on a pressure point. He lets go of BC, drops the bottle from his other hand, and falls to one knee.

"Ouch! Shit, man, that hurt. I was just asking? What kind of priest beats you up, anyway?"

Drex pipes in, "Oh, I went to Jesuit schools. Trust me, I knew quite a few." He pulls BC aside and strategically stands between BC and the drunk getting back on his feet. He speaks low to BC, "What's up?"

"I don't know. But I better go. They know I'm here, obviously."

"Obviously," Drex agrees. "Or they had every captain make the same announcement and now they're waiting to see if and where you show up. It's what I'd do, anyways."

"Good point." BC has to admit.

"I know how they think. I was a UTZ grunt for a bit. Anyways..."

"I'll be back," BC says.

Drex shrugs, "Okay."

Now... where's that confounded bridge?

BC finds the door he came in through and traces his way towards what he thinks is the front of the ship.

The bridge is near the front, usually, right?

BC spies a door with an armed guard in front of it.

That looks promising. Got to get close enough to read...

"Can I help you?" the guard challenges BC.

"Sure. They just paged me? Bernard Campion? I'm looking for the bridge." He explains.

"You found it, see?" the guard moves aside so BC can read "BRIDGE" on the door in block letters. "So you're Father Bernard Campion?"

"Yes?"

He steps even further aside, nods toward the door. "Go ahead in."

"Thanks." BC looks for but doesn't see door controls. He turns to the guard, nearly bumps into him as the guard leans forward to press on a small unmarked panel in the wall next to the door.

"Sorry." BC apologizes.

"Not a problem. There you go," the guard says. The door slides open.

BC steps through into a large open room with a low ceiling.

BC can see out into deep space through windows that make up the upper half of the three walls he's facing. The lower halves of all three are lined with consoles, manned by bridge personnel. There's a bustle as people get up from their consoles, cross the room and consult with each other.

Compared to the Paladin, this is palatial!

A large, freestanding console dominates the center of the room, two sections surrounding a chair in their center. A well-groomed UTZ captain gets up out of the chair and approaches BC.

"Father Bernard Campion?" he asks.

"Yes?"

"Pleased to meet you." He extends his right hand. "I'm Taka Yamano, Commander of Mission Alpha at Fortune Station. Welcome aboard my ship. I didn't know you'd be aboard, but there was a mad scramble to get off that old heap, eh?"

"Yeah. I mean, I hope that's okay."

"Not a problem," he says. "I was briefed on all aspects of Fortune Station before we came out here. Guess you did the initial legwork for us, eh?"

"You could say that."

And, you did. Not quite how I would have put it...

"Good work! They never expected us! And with their old leader dead, and you as their absentee leader... that was a stroke of pure genius, by the way, Father. Well, we just came in, herded them up, sent 'em home and took over. You made it too easy for us! Good work!"

He seems pretty happy about it. I feel like shit. I set the cult up and I didn't even know it. Didn't even think about it. I used to be able to see this kind of thing before it happened. I used to know how devious minds operated. I was one. I AM one, dammit. Just out of practice, maybe.

When BC doesn't answer, Yamano continues. "I just found out you were on board and I wanted to meet you. We've been recalled to the Moon. Though you might like to join us on the bridge for the trip."

Guess impressing this guy has its privileges...

"Sure. I was heading to the Moon anyway. Or trying to when the UIN attacked and drove us out here. I want to go to the Moon."

"Oo, I don't know if you really want to be there right now. The attack on us out at Fortune is a side action. The UIN is hitting the Moon and Earth both pretty hard right now, and hitting some orbitals, too. The UTZ is calling back all ships, even those like us engaged in combat already. Not a good sign," Yamano cautions.

"They haven't attacked in a while," BC thinks out loud.

"Yeah. Saving up to buy us all a nice Christmas Present. Merry Fucking Christmas. Oh, sorry, Father."

"Don't be. Merry Fucking Christmas indeed, Captain Yamano," BC agrees.

Chapter Thirty

Captain Yamano seems to enjoy having BC on the bridge. Whenever there's a lull in activity, he explains what's going on to BC.

"There's still fighting going on at Luna Prime, that's where we're going," Yamano tells him. "They're still hitting some Earth targets, too: Sydney, Hong Kong, Manila. They've been dipping up and down from orbit. They hit Moscow, Berlin, London, New York, LA, Tokyo, all the major cities. 'Death swooping down from the skies,' I heard one guy call it." Yamano's brow furrows, "This is bad, Father, all out war. They have to have more transpace ships than we thought. Shit. Look at that... we're coming up on the Moon," something catches his eye, "hold on, Father! Grab a seat... you can sit over their by the nav console. Strap in, in case we lose G."

An insistent, pinging alarm sounds. Red emergency lights come on around the bridge.

BC bolts to the chair the captain indicated. Out the window ahead he can see the Moon, about the size of someone's head at this distance.

Two small explosions flare up in the space around the Moon. BC can see angry black and orange hot points glowing on the lunar surface, but not much else.

Hard to make out Luna Prime. That can't be good.

Those small explosions. Weapons fire. Not just that, though. To see it this far away, those have to be ships exploding...

"Damn." Yamano turns to BC. "That one on the right was the DeGaulle. I just hope that other one was one of theirs," the captain says.

BC turns in his chair to face the captain. "The heavy cruiser DeGaulle?"

"The former heavy cruiser, unfortunately. This is bad." The captain stops talking as he studies the readouts around him, a mask of concentration freezing his features with furrowed brow.

BC looks back out the front viewport. The moon has surged closer, looms larger than the limits of the viewing area, horrid black smears glowing fierce orange red like open wounds marring the surface. BC sees something flash by, sees metallic rain sparkling outside.

Must have been a missile. And countermeasures.

"Pull us up and away off the elliptic a hundred degrees. Now!" Yamano yells.

BC watches the moon drop out of sight in the viewports as their ship surges up and ahead in a burst of speed. BC feels the Gs pushing him down in his chair despite the artificial gravity.

"Rear guns, I want answering fire on that missile launcher yesterday!" Yamano calls out. "Launch more countermeasures, we haven't covered this position."

Shit... this is bad. I've never seen it this bad before. The moon looks like Hell.

"They're probably going to need you down on Luna Prime, Father, or what's left of it. I'm getting a report here of heavy casualties and wounded."

"How bad is it?" BC has to ask.

"They hit the main dome of Luna Prime," Yamano says, "destroyed the central section." The captain is listening to some com source BC can't hear and relaying the information.

He looks directly at BC. "They hit the Vatican section pretty hard, I'm afraid, Father. It's being mentioned as one of the hardest hit areas." Yamano tries to cheer him up, "Guess you're lucky you're with us here, huh? Well, let's hope..." Yamano is cut off.

"Captain, we're being hailed by the *King*," an officer tells him. The captain nods back.

"Go ahead, King. Yamano on the Eisenhower, fresh back from Fortune. How can we help?"

"Nice to see you, Ike," the com sputters. The signal is just barely holding together.

BC can hear explosions in the background on the com.

"We're picking up a UIN flanking action around the darkside," the com sputters.

"Hey Ike, why don't you come on over and help us stop them from hitting our line's blind side. Sending coordinates, see you soon, King out." Another background explosion is cut off as the message ends.

"Nav, helm, get us over there. Tactical, I need some scans in that area. Bridge, kill the white light in here, we're going darkside."

Regular lighting blips off at the captain's command. The bridge is now lit only by the red alert lighting.

Cool. Just like the movies. *Except here we can die.*

Maybe nothing like the movies, come to think of it.

BC watches the moon go from orb to crescent all the while getting larger in the forward viewport.

Going in...

He sees extensive damage to sites on the surface of the dark side as they get closer. He thinks about what Yamano told him.

Man, did they hit us hard. The atrium of Luna Prime. All those good restaurants and bars... and our section. I wanted to forget that, pretend I didn't hear it. God, I hope everybody got to safety in the shelters. I have no idea how much advance warning they got. Merry Christmas from your friends in the UIN. Happy Anniversary.

BOOM-ANG-THUD!

A blast shakes the bridge. The entire bridge crew snap into a spurt of precise activity as they take battle stations in earnest.

"We've got company!" someone shouts. "That was a hit!"

"Tell me something we both don't already know, Chargon," Yamano says, cool and sarcastic. "Damage?"

"Minimal," an officer on BC's right reports.

"Good. That's what I wanted to hear. Okay, you guys got one free shot, you don't get another one," the captain tells the enemy. Then he turns to BC. "Hey there, Father, how you doin'? Ever ride a cruiser into battle before?"

BC musters a smile. "I'm, uh, I'm okay. Can't say as I have, captain."

"First time for everything, huh?"

"Captain, we've got missiles locking on!" the guy BC now knows is Chargon shouts.

Yamano turns to face front.

"Return fire!" he barks. "Countermeasures!"

"Another one coming in from starboard, sir!" Chargon reports.

"I'm on it, captain," the guy on BC's right tells Yamano. "Starboard side batteries firing."

"Good. Keep those missile away from us. No lasers yet? Funny. They may not have them on every ship. Missiles are easier to mount, easier to come by, too," Yamano thinks out loud.

BC watches the bridge crew in their ballet of battle.

It is almost a dance, the way they work together to run the ship. They're the interactive human brain for the cruiser's killing machine. Kill or be killed.

They close in on the UIN ship that fired on them. As the ship gets close enough for BC to see some detail it erupts into and orange cloud of debris and quickly extinguished flame under the nearly invisible laser fire from their cruiser.

Another UIN ship suddenly appears from behind and to the left, bearing down on them. The *Eisenhower's* lasers are soon focussed on the new intruder and it is obliterated in turn, only to be followed by a third, right behind it. It too quickly disintegrates under the laser fire from their cruiser.

"I've got a fix on another two, maybe three of them," the officer to BC's right tells the captain after they've taken out the third UIN vessel.

"Try to keep us between them and the moon. There

are still civilians alive down there. Let's see if we can't keep more of our people from being killed." The captain pauses, thinking. "Don't let us get too close to the surface. We need to be able to maneuver. If they get too close to us, or head towards the surface, slice 'em and dice 'em," he orders.

"Captain, The *King* on the com!" Chargon says.

"Go ahead, *King*," Yamano authorizes.

"*Eisenhower*, you are a sight for sore eyes! Good to see you. You're hot, good shooting!" the com sputters, stronger than the last time.

"Who else we got here, *King*?" Yamano asks.

"Well, we had the *Kennedy*, but they're gone, back for repairs. The UIN first wave took out the *Blair*... down with all hands, the poor bastards. But The *Blair* took out a huge UIN Transpace Transport ship, one we hadn't see before, before she went down. They used the big ship to ferry smaller ones here from Mars. If the *Blair* hadn't stopped them, they woulda been able to bring in more ships."

"The *Blair* took it out, huh?" the captain asks the com.

"Yeah, but not before it unloaded it's last batch of assault craft. We got another one coming in!" the com clicks off.

"We got it, captain. Coming up from the surface, didn't see that one on the scans! Incoming!"

BOOM-THUD-ANG

"I want that ship! Get some fire on that fucker!" Yamano yells. The UIN ship explodes in their viewport.

BC watches the battle blur by. Their ship is hit, but not badly damaged as they mop up the failed UIN flanking action on the darkside. Then Yamano brings the *Eisenhower* back around near Luna Prime.

The UTZ line has been holding the main UIN advance at bay in the space around Luna Prime. As The *Eisenhower* approaches the UTZ line, more UIN ships appear, probably the last of the UIN flankers.

The *Ike* engages a couple of these straggling assault ships, but they're no match for the UTZ Heavy Cruiser. The

Eisenhower takes some damage, but deals out more. Both ships are destroyed.

. The *Eisenhower,* two other heavy cruisers, and several smaller support craft are all that are left of the UTZ forces by the time the *Ike* arrives on the line. To BC, the battle seems to be all but over, with the exception of a UIN straggler here and there like the two The *Eisenhower* had taken out earlier. But the bridge of The *Ike* remains tense and alert. The crew is using every scanner at their disposal searching for enemy ships. Eyes wide open. BC figures the scene is the same on the bridges of the other cruisers as well.

The *King* had tried to follow them from the dark side, but ended up touching down for repairs at a nearby outpost instead when their damage proved too extensive for them to continue. They'll live to fight another day, Yamano had quipped. BC heard him mention something about another cruiser coming back from action darkside, too.

BC sits in his chair and listens. He knows the battle is really over when all of a sudden everyone seems to simultaneously exhale a breath they didn't know they were holding. No one says anything, but it's been a while since they've seen an enemy ship, and all of a sudden everything is All Right. A relative calm descends over the bridge.

I guess we won. There's more of us than them. But the cost seems incredibly high. What is the UIN doing?

The white lighting comes back on. BC realizes Chargon is reciting a list of ship's damages to Captain Yamano and begins to pay attention.

"...about seventy percent. It's okay, not great, but okay. And the other one, well... it'll probably blow up if we push it beyond minimal directional firing. But we'll need it for that, because most of the starboard side directional engines are out. We suffered most of our hull breaches on the starboard side, some explosive dee, mostly confined to deck two."

"Casualties?" Yamano asks.

"Two," he's told. "Endoway is gone, sucked right out

of C corridor on deck two. LeClair was killed when Engine Two flared."

"Roger." Yamano massages his brow, closes his eyes.

"Orders, sir?" the helmsman asks.

"Right." Yamano lowers his hands, opens his eyes. "Take us in to Luna Prime, Reagan Station. Take us down, Mr. Chargon."

BC leans forward to see what he can of Luna Prime out of the viewports as they approach. What he sees makes him feel sick, sour and twisted in the pit of his stomach. The entire station is a charred mess. Twisted metal beams jut up out of melted piles of what were once walls, ceilings, floors. New craters mar the surface.

One of those craters is where I used to live. I can only hope everyone made it to some kind of shelter. But I'm not sure anywhere was safe from that blast, by the look of it. Might have been a nuke! Would they dare? Man, this is the most destruction I've ever seen, maybe worse than some of the Earth attacks back when I was a kid. This was major, an all out blitz.

"There were a lot of casualties down there," Yamano says at BC's side, startling him out of his thoughts.

I never heard him approach... must be slipping. Might be shock. Caught me daydreaming, or, what, day-nightmaring?

"Looks like it." BC says.

"I'm sorry. I know you were based here. Maybe you were lucky to be with us instead of here when the attack came," Yamano says. He looks out at the ruins with BC.

"They threw everything they had at us, seems like," Yamano ponders aloud.

"Looks that way. Merry Christmas, huh?"

"They won't forget the massacre." It's a statement.

"Not likely," BC agrees.

"Captain, we're down. Into what's left, anyway. We're improvising an airlock using our ship-to-ship facilities. Should be able to disembark in twenty minutes," the com says.

Chapter Thirty One

BC thanks Captain Yamano and makes his way off The *Eisenhower* and back onto Luna Prime through the makeshift airlock.

I can breathe, guess that means it works.

This is not the way I saw myself getting back here. I figured little trip to deposit Fiza, then right back in time for Christmas, no worries. How wrong can a man be?

Luna Prime's spaceport is in chaos. Armed UTZ guards move in patrols through the confused crowd. LSC's are doing their best to move among the people, comforting them, telling them where they can go to get help. Most of those wandering through the spaceport seem a little dazed, still in shock from the terrible, shattering force of the attacks.

BC spots Governor Edwards in the crowd, doing his best to help the cause.

BC makes his way up to Edwards. He finds Edwards staring off into space while a UTZ officer reports to him. It takes over a minute for Edwards to turn, see BC, and have it register who it is standing there. Then his eyes snap alert and brighten.

"BC!" Edwards says, surprised and smiling. Then his smile drops, his eyes darken and dim with sadness. BC tries for comfort.

"Marc, I can't believe this, that they'd do this."

"I guess I know better what you've been talking about now, huh?" Edwards shakes his head. "Why? Why did they... they never hit us like this before. We're not on their side, but we're not their enemy. Why us?"

"I don't know, Marc. I just don't know. Why kill anybody this way? Deep and ancient hatreds. It is Christmas, you know."

"I know. They'll never forget that. I don't think they should. But that wasn't even us! Not the Luna Free State!

We didn't kill them. Why us? Why today?"

"Maybe it was us. The Vatican, I mean. Our fault. I saw the crater where the mission used to be."

Marc Edwards lowers his head, then looks back up, eye to eye with BC. He clears his throat and prepares to pass along grim news.

"The Cardinal is dead, BC. I helped identify him after the first wave of attacks. I'm sorry. The Reverend Swan is still missing, but presumed dead. The Vatican Mission was hit first, and hard."

"Was it a nuke?"

"No. I think they were flinging captured asteroids at us at first."

Damn, that's hardcore. Oh, man, not now!

A headache comes on and overwhelms BC where he stands. Pain shoots through his skull. He closes his eyes, squeezes the bridge of his nose between his thumb and right pointer.

A bad one! Gotta be the crazy stress.

"You okay, BC?" Edwards asks, concerned.

"Yeah, I think, it's just a lot, getting one of those headaches again." BC says, and looks around for somewhere to sit. Quickly.

"Here, man, sit down. Sit down," Edwaqrds says, helping him to a chair and clearing off debris so BC can plop down. BC sits, head in his hands, as the headache grows. He rubs his temples but it doesn't help.

So much pain this time! Shit! What sort of permanent damage did those cult drugs do to my brain? This is their revenge for my letting them down.

"BC?" Edwards is leaning over him, worried.

"I'll be okay, just give me a sec."

I hope I'll be okay. They tell me again and again there are no tumors or growths but then what aw fuck what ouch ow!

"Have you heard about the Earth attacks?" Edwards asks him.

BC tries to concentrate, lowers his right hand from

his head and opens his right eye to look at Edwards. "Not in any detail. Have you heard any reports?"

"It was bad, BC. They may still be attacking. I haven't heard any recent updates. We were lucky to get the small defence group we did from the UTZ when we requested it. Most of the UTZ fleet were defending Earth."

"What have you heard?"

"They threw everything they had at us. And they had more than anybody knew. They've been majorly stockpiling on Mars. They did major damage to Sydney, London, New York, Los Angeles, Tokyo, Lima, and Vatican City." Edwards pauses as something else occurs to him. He leans in a little closer. "Pope Peter is dead, BC. It happened before the attacks. We got the news right after you left with that woman Fiza. His death was confirmed this morning. I'm sorry."

I'm sorry... I'm sorry... I'm sorry...

The words echo in his brain. BC's head feels like it's about to explode, as if his brain is expanding, trying to break out of the confines of his skull. He closes his eye. The pain is intense.

I'm sorry... I'm sorry... I'm sorry... I'm sorry... I'm sorry...

The words keep echoing in BC's head. Then the floor falls away.

BC keeps falling, falling, dropping faster, free falling.
Everything is gone. The world falls away.

BC opens his eyes. The world around him contracts down into a small marble that shrinks into a pinpoint of light and then -pop- dissappears.

Everyone is dead. The Cardinal. Swan. Who knows who else. M'Bekke? Marino?

BC doesn't realize he's passed out until he comes to lying on his back on a couch.

In Edward's office. Still here, still intact.

Edwards is sitting behind a desk across the room from BC and notices him stirring. He smiles and gets up to come over.

"BC! You're back!"

"Where did I go?"

"You tell me! You went... I don't know. Catatonic or something."

BC sits up and rubs his temples. The headache has passed.

I still feel like I'm hungover. I should have more fun if I'm going to end up suffering like this. How long has it been?

"How long was I out for?"

"You were staring straight ahead, but you weren't seeing anything. You wouldn't respond to anything. It's been almost a day. I had them bring you here so you weren't left sitting staring into space in the middle of the spaceport. Not that you were the only one shell shocked."

"Thanks, Marc," BC says in a mumble.

Still groggy.

"How's your head?" Edwards asks, sitting down in a nearby chair.

"S'okay," BC laughs, "least of my worries. Everyone I know and work with and for is dead. Where I lived and worked is gone. And I'm still here, somehow."

"So am I, man. So am I. Hey, Doctor O'Neel says it may have overwhelmed you, everything hitting you at once, mental overload or something. Brought on your headache. Sounded like a good explanation to me."

"I suppose."

I gotta see another neurologist or someone about these headaches. That last was a doozy.

"They announced a new pope while you were out of it!" Edwards says, trying to cheer up BC.

"Wha?"

"Pope Linus!" Edwards tells him. "They broadcast it about two hours ago."

"Really? Who is he?"

"I told you, Linus. Are you sure you're okay?" Edwards sounds concerned.

"No, no, man, that's not what I mean." BC shakes his head, chuckles. "Popes take on a saint's name when they

255

become pope. 'Linus' isn't his real name. So I wonder who he is."

"Oh, I get it," Edwards says, nodding. He gets up, walks back over to his desk and sits down.

BC's feeling better, so he stands up.

No dizziness, good. Legs feel solid. Not jelly.

"Do you have a report, something I can read, look at?" BC asks.

Edwards stands up, motions for BC to come over.

"The story's still on my screen. Go ahead, take a look." He steps back and lets BC sit down to read the news.

Linus the Second has been elevated to the Papacy after the convening of an emergency meeting of the College of Cardinals. He was made pope on Christmas day.

He was pope before I even knew Peter was dead. And Giusseppe Fioreni is now Linus the Second. Who the fuck is Giusseppe Fioreni? Where's the bio link? Oh there...

Fioreni was a leader in the old Roman Catholic Church until the time of the Great Reunification. He was a lead member of the Vatican team in the ecumenical councils that led to the reunification.

Sounds old school Catholic. Wonderful.

BC keeps reading. Fioreni was evidently a surprise choice, and from the sounds of the article one of only a couple of candidates to come forward. Massive losses were suffered on Christmas Eve when the UIN attacked Vatican City unannounced, thinning the ranks of those who would be pope. The College of Cardinals is now much smaller, evidently, having been gathered at the Vatican for the Papal vote when the attacks commenced.

"Linus the Second, huh?" BC mumbles.

"What was that?" Edwards asks from behind him.

"Nothing. Just trying to get used to the idea of a new boss."

"So, do you know this new guy?" Edwards asks.

"Not at all. Never met the man. He and I didn't run in the same circles. I'm sure he'll be fine, though, if the cardinals chose him that quickly."

"Gotta pick up the pieces and move on," Edwards muses.

"Yeah, but the church never moves that fast. It's funny. Funny peculiar, not funny ha ha. Especially where Pope Peter died before the attacks."

"Yeah, that part was never made too clear," Edwards agrees. He walks around the desk, paces across the room.

BC changes the subject. "Hey, I noticed something."

"What's that?" Edwards turns and paces back.

"You're still in charge here. There are no UIN soldiers herding us into containment areas. Did we win?"

"If you can call this winning. They threw everything they had at us, and we held them back. We took a beating, we're hurt, and a lot of people are dead. But we are still here. We stopped them, BC.

"They lost a lot of ships, wasted a lot of lives on their side. Some of them got away, limped off, but they accomplished nothing. Nothing has changed. Except there's a lot of people dead who weren't before. All of this for nothing. It's so fucking pointless, BC. Nothing's changed!" Edwards can't help but get worked up.

BC looks down at the desk screen, flips to the item before the piece on the new pope. It's an updated doc on the confirmed dead. Swan is on the list. The Cardinal, too.

"Nothing? Everything's changed, Marc." BC finds himself growing angry. "Aside from you, Marc, most of the people I know are now dead. This makes it a personal war for me, now. I feel like they're waging war on *me*. They killed all these people I cared about and it got them nothing."

It was never personal before. Just my job. Who do I work for now?

"Tell you what, Marc. I'm going to give them something for their trouble, for all the trouble they brought down on us. I don't know what or how yet, or where, when, any of that, but they've made me their enemy! It's never felt this personal to me before. When I figure out what I'm going to do, you'll be the first to know..."

BC is interrupted by the door bell. It rings again

quickly. Before Edwards can answer it, the door whips open. Daniel McEntyre bursts in.

"Marc, this has..." he starts to say. He stops in his tracks when he sees BC sitting behind the desk where he expected to see Edwards. His head whips back and forth as he looks for Edwards. When he spots him he demands, pointing at BC, "What is he doing here?!"

BC is up from behind the desk before his mind knows his body is moving. All his anger at the UIN is concentrating in his right fist as he pulls it back.

Fuck it.

BC lets a solid right fly. His fist connects flat with McEntyre's jaw. McEntyre's head snaps back. McEntyre stumbles back, falls into the closing door, then slides to the floor holding his jaw. BC shakes his hand.

Damn. That felt good. May have broken something...

"Sorry, Marc," BC apologizes. He steps over McEntyre and into the doorway, then turns to look down at his victim.

"Don't even think of pressing any charges," BC tells McEntyre, "or I'll bring up your tackle you laid on me back on the day you had your wife killed. Oh wait, no, that's right, I assssassssinated her, right? Fuck you." BC turns back, walks out the door and down the corridor.

I have no idea where I'm going. There's no place left to go to. I'd like to get some air. But what am I gonna do, go out for a walk? That doesn't work here. The only thing close was the dome, and that's gone now, too.

The air tastes stale. Recyclers aren't what they used to be, must have been hit. The main dome was a big part of the atmosphere system, come to think of it. Maybe we're running on old back ups.

BC stops walking when he reaches an emergency airlock door. All the door panels are lit up bright red. There's no air on the other side. BC can see through the doors ahead to a wreck of a corridor. The corridor extends a short way ahead, then is simply flattened down and melted into spiky modern art.

But its not art. Not some sculptor's nightmare made